Dear Reader,

In life, nothing ventured, nothing gained—and the same is true in love.

In this collection, the incredible Nora Roberts brings us two classics that explore how quickly our fortunes can shift if we keep our hearts open.

Stephen Nickodemus had known many beautiful women, but Rebecca Malone caught his eye from the moment he saw her. She had a kind of electricity about her—ready to face anything. The *Impulse* came suddenly to send champagne to her table, and he knew it was the beginning of something wonderful….

Obviously ex-socialite Eden Carlborough didn't know a thing about running a girls' camp, but Chase Elliott admired her determination—and that wasn't all he liked about her! The instant she fell from his apple tree and into his arms, Chase knew his heart was in trouble, because Eden was all *Temptation!*

Sit back, relax and take the plunge with our heroes and heroines as they discover that change is good, and quite often life-changing!

The Editors

Silhouette Books

NORA ROBERTS

Windfall

Published by Silhouette Books

America's Publisher of Contemporary Romance

SILHOUETTE BOOKS

WINDFALL

ISBN-13: 978-0-373-28595-2

Copyright © 2009 by Harlequin Books S.A.

The publisher acknowledges the copyright holder of the individual works as follows:

IMPULSE
Copyright © 1989 by Nora Roberts

TEMPTATION
Copyright © 1987 by Nora Roberts

Recycling programs for this product may not exist in your area.

Visit Silhouette Books at www.eHarlequin.com

Printed in U.S.A.

CONTENTS

IMPULSE

Chapter 1

She knew it was crazy. That was what she liked best about it. It was crazy, ridiculous, impractical and totally out of character. And she was having the time of her life. From the balcony of her hotel suite Rebecca could see the sweep of the beach, the glorious blue of the Ionian Sea, blushed now with streaks of rose from the setting sun.

Corfu. Even the name sounded mysterious, exciting, glamorous. And she was here, really here. Practical, steady-as-a-rock Rebecca Malone, who had never traveled more than five hundred miles from Philadelphia, was in Greece. Not just in Greece, she thought with a grin, but on the exotic island of Corfu, in one of the most exclusive resorts in Europe.

First-class, she thought as she leaned out to let the sweet breeze ruffle over her face. As long as it lasted, she was going first-class.

Her boss had thought she was suffering from temporary insanity. Edwin McDowell of McDowell, Jableki and Kline was never going to understand why a promising young CPA would resign from her position with one of the top accounting firms in Philadelphia. She'd made a good salary, she'd enjoyed excellent benefits, and she'd even had a small window in her office.

Friends and associates had wondered if she'd suffered a breakdown. After all, it wasn't normal, and it certainly wasn't Rebecca's style to quit a solid, well-paying job without the promise of a better one.

But she'd given her two weeks' notice, cleared out her desk and had cheerfully walked out into the world of the unemployed.

When she'd sold her condo and then in one frantic week, auctioned off every possession she owned—every stick of furniture, every pot and pan and appliance—they'd been certain she'd gone over the edge.

Rebecca had never felt saner.

She owned nothing that didn't fit in a suitcase. She no longer had any tax-deferred investments or retirement plans. She'd cashed in her certificates of deposit, and the home entertainment center she'd thought she couldn't live without was now gracing someone else's home.

It had been more than six weeks since she'd even looked at an adding machine.

For the first—and perhaps the only—time in her life, she was totally free. There were no responsibilities, no pressures, no hurried gulps of cold coffee. She hadn't packed an alarm clock. She no longer owned one. Crazy? No. Rebecca shook her head and laughed into the breeze. For as long as it lasted, she was going to grab life with both hands and see what it had to offer.

Aunt Jeannie's death had been her turning point. It had come so suddenly, so unexpectedly, leaving Rebecca without any family. Aunt Jeannie had worked hard for most of her sixty-five years, always punctual, always responsible. Her position as head librarian had been her whole life. She'd never missed a day, never failed to do her duty. Her bills had been paid on time. Her promises had always been kept.

More than once Rebecca had been told she took after her mother's older sister. She was twenty-four, but she was—had been—as solid and sturdy as her maiden aunt. Two months into retirement, two months after dear Aunt Jeannie began to make plans to travel, to enjoy the rewards she'd worked so hard to earn, she was gone.

After Rebecca's grief had come the anger, then the frustration, then slowly, the realization that she was traveling the same straight road. She worked, she slept, she fixed well-balanced meals that she ate alone. She had a small circle of friends who knew she could be counted on in a crisis. Rebecca would always find the best and most practical answer. Rebecca would never drop her own problems in your lap—because she didn't have any. Rebecca, bless her, was a port in any storm.

She hated it, and she'd begun to hate herself. She had to do something.

And she was doing it.

It wasn't running away as much as it was breaking free. All her life she'd done what was expected of her and tried to make as few waves as possible while doing it. All through school a crushing shyness had kept her more comfortable with her books than with other teen-agers. In college a need to succeed and justify her aunt's faith had locked her tightly into her studies.

She had always been good with figures—logical, thorough, patient. It had been easy, perhaps too easy, to pour herself into that one area, because there, and really only there, had she felt confident.

Now she was going to discover Rebecca Malone. In the weeks or months of freedom she had, she wanted to learn everything there was to know about the woman within. Perhaps there wasn't a butterfly inside the cocoon she'd wrapped herself in so comfortably, but whatever she found—whoever she found—Rebecca hoped she would enjoy her, like her, perhaps even respect her.

When the money ran out, she'd get another job and go back to being plain, practical Rebecca. Until that time she was rich, rootless and ready for surprises.

She was also hungry.

Stephen saw her the moment she entered the restaurant. It wasn't that she was particularly striking. Beautiful women passed through the world every day and they usually warranted a glance. But there was something about the way this one walked, as if she were ready for anything, even looking forward to it. He stopped, and because business was slow at this hour he took a second, longer look.

She was tall for a woman, and more angular than slender. Her skin was pale, and that made him think she had only just arrived at the resort or was shy of the sun. The white sundress that left her shoulders and back bare accented the lack of color and gave dramatic contrast to her short cap of raven hair.

She paused, then seemed to take a deep breath. Stephen could almost hear her satisfied sigh. Then she smiled at the headwaiter, and followed him to her table, tossing her head back, so that her hair, which she wore arrow-straight, swung away from her chin.

A nice face, Stephen concluded. Bright, intelligent, eager. Especially the eyes. They were pale, an almost translucent gray. But there was nothing pale in their expression. She smiled at the waiter again, then laughed and looked around the restaurant. She looked as if she'd never been happier in her life.

She saw him. When Rebecca's gaze first skimmed over the man leaning against the bar, her automatic shyness kicked in and had her looking away. Attractive men had stared at her before—though it wasn't exactly a daily event. She'd never been able to handle it with the aplomb—or even cynicism—of most of her contemporaries. To cover her momentary embarrassment, she lifted her menu.

He hadn't meant to linger more than a few moments longer, but the impulse came suddenly. Stephen flicked a hand at the waiter and had him scurrying over, nodding quickly at Stephen's murmured request and hurrying off. When he returned it was to deliver a bottle of champagne to Rebecca's table.

"Compliments of Mr. Nickodemus."

"Oh." Rebecca followed the waiter's gaze over to the man by the bar. "Well, I—" She brought herself up short before she could stammer. A sophisticated woman wouldn't stutter over a gift of champagne, she reminded herself. She'd accept it graciously, with dignity. And maybe—if she wasn't a complete fool—she'd relax enough to flirt with the man who offered it.

Stephen watched the expressions pass across her face. Fascinating, he mused, and realized that the vague boredom he'd been feeling had vanished. When she lifted her head and smiled at him, he had no idea that her heart was pounding. He saw only a casual invitation, and he answered it.

He wasn't just attractive, Rebecca realized as he crossed to her table. He was gorgeous. Eye-popping, mouth-dropping gorgeous. She had an image of Apollo and ancient Greek warriors. Thick blond hair streaked by the sun fell over the collar of his shirt. Smooth, bronzed skin was marred—and somehow enhanced—by a faint scar under his jawline. A strong jaw, she thought. A strong face, with the darkest, deepest blue eyes she'd ever seen.

"Good evening, I'm Stephen Nickodemus." His voice wasn't accented, it was rounded, rich. He might have come from anywhere. Perhaps it was that, more than anything else, that intrigued her.

Lecturing herself on poise and image, she lifted her hand. "Hello. I'm Rebecca, Rebecca Malone." She felt a quick flutter when he brushed his lips over her knuckles. Feeling foolish, she drew her hand away and balled it in her lap. "Thank you for the champagne."

"It seemed to suit your mood." He studied her, wondering why he was getting such a mix of signals. "You are by yourself?"

"Yes." Perhaps it was a mistake to admit it, but if she was going to live life to the fullest she had to take some risks. The restaurant wasn't crowded, but they were hardly alone. Take the plunge, she told herself, and tried another smile. "The least I can do is offer you a glass."

Stephen took the seat across from her, brushing the waiter aside to pour the wine himself. "You are American?"

"It shows."

"No. Actually, I thought you were French until you spoke."

"Did you?" That pleased her. "I've just come from Paris." She had to force herself not to touch her hair. She'd had it cut, with trepidation and delight, in a French salon.

Stephen touched his glass to hers. Her eyes bubbled with life as cheerfully as the wine. "Business?"

"No, just pleasure." What a marvelous word, she thought. *Pleasure.* "It's a wonderful city."

"Yes. Do you go often?"

Rebecca smiled into her glass. "Not often enough. Do you?"

"From time to time."

She nearly sighed at that. Imagine anyone speaking of going to Paris "from time to time." "I nearly stayed longer, but I'd promised myself Greece."

So she was alone, restless, and on the move. Perhaps that was why she had appealed to him, because he was, too. "Is Corfu your first stop?"

"Yes." She sipped at her drink. A part of her still believed it was all a dream. Greece, champagne, the man. "It's beautiful. Much more beautiful than I imagined it could be."

"It's your first trip, then?" He couldn't have said why that pleased him. "How long do you stay?"

"As long as I like." She grinned, savoring the feeling of freedom. "And you?"

He lifted his glass. "Longer, I think, than I had planned." When the waiter appeared at his side, Stephen handed over the menu, then spoke to him in soft, quick Greek. "If you don't object, I'd like to guide you through your first meal on the island."

The old Rebecca would have been too nervous to sit through a meal with a stranger. The new Rebecca took a second, deeper sip of champagne. "I'd love it. Thank you."

It was easy. Easy to sit, to laugh, to sample new and exotic tastes. She forgot that he was a stranger, forgot that the world she was living in now was only temporary. They didn't speak of anything important—only of Paris, and the weather, and the wine. Still, she was sure it was the most interesting conversation of her life. He looked at her when he spoke to her, looked at her as though he were delighted to spend an hour talking of nothing. The last man she'd had dinner with had wanted her to give him a discount when she did his taxes.

Stephen wasn't asking her for anything more than her company for dinner. When he looked at her it seemed unlikely that he'd care if she knew how to fill out Schedule C.

When he suggested a walk along the beach, she agreed without a qualm. What better way to end an evening than a walk in the moonlight?

"I was looking out at this from my window just before dinner." Rebecca stepped out of her shoes, then dangled them from her fingers as she walked. "I didn't think it could look more beautiful than it did at sunset."

"The sea changes, like a woman, in the light." He paused to touch a flame to the end of a slim cigar. "So men are drawn to her."

"Are you? Drawn to the sea?"

"I've spent my time on her. I fished in these waters as a boy."

She'd learned at dinner that he'd grown up traveling the islands with his father. "It must have been exciting, moving from place to place, seeing new things almost every day."

He shrugged. He'd never been sure whether the restlessness had been born in him or had been a product of his upbringing. "It had its moments."

"I love to travel." Laughing, she tossed her shoes aside, then stepped into the surf. The champagne was making her head swim and the moonlight felt as soft as rain. "I adore it." She laughed again when the spray washed up to dampen her skirts. The Ionian Sea. She was standing in it. "On a night like this I think I'll never go home."

She looked so vibrant, so alive, standing in the surf with her white skirts billowing. "Where's home?"

She glanced over her shoulder. The flirtatious look was totally unplanned and completely devastating. "I haven't decided. I want to swim." On impulse, she dived into the surf.

Stephen's heart stopped when she disappeared. He'd already kicked off his shoes and started forward when she rose up again. For a second time, his heart stopped.

She was laughing, her face lifted to the moonlight. Water cascaded from her hair, from her skin. The drops that clung to her were the only jewels she wore. Beautiful? No, she wasn't beautiful. She was electric.

"It's wonderful. Cool and soft and wonderful."

With a shake of his head, he stepped in far enough to take her hand and pull her toward shore. She was a little mad, perhaps, but engagingly so. "Are you always so impulsive?"

"I'm working on it. Aren't you?" She combed her hand through her dripping hair. "Or do you always send champagne to strange women?"

"Either way I answer that could be trouble. Here." He shrugged out of his jacket and draped it over her shoulders. Unframed, washed clean, her face glowed in the moonlight. There was a graceful kind of strength in it, to the sweep of cheekbone, the slightly pointed chin. Delicate— except for the eyes. One look there showed power, a power that was still. "You're irresistible, Rebecca."

She stared at him, confused all over again, as he gathered the neck of the jacket close around her throat. "I'm wet," she managed.

"And beautiful." With his hands still on the jacket, he brought her toward him. "And fascinating."

That made her laugh again. "I don't think so, but thanks. I'm glad you sent me the champagne and guided me through my first meal." Her nerves began to jangle. His eyes stayed on hers, journeying only once to her mouth, which was still damp from the sea. Their bodies were close, close enough to brush. Rebecca began to shiver, and she knew it had nothing to do with wet clothes and the breeze.

"I should go in…change my dress."

There was something about her. The impulsiveness,

the easy flirtatiousness, hid an unmistakable innocence that baffled and attracted him. Whatever it was, he wanted more.

"I'll see you again."

"Yes." She prayed for her heartbeat to slow. "It's not a very big island."

He smiled at that, slowly. She felt, with a mixture of relief and regret, the relaxation of his hands. "Tomorrow. I have business early. I'll be done by eleven, if that suits you. I'll show you Corfu."

"All right." Better judgment and nerves be damned. She wanted to go with him. "I'll meet you in the lobby." Carefully, because she suddenly wasn't sure she could manage it, she stepped back. Moonlight silhouetted him against the sea. "Good night, Stephen."

She forgot to be sophisticated and dashed toward the hotel.

He watched her go. She puzzled him, puzzled him as no woman had since he'd been a boy and too young to understand that a woman was not meant to be understood. And he wanted her. That wasn't new, but the desire had come with surprising speed and surprising force.

Rebecca Malone might have started out as an impulse, but she was now a mystery. One he intended to solve. With a little laugh, he bent to scoop up the shoes she'd forgotten. He hadn't felt quite so alive in months.

Chapter 2

Stephen wasn't the kind of man who rearranged his schedule to spend the day with a woman. Especially a woman he barely knew. He was a wealthy man, but he was also a busy man, driven by both pride and ambition to maintain a high level of involvement in all his projects. He shouldered responsibility well and had learned to enjoy the benefits of hard work and dedication.

His time on Corfu wasn't free—or rather hadn't been planned as free. Mixing business and pleasure wasn't his style. He pursued both, separately, with utter concentration. Yet he found himself juggling appointments, meetings, conference calls, in order to have the afternoon open for Rebecca.

He supposed any man would want to get to know a woman who flirted easily over a champagne flute one moment and dived fully dressed into the sea the next.

"I've postponed your meeting with Theoharis until five-thirty this evening." Stephen's secretary scribbled on a notepad she had resting on her lap. "He will meet you for early cocktails in the suite. I've arranged for hors d'oeuvres and a bottle of ouzo."

"Always efficient, Elana."

She smiled and tucked a fall of dark hair behind her ear. "I try."

When Stephen rose to pace to the window, she folded her hands and waited. She had worked for him for five years, she admired his energy and his business acumen, and—fortunately for both of them—had long since gotten over an early crush. There was often speculation about their personal relationship, but though he could be friendly—even kind when it suited him—with Stephen, business was business.

"Contact Mithos in Athens. Have him telex that report by the end of the day. And I want to hear from Lereau by five, Paris time."

"Shall I call and give him a nudge?"

"If you think it's necessary." Restless, he dug his hands in his pockets. Where had this sudden discontent come from? he wondered. He was wealthy, successful, and free, as always, to move from place to place. As he stared out at the sea, he remembered the scent of Rebecca's skin. "Send flowers to Rebecca Malone's suite. Wildflowers, nothing formal. This afternoon."

Elana made a note, hoping she'd get a look at this Rebecca Malone before long. She had already heard through the grapevine that Stephen had had dinner with an American woman. "And the card?"

He wasn't a man for poetry. "Just my name."

"Anything else?"

"Yes." He turned and offered her a half smile. "Take some time off. Go to the beach."

Pad in hand, she rose. "I'll be sure to work it in. Enjoy your afternoon, Stephen."

He intended to. As she left him, Stephen glanced at his watch. It was fifteen minutes before eleven. There was work he could do to fill in the time, a quick call that could be made. Instead, he picked up Rebecca's shoes.

After three tries, Rebecca settled on an outfit. She didn't have an abundance of clothes, because she'd preferred to spend her funds on travel. But she had splurged here and there on her route through Europe. No tidy CPA suits, she thought as she tied a vivid fuchsia sash at the waist of her sapphire-colored cotton pants. No sensible shoes or pastel blouses. The last shock of color came from a primrose-hued blouse cut generously to layer over a skinny tank top in the same shade as the slacks.

The combination delighted her, if only because her firm had preferred quiet colors and clean lines.

She had no idea where she was going, and she didn't care.

It was a beautiful day, even though she'd awoken with a dull headache from the champagne, and the disorientation that went with it. A light, early breakfast on her terrace and a quick dip in the sea had cleared both away. She still had trouble believing that she could lounge through a morning as she pleased—and that she'd spent the evening with a man she'd just met.

Aunt Jeannie would have tut-tutted and reminded her of the dangers of being a woman alone. Some of her friends would have been shocked, others envious. But they would all have been astonished that steady Rebecca had strolled in the moonlight with a gorgeous man with a scar on his jawline and eyes like velvet.

If she hadn't had his jacket as proof, she might have thought she'd dreamed it. There had never been anything wrong with her imagination—just the application of it. Often she'd pictured herself in an exotic place with an exotic man, with moonlight and music. Imagined herself, she remembered. And then she'd turned on her calculator and gotten down to business.

But she hadn't dreamed this. She could still remember the giddy, half-terrified feeling that had swarmed through her when he'd gathered her close. When his mouth had been only an inch from hers and the sea and the champagne had roared in her head.

What if he had kissed her? What tastes would she have found? Rich, strong ones, she mused, almost able to savor them as she traced a fingertip over her lips. After just one evening she was absolutely certain there would be nothing lukewarm about Stephen Nickodemus. She wasn't nearly so certain about Rebecca.

She probably would have fumbled and blushed and stammered. With a shake of her head, she pulled a brush through her hair. Exciting men didn't tumble all over themselves to kiss neat, practical-minded women.

But he'd asked to see her again.

Rebecca wasn't certain whether she was disappointed or relieved that he hadn't pressed his advantage and kissed her. She'd been kissed before, held before, of course. But she had a feeling—a very definite feeling—that it wouldn't be the same with Stephen. He might make her want more, offer more, than she had with any other man.

Crossing bridges too soon, she decided as she checked the contents of her big straw bag. She wasn't going to have an affair with him, or with anyone. Even the new, improved Rebecca Malone wasn't the type for a casual affair. But maybe— She caught her lower lip between her teeth. If the time was right she might have a romance she'd remember long after she left Greece.

For now, she was ready, but it was much too early to go down. It would hardly make her look like a well-traveled woman of the world if she popped down to the lobby and paced for ten minutes. This was her fantasy, after all. She didn't want him to think she was inexperienced and overeager.

Only the knock on the door prevented her from changing her mind about her outfit one more time.

"Hello." Stephen studied her for a moment, unsmiling. He'd nearly been certain he'd exaggerated, but she was just as vibrant, just as exciting, in the morning as she had been in the moonlight. He held out her shoes. "I thought you might need these."

She laughed, remembering her impulsive dunk in the sea. "I didn't realize I'd left them on the beach. Come in a minute." With a neatness ingrained in her from childhood, she turned to take them to the bedroom closet. "I'm ready to go if you are."

Stephen lifted a brow. He preferred promptness, but he never expected it in anyone but a business associate. "I've got a Jeep waiting. Some of the roads are rough."

"Sounds great." Rebecca came out again, carrying her bag and a flat-brimmed straw hat. She handed

Stephen his jacket, neatly folded. "I forgot to give this back to you last night." Should she offer to have it cleaned? she wondered when he only continued to look at her. Fiddling with the strap of her bag, she decided against it. "Does taking pictures bother you?"

"No, why?"

"Good, because I take lots of them. I can't seem to stop myself."

She wasn't kidding. As Stephen drove up into the hills, she took shots of everything. Sheep, tomato plants, olive groves and straggly sage. He stopped so that she could walk out near the edge of a cliff and look down at a small village huddled near the sea.

She wouldn't be able to capture it on film; she wasn't clever enough. But she knew she'd never forget that light, so pure, so clear, or the contrast between the orange tiled roofs and the low white-washed walls and the deep, dangerous blue of the water that flung itself against the weathered rock that rose into harsh crags. A stork, legs tucked, glided over the water, where fishing boats bobbed.

There were nets drying on the beach and children playing. Flowers bloomed and tangled where the wind had planted them, more spectacular than any planned arrangement could ever be.

"It's beautiful." Her throat tightened with emotion, and with a longing she couldn't have defined. "So calm. You imagine women baking black bread and the men coming home smelling of fish and the sea. It looks as though it hasn't changed in a hundred years."

"Very little." He glanced down himself, surprised and more than a little pleased that she would be touched by something so simple. "We cling to antiquity."

"I haven't seen the Acropolis yet, but I don't think it could be any more spectacular than this." She lifted her face, delighted by the way the wind whipped at it. Here, high above the sea, she absorbed everything—the salty, rough-edged bite of the wind, the clarity of color and sound, and the man beside her. Letting her camera dangle from its strap, she turned to him. "I haven't thanked you for taking the time to show me all of this."

He took her hand, not to raise it to his lips, just to hold it. It was a link he hadn't known he wanted. "I'm enjoying seeing the familiar through someone else's eyes. Your eyes."

Suddenly the edge of the cliff seemed too close, the sun too hot. Could he do that just by touching her? With an effort, Rebecca smiled, keeping her voice light. "If you ever come to Philadelphia, I'll do the same for you."

It was odd. She'd looked almost frightened for a moment. Fragile and frightened. Stephen had always carefully avoided women who were easily bruised. "I'll consider that a promise."

They continued to drive, over roads that jarred and climbed and twisted. She saw her first of the *agrimi*, the wild goat of Greece, and the rocky pastures dotted with sturdy sheep. And everywhere, rich and defiant, was the intense color of flowers.

He didn't complain when she asked him to stop so that she could snap pictures of tiny blue star blossoms that pushed their way through cracks in the rock. He listened to her delight as she framed a thick, thorny stem topped with a ragged yellow flower. It made him realize, and regret, that it had been years since he'd taken the time to look closely at the small, vital things that grew around him.

He looked now at Rebecca standing in the sunlight, her hat fluttering around her face and her laugh dancing on the air.

Often the road clung to cliffs that plunged dizzily into the sea. Rebecca, who was too timid to fight rush-hour traffic, found it exhilarating.

She felt almost like another person. She *was* another person, she thought, laughing as she held on to her hat to keep the wind from snatching it away.

"I love it!" she shouted over the wind and the noise of the engine. "It's wild and old and incredible. Like no place I've ever been."

Still laughing, she lifted her camera and snapped his picture as he drove. He wore sunglasses with amber lenses and had a cigar clamped between his teeth. The wind blew through his hair and chased the smoke behind them. He stopped the Jeep, took the camera and snapped a picture of her in turn.

"Hungry?"

She dragged her tousled hair back from her face. "Starving."

He leaned over to open her door. A current passed through her, sharp and electric, strong enough to make him pause with his arm across her body and his face close to hers. It was there again, he thought as he waited and watched. The awareness, ripe and seductive. And the innocence, as alluring as it was contradictory. In a test—a test for both of them—he lifted a hand to stroke her cheek. It was as soft as her scent.

"Are you afraid of me, Rebecca?"

"No." That was true; she was nearly sure of it. "Should I be?"

He didn't smile. Through the amber lenses she saw that his eyes were very intense. "I'm not entirely sure." When he pulled away he heard her release an unsteady breath. He wasn't feeling completely steady himself. "We'll have to walk a little first."

Confused, her mind churning, she stepped out onto the dirt path. A woman on a simple date didn't tremble every time a man got close, Rebecca told herself as Stephen lifted the picnic basket out of the back. She was behaving like a teenager, not a grown woman.

Troubled by his own thoughts, Stephen stopped beside her. He hesitated, then held out a hand. It felt good, simply good, when she put hers in it.

They walked through an olive grove in a companionable silence while the sun streamed down on dusty leaves and rocky ground. There was no sound of the sea here, but when the wind was right she could hear the screech of a gull far away. The island was small, but here it seemed uninhabited.

"I haven't had a picnic in years." Rebecca spread the cloth. "And never in an olive grove." She glanced around, wanting to remember every leaf and pebble. "Are we trespassing?"

"No." Stephen took a bottle of white wine from the basket. Rebecca left him to it and started rummaging in search of food.

"Do you know the owner?"

"I'm the owner." He drew the cork with a gentle pop.

"Oh." She looked around again. It should have occurred to her that he would own something impressive, different, exciting. "It sounds romantic. Owning an olive grove."

He lifted a brow. He owned a number of them, but he had never thought of them as romantic. They were simply profitable. He offered her a glass, then tapped it with his own. "To romance, then."

She swept down her lashes, battling shyness. To Stephen, the gesture was only provocative. "I hope you're hungry," she began, knowing she was talking too fast. "It all looks wonderful." She took a quick sip of wine to ease her dry throat, then set it aside to finish unpacking the basket.

There were sweet black olives as big as a man's thumb, and there was a huge slab of sharp cheese. There were cold lamb and hunks of bread, and fruit so fresh it could have been just plucked from the stem.

Gradually she began to relax again.

"You've told me very little about yourself." Stephen topped off her wine and watched her bite into a ripe red plum. "I know little more than that you come from Philadelphia and enjoy traveling."

What could she tell him? A man like him was bound to be bored with the life story of the painfully ordinary Rebecca Malone. Lies had never come easily to her, so she skirted between fact and fiction. "There's little more. I grew up in Philadelphia. I lost both of my parents when I was a teenager, and I lived with my aunt Jeannie. She was very dear, and she made the loss bearable."

"It's painful." He flicked his lighter at the end of a cigar, remembering not only the pain, but also the fury he had felt when his father had died and left him orphaned at sixteen. "It steals childhood."

"Yes." So he understood that. It made her feel close to him, close and comfortable. "Maybe that's why I like to travel. Every time you see a new place you can be a child again."

"So you don't look for roots?"

She glanced at him then. He was leaning back against the trunk of a tree, smoking lazily, watching carefully. "I don't know what I'm looking for."

"Is there a man?"

She moved her shoulders, determined not to be embarrassed. "No."

He took her hand, drawing her closer. "No one?"

"No, I…" She wasn't certain what she would have said, but could say nothing at all when he turned her palm upward and pressed his lips to its center. She felt the fire burst there, in her hand, then race everywhere.

"You're very responsive, Rebecca." He lowered her hand but kept it in his. He could feel the heat, but he wasn't sure whether it had sprung to her skin or to his own. "If there's no one, the men in your Philadelphia must be very slow."

"I've been too…busy."

His lips curved at that. There was a tremor in her voice, and there was passion in her eyes. "Busy?"

"Yes." Afraid she'd make a fool of herself, she drew her hand back. "This was wonderful." Trying to calm herself, she pushed a hand through her hair. "You know what I need?"

"No. Tell me."

"Another picture." She sprang to her feet and, steadier, grinned. "A memento of my first picnic in an olive grove. Let's see…you can stand right over there. The sun's good in front of that tree, and I should be able to frame in that section of the grove."

Amused, Stephen tapped out his cigar. "How much more film do you have?"

"This is the last roll—but I have scads back at the hotel." She flicked him a quick laughing glance. "I warned you."

"So you did." Competent hands, he thought as he watched her focus and adjust. He hadn't realized he could be as attracted to competence as he was to beauty. She mumbled to herself, tossing her head back so that her hair swung, then settled. His stomach tightened without warning.

Good God, he wanted her. She'd done nothing to make him burn and strain this way. He couldn't accuse her of taunting or teasing, and yet…he felt taunted. He felt teased. For the first time in his life he felt totally seduced by a woman who had done nothing more than give him a few smiles and a little companionship.

Even now she was chattering away as she secured her camera to the limb of a tree. Talking easily, as though they were just friends, as though she felt nothing more than a light, unimportant affection. But he'd seen it. Stephen felt his blood heat as he remembered the quick flash of arousal he'd seen on her face. He'd see it again. And more.

"I'm going to set the timer," Rebecca went on, blissfully unaware of Stephen's thoughts. "All you have to do is stand there. Once I get this damn thing set, I'm going to run over so it'll take one of both—There." She interrupted herself, crossed her fingers and ran to Stephen's side in a dash. "Unless I messed up, it'll snap all by itself in—"

The rest of the words slid down her throat as he crushed her against him and captured her mouth.

Chapter 3

Heat. Light. Speed. Rebecca felt them, felt each separate, distinct sensation. Urgency. Demand. Impatience. She tasted them, as clearly as wild honey, on his lips. Though she'd never experienced it, she had known exactly what it would be like to be with him, mouth to mouth and need to need.

In an instant the world had narrowed from what could be seen and understood to a pure, seamless blanket of emotion. It cloaked her, not softly, not in comfort, but tightly, hotly, irresistibly. Caught between fear and delight, she lifted a hand to his cheek.

God, she was sweet. Even as he dragged her closer, aroused by the simplicity of her acceptance, he was struck by—disarmed by—her sweetness. There had been a hesitation, almost too brief to be measured, before her lips had parted beneath his. Parted, invited, accepted.

There was a sigh, so soft it could barely be heard, as she stroked her hands up his back to his shoulders. Curious, simple, generous. A man could drown in such sweetness, fall prisoner to such pliancy. And be saved by it. Beneath the patterned shade of the olive tree, she gave him more than passion. She gave him hope.

Charmed, he murmured some careless Greek phrase lovers might exchange. The words meant nothing to her, but the sound of them on the still air, the feel of them stroking across her lips…seduction. Glorious seduction.

Pleasure burst in her blood, in her head, in her heart, thousands of tiny bubbles of it, until she was straining against him.

The quiet explosion rocked him. It tightened his chest, fuddled his mind. She fitted into his arms as if she'd been born for him. As if, somehow, they had known each other before, loved before, hungered before. Something seemed to erupt between them, something molten, powerful, dangerous. But it wasn't new. It was ancient, a whispering echo of ageless passions.

She began to tremble. How could this be so right, so familiar? It wasn't possible to feel safe and threatened at the same time. But she did. She clung to him while a dim, floating image danced through her head. She had kissed him before. Just like this. As her mind spun, she heard her own mindless murmurs answer his. As freely, as inescapably as the sun poured light, response flowed from her. She couldn't stop it. Frightened by her sudden loss of control, she struggled against him, against herself.

He slipped his hands up to her shoulders, but not to free her, to look at her. To look at how their coming together had changed her. It had changed him. Passion had made her eyes heavy, seductive. Fear had clouded them. Her lips were full, softened and parted by his. Her breath shivered through them. Under his hands he could feel the heat of her skin and the quick, involuntary trembling of her muscles.

No pretense here, he decided as he studied her. He was holding both innocence and delight in his hands.

"Stephen, I—"

"Again."

Then his face filled her vision and she was lost.

Differently. Should she have known that one man could hold one woman in so many different ways? That one man could kiss one woman with such stunning variety? There was gentleness now, as familiar and as novel as the urgency. His lips persuaded rather than demanded. They savored instead of devouring. Her surrender came as quietly, and as unmistakably, as her earlier passion. The trembling stopped; the fear vanished. With a complete trust that surprised them both, she leaned against him, giving.

More aroused by her serenity than by the storm that had come before, Stephen pulled back. He had to, or what had begun would finish without either of them saying a word. As he swore and pulled out a cigar, Rebecca placed a hand on the olive tree for support.

Moments, she thought. It had been only moments, and yet she felt as though years had passed, racing backward or forward, perhaps spinning in circles. In a place like this, with a man like this, what difference did it make what year it was? What century?

Half terrified, she lifted a hand to her lips. Despite her fear, they curved under her touch. She could still taste him. Still feel him. And nothing, nothing, would ever be quite the same again.

He stared out at the rough and dusty land he'd known as a boy, and beyond, to the stark, tumbling rocks where he and other wild things had climbed.

What was he doing with her? Furious with himself, he drew on the cigar. What was he feeling? It was new, and far from comfortable. And it was comfort he preferred, he reminded himself. Comfort and freedom. Bringing himself under control, he turned to her again, determined to treat what had happened as a man should—lightly.

She just stood there, with the sun and the shade falling over her. There was neither recrimination nor invitation in her eyes. She didn't flinch or step forward, but merely stood, watching him with the faintest of smiles, as if… As if, Stephen realized, she knew what questions he was asking himself—and the answers.

"It grows late."

She felt the ache and fought not to let it show on her face. "I guess you're right." She dragged a hand through her hair—it was the first sign of her agitation—then walked over to pick up her camera. "I should have a picture to remember all this by," she said, forcing brightness into her voice. Her breath caught when his fingers closed over her arm and whirled her around.

"Who are you?" he demanded. "What are you?"

"I don't know what you mean." The emotion burst out before she could stop it. "I don't know what you want."

With one jerk he had her tumbling against him. "You know what I want."

Her heart was in her throat, beating wildly. She found

it strange that it was not fear but desire that she felt. She hadn't known she was capable of feeling a need that was so unreasonable, so reckless. It was almost purifying to experience it, and to see it mirrored in his eyes.

"It takes more than one afternoon." Didn't it? Her voice rose as she tried to convince herself. "It takes more than a picnic and a walk in the moonlight for me."

"One moment the temptress, the next the outraged innocent. Do you do it to intrigue me, Rebecca?" She shook her head, and his fingers tightened. "It works," he murmured. "You've hardly been out of my mind since I first saw you. I want to make love with you, here, in the sun."

Color flooded her face, not because she was embarrassed, but because she could imagine it, perfectly. And then what? Carefully she leveled her breathing. Whatever impulses she had followed, whatever bridges she had burned, she still needed answers.

"No." It cost her to go against her own needs and say it. "Not when I'm unsure and you're angry." She took a deep breath and kept her eyes on him. "You're hurting me, Stephen. I don't think you mean to."

Slowly he released her arm. He was angry, furious, but not at her refusal. The anger stemmed from the need she pulled from him, a need that had come too fast and too strong for him to channel. "We'll go back."

Rebecca merely nodded, then knelt to gather the remains of the picnic.

He was a busy man, much too busy to brood about a woman he barely knew and didn't understand at all. That was what Stephen told himself. He had reports to read, calls to make and paperwork—which he had both a talent and a distaste for—to deal with. A couple of simple kisses weren't enough to take a man's mind off his work.

But there hadn't been anything simple about them. Disgusted, Stephen pushed away from his desk and wandered to the terrace doors. He'd left them open because the breeze, and the fragrances it brought, helped him forget he was obligated to be inside.

For days he'd worked his way through his responsibilities, trying to ignore the nagging itch at the back of his mind—the itch that was Rebecca. There was no reason for him to stay on Corfu. He could have handled his business in Athens, or Crete, or in London, for that matter. Still, he'd made no plans to leave, though he'd also made no attempt to approach her.

She…concerned him, he decided. To be drawn to an attractive woman was as natural as breathing. To have the attraction cause discomfort, confusion, even annoyance was anything but natural. A taste of her hadn't been enough. Yet he hesitated.

She was…mysterious. Perhaps that was why he couldn't push her from his mind. On the surface she appeared to be an attractive, free-spirited woman who grabbed life with both hands. Yet there were undercurrents. The hints of innocence, of shyness. The sweetness. The complexity of her kept him wondering, thinking, imagining.

Perhaps that was her trick. Women had them…were entitled to them. It was a waste of time to begrudge them their illusions and their feminine magic. More than a waste of time, it was foolish, when a man could enjoy the benefits. But there was more, and somehow less, to Rebecca than innate feminine magic.

When he had kissed her, though it had been the first time, it had been like coming back to a lover, to a love, after a painful separation. When his lips had found hers, something had filled him. A heat, an impatience, a knowledge.

He knew her, knew more than her name and her background and the color of her eyes. He knew all of her. Yet he knew nothing.

Fantasies, he told himself. He didn't have time for them. Leaning a hip against the railing, he lit a cigar and watched the sea.

As always, it pulled at him, bringing back memories of a childhood that had been careless and too short. There were times, rare times, when he allowed himself to regret. Times when the sun was a white flash of heat and the water was blue and endless. His father had taught him a great deal. How to fish, how to see both beauty and excitement in new places, how to drink like a man.

Fifteen years, Stephen thought, a smile ghosting around his mouth. He still missed him, missed the companionship, the robust laughter. They had been friends, as well as parent and child, with a bond as easy, and as strong, as any Stephen had ever known. But his father had died as he would have wanted to, at sea and in his prime.

He would have taken one look at Rebecca, rolled his eyes, kissed his fingers and urged his son to enjoy. But Stephen wasn't the boy he had once been. He was more cautious, more aware of consequences. If a man dived into the sea, he should know the depth and the currents.

Then he saw her, coming from the sea. Water ran down her body, glistening in the strong sun, sparkling against skin that had warmed in the last few days to a dusky gold. As he looked, as he wanted, he felt his muscles clench, one by one, shoulders, stomach, thighs. Without his being aware, his fingers tightened, snapping the cigar in two. He hadn't known that desire could arouse a reaction so akin to anger.

She stopped, and though he knew she was unaware of him, she might easily have been posing. To taunt, to tease, to invite. As drops of water slid down her, she stretched, lifting her face skyward. Her skimpy suit rested low over her boyish hips, shifted enticingly over the subtle curve of her breasts. At that moment, she was totally absorbed in her own pleasure and as unselfconscious as any young animal standing in the sun. Nothing had ever been so alluring.

Then, slowly, seductively, she combed her fingers through her hair, smiling, as if she enjoyed the wet, silky feel of it. Watching her, he felt the air back up and clog in his lungs. He could have murdered her for it, for making him want so unreasonably what he did not yet understand.

She plucked a long, mannish T-shirt from a straw bag and, after tugging it on, strolled barefoot into the hotel.

He stood there, waiting for the need to pass. But it built, layered with an ache that infuriated him and a longing that baffled him.

He should ignore her. Instinct warned him that if he didn't his life would never be the same. She was nothing more than a distraction, a momentary impulse he should resist. He should turn away, go back to work. He had commitments, obligations, and no time to waste on fantasies. With an oath, he tossed the broken cigar over the rail.

There were times, he thought, when a man had to trust in fate and dive in.

Chapter 4

Rebecca had hardly shut the door behind her before she turned back to answer the knock. The sun and the water had left her pleasantly tired, but all thoughts of a lazy catnap vanished when she saw Stephen.

He looked wonderful. Cool, a little windblown, intense. For days she'd wondered about him, wondered and wished. She felt her pulse skip and her lips curve just at the sight of him. With an effort, she kept her voice breezy.

"Hello. I wasn't sure you were still on the island."

It wasn't really a lie, she told herself. An offhand inquiry had assured her that Mr. Nickodemus hadn't checked out, but she hadn't actually seen him.

"I saw you come up from the beach."

"Oh." Unconsciously she tugged at the hem of her cover-up. To Stephen the small gesture was one more contradictory signal. "I can't seem to get enough of the sun and the sea. Would you like to come in?"

By way of an answer he stepped through and shut the door behind him. It made a very quiet, a very final sound. Rebecca's carefully built poise began to crumble. "I never thanked you for the flowers." She made a gesture indicating the vase near the window, then brought her hands back together and linked them in front of her. "They're still beautiful. I…I thought I might run into you, in the dining room, on the beach, or…" Her words trailed off when he lifted a hand to her hair.

"I've been busy." He watched her eyes, eyes that were as clear as rainwater, blur at the slight touch. "Business."

It was ridiculous, she knew, but she wasn't at all sure she could speak. "If you have to work, I doubt you could pick a more beautiful place."

He stepped closer. She smelled of the water and the sun. "You're enjoying the resort, and the island."

Her hand was in his now, caught lightly. It took only that to make her knees weak. "Yes, very much."

"Perhaps you'd like to see it from a different perspective." Deliberately, wanting to test them both, he lifted her hand to his lips. He grazed her knuckles—it was barely a whisper of contact—and felt the jolt. She felt it, and he could see that she did, so it couldn't just be his imagination. "Spend the day with me tomorrow on my boat."

"What?"

He smiled, delighted with her response. "Will you come with me?"

Anywhere. Astonished, she stepped back. "I haven't any plans."

"Good." He closed the distance between them again. Her hands fluttered up in flustered defense, then settled again when he made no attempt to touch her. "Then I'll make them for you. I'll come for you in the morning. Nine?"

A boat. He'd said something about a boat. Rebecca drew in a deep breath and tried to pull herself together. This wasn't like her—going off into daydreams, feeling weak-kneed, being flooded with waves of desire. And it felt wonderful.

"I'd like that." She gave him what she hoped was an easy woman-of-the-world smile.

"Until tomorrow, then." He started for the door, then turned, a hand on the knob. "Rebecca, don't forget your camera."

She waited until he'd closed the door before she spun in three quick circles.

When Stephen had said "boat," Rebecca had pictured a trim little cabin cruiser. Instead, she stepped onto the glossy mahogany deck of a streamlined hundred-foot yacht.

"You could live on this," Rebecca said, then wished she'd bitten her tongue. But he only laughed.

"I often do."

"Welcome aboard, sir," a white-uniformed man with a British accent said.

"Grady. This is my guest, Miss Malone."

"Ma'am." Grady's cool British reserve didn't flicker for an instant, but Rebecca felt herself being summed up.

"Cast off when you're ready." Stephen took Rebecca's arm. "Would you like a tour?"

"Yes." A yacht. She was on a yacht. It took all her willpower to keep her camera in the bag. "I'd love to see it all."

He took her below, through four elegantly appointed cabins. Her comment about living on board had been said impulsively, but she could see now that it could be done easily, even luxuriously.

Above there was a large glassed-in cabin in which one could stretch out comfortably, out of the sun, and watch the sea, whatever the weather. She had known that there were people who lived like this. Part of her job had been to research and calculate so that those who did paid the government as little as possible. But to be there, to see it, to be surrounded by it, was entirely different from adding figures on paper.

There was a masculine feel to the cabin, to the entire boat—leather, wood, muted colors. There were shelves filled with books and a fully stocked bar, as well as a stereo system.

"All the comforts of home," Rebecca murmured, but she'd noted that there were doors and panels that could be secured in case of rough weather. What would it be like to ride out a storm at sea, to watch the rain lash the windows and feel the deck heave?

She gave a quick gasp when she felt the floor move. Stephen took her arm again to steady her.

"We're under way." Curious, he turned her to face him. "Are you afraid of boats?"

"No." She could hardly admit that the biggest one she'd been on before this had been a two-passenger canoe at summer camp. "It just startled me." Under way, she thought as she prayed that her system would settle. It was such an exciting, adventurous word. "Can we go out on deck? I'd like to watch."

It was exciting. She felt it the moment the wind hit her face and rushed through her hair. At the rail, she leaned out, delighted to see the island shrink and the sea spread. Because she couldn't resist and he didn't laugh at her, she took half a dozen pictures as the boat sped away from land.

"It's better than flying," she decided. "You feel a part of it. Look." With a laugh, she pointed. "The birds are chasing us."

Stephen didn't bother to glance at the gulls that wheeled and called above the boat's wake. He preferred to watch the delight and excitement bloom on her face. "Do you always enjoy so completely?"

"Yes." She tossed her hair away from her face, only to have the wind rush it back again. With another laugh, she stretched back from the railing, her face lifted to the sun. "Oh, yes."

Irresistible. With his hands at her waist, he spun her toward him. It was like holding a live wire. The shock rippled from her to him, then back again. "Everything?" His fingers spread over her back and, with the slightest pressure, moved her forward until their thighs met.

"I don't know." Instinctively she braced her hands on his shoulders. "I haven't tried everything." But she wanted to. Held close, with the sound of the water and the wind, she wanted to. Without giving a thought to self-preservation, she leaned toward him.

He swore, lightly, under his breath. Rebecca jolted back as if he had shouted at her. Stephen caught her hand as he nodded to the steward, who had just approached with drinks. "Thank you, Victor. Just leave everything." His voice was smooth enough, but Rebecca felt the tension in his hand as he led her to a chair.

He probably thought she was a fool, she decided. All but tumbling into his arms every time he touched her. He was obviously a man of the world—and a kind man, she added as she sipped her mimosa. Not all powerful men spoke kindly to those who worked for them. Her lips curved, a little wryly, as she sipped again. She knew that firsthand.

His body was in turmoil. Stephen couldn't remember, even in his youth, having had a woman affect him so irrationally. He knew how to persuade, how to seduce— and always with finesse. But whenever he was around this woman for more than five minutes he felt like a stallion being spurred and curbed at the same time.

And he was fascinated. Fascinated by the ease with which she went into his arms, by the trust he saw when he looked down into her eyes. As he had in the olive grove, he found himself believing he'd looked into those eyes, those rainwater-clear eyes, a hundred times before.

Still churning, he took out a cigar. The thought was fanciful, but his desire was very real. If there couldn't be finesse, perhaps there could be candor.

"I want you, Rebecca."

She felt her heart stop, then start up again with slow, dull throbs. Carefully she took another sip, then cleared her throat. "I know." It amazed her, flattered her, terrified her.

She seemed so cool. He envied her. "Will you come with me, to my cabin?"

She looked at him then. Her heart and her head were

giving very different answers. It sounded so easy, so…natural. If there was a man she could give herself to, wholly, he was with her now. Complications, what complications there were, were her own.

But no matter how far she had run from Philadelphia and her own strict upbringing, there were still lines she couldn't cross.

"I can't."

"Can't?" He lit his cigar, astonished that they were discussing making love as though it were as casual a choice as what dinner entrée to chose. "Or won't?"

She drew a breath. Her palms were damp on the glass, and she set it down. "Can't. I want to." Her eyes, huge and lake-pale, clung to his. "I very much want to, but…"

"But?"

"I know so little about you." She picked up her glass again because her empty hands tended to twist together. "Hardly more than your name, that you own an olive grove and like the sea. It's not enough."

"Then I'll tell you more."

She relaxed enough to smile. "I don't know what to ask."

He leaned back in his chair, the tension dissolving as quickly as it had built. She could do that to him with nothing more than a smile. He knew no one who could excite and solace with so little effort.

"Do you believe in fate, Rebecca? In something un-expected, even unlooked-for, often a small thing that completely and irrevocably changes one's life?"

She thought of her aunt's death and her own unchar-acteristic decisions. "Yes. Yes, I do."

"Good." His gaze skimmed over her face, quickly,

then more leisurely. "I'd nearly forgotten that I believe it, too. Then I saw you, sitting alone."

There were ways and ways to seduce, she was discovering. A look, a tone, could be every bit as devastating as a caress. She wanted him more in that moment than she had ever known she could want anything. To give herself time, and distance, she rose and walked to the rail.

Even her silence aroused him. She had said she knew too little about him. He knew even less of her. And he didn't care. It was dangerous, possibly even destructive, but he didn't care. As he watched her with the wind billowing her shirt and her hair he realized that he didn't give a damn about where she had come from, where she had been, what she had done.

When lightning strikes, it destroys, though it blazes with power. Rising, he went to her and stood, as she did, facing the sea.

"When I was young, very young," he began, "there was another moment that changed things. My father was a man for the water. He lived for it. Died for it." When he went on it was almost as if he were speaking to himself now, remembering. Rebecca turned her head to look at him. "I was ten or eleven. Everything was going well, the nets were full. My father and I were walking along the beach. He stopped, dipped his hand into the water, made a fist and opened it. 'You can't hold it,' he said to me. 'No matter how you try or how you love or how you sweat.' Then he dug into the sand. It was wet and clung together in his hand. 'But this,' he said, 'a man can hold.' We never spoke of it again. When my time came, I turned my back on the sea and held the land."

"It was right for you."

"Yes." He lifted a hand to catch at the ends of her hair. "It was right. Such big, quiet eyes you have, Rebecca," he murmured. "Have they seen enough, I wonder, to know what's right for you?"

"I guess I've been a little slow in starting to look." Her blood was pounding thickly. She would have stepped back, but he shifted so that she was trapped between him and the rail.

"You tremble when I touch you." He slid his hands up her arms, then down until their hands locked. "Have you any idea how exciting that is?"

Her chest tightened, diminishing her air even as the muscles in her legs went limp. "Stephen, I meant it when I said…" He brushed his lips gently over her temple. "I can't. I need to…" He feathered a kiss along her jawline, softly. "To think."

He felt her fingers go lax in his. She was suddenly fragile, outrageously vulnerable, irresistibly tempting. "When I kissed you the first time I gave you no choice." His lips trailed over her face, light as a whisper, circling, teasing, avoiding her mouth. "You have one now."

He was hardly touching her. A breath, a whisper, a mere promise of a touch. The slow, subtle passage of his lips over her skin couldn't have been called a kiss, could never have been called a demand. She had only to push away to end the torment. And the glory.

A choice? Had he told her she had a choice? "No, I don't," she murmured as she turned to find his lips with hers.

No choice, no past, no future. Only now. She felt the present, with all its needs and hungers, well up inside her. The kiss was instantly hot, instantly desperate. His heart pounded fast and hard against hers, thunderous now, as he twisted a hand in her hair to pull her head back. To plunder. No one had ever taken her like this. No one had ever warned her that a touch of violence could be so exciting. Her gasp of surprise turned into a moan of pleasure as his tongue skimmed over hers.

He thought of lightning bolts again, thought of that flash of power and light. She was electric in his arms, sparking, sizzling. Her scent, as soft, as seductive, as a whisper, clouded his mind, even as the taste of her heightened his appetite.

She was all woman, she was every woman, and yet she was like no other. He could hear each quick catch of her breath above the roar of the motor. With her name on his lips, he pressed them to the vulnerable line of her throat, where the skin was heated from the sun and as delicate as water.

She might have slid bonelessly to the deck if his body hadn't pressed hers so firmly against the rail. In wonder, in panic, she felt his muscles turn to iron wherever they touched her. Never before had she felt so fragile, so at the mercy of her own desires. The sea was as calm as glass, but she felt herself tossed, tumbled, wrecked. With a sigh that was almost a sob, she wrapped her arms around him.

It was the defenselessness of the gesture that pulled him back from the edge. He must have been mad. For a moment he'd been close, much too close, to dragging her down to the deck without a thought to her wishes or to the consequences. With his eyes closed, he held her, feeling the erratic beat of her heart, hearing her shallow, shuddering breath.

Perhaps he was still mad, Stephen thought. Even as

the ragged edges of desire eased, something deeper and far more dangerous bloomed.

He wanted her, in a way no man could safely want a woman. Forever.

Fate, he thought again as he stroked her hair. It seemed he was falling in love whether he wished it or not. A few hours with her and he felt more than he had ever imagined he could feel.

There had been a few times in his life when he had seen and desired on instinct alone. What he had seen and desired, he had taken. Just as he would take her. But when he took, he meant to keep.

Carefully he stepped back. "Maybe neither of us has a choice." He dipped his hands into his pockets. "And if I touch you again, here, now, I won't give you one."

Unable to pretend, knowing they were shaking, she pushed her hands through her hair. She didn't bother to disguise the tremor in her voice. She wouldn't have known how. "I won't want one." She saw his eyes darken quickly, dangerously, but she didn't know his hands were balled into fists, straining.

"You make it difficult for me."

A long, shuddering breath escaped her. No one had ever wanted her this way. Probably no one ever would again. "I'm sorry. I don't mean to."

"No." Deliberately he relaxed his hands. "I don't think you do. That's one of the things about you I find most intriguing. I will have you, Rebecca." He saw something flicker in her eyes…. Excitement? Panic? A combination of the two, perhaps. "Because I'm sure of it, because I know you're sure of it, I'll do my best to give you a little more time."

Her natural humor worked through the sliver of unease she felt. "I'm not sure whether I should thank you politely or run like hell."

He grinned, surprising himself, then flicked a finger down her cheek. "I wouldn't advise running, *matia mou*. I'd only catch you."

She was sure of that, too. One look at his face, even with the smile that softened it, and she knew. Kind, yes, but with a steely underlying ruthlessness. "Then I'll go with the thank-you."

"You're welcome." Patience, he realized, would have to be developed. And quickly. "Would you like to swim? There's a bay. We're nearly there."

The water might, just might, cool her off. "I'd love it."

Chapter 5

The water was cool and mirror-clear. Rebecca lowered herself into it with a sigh of pure pleasure. Back in Philadelphia she would have been at her desk, calculator clicking, the jacket of her neat business suit carefully smoothed over the back of her chair. Her figures would always tally, her forms would always be properly filed.

The dependable, efficient Miss Malone.

Instead, she was swimming in a crystal-clear bay, letting the water cool and the sun heat. Ledgers and accounts were worlds away. Here, as close as a handspan, was a man who was teaching her everything she would ever want to know about needs, desires, and the fragility of the heart.

He couldn't know it, she thought. She doubted she'd ever have the courage to tell him that he was the only one who had ever made her tremble and burn. A man as physically aware as he would only be uncomfortable knowing he held an inexperienced woman in his arms.

The water lapped around her with a sound as quiet as her own sigh. But he didn't know, because when she was in his arms she didn't feel awkward and inexperienced. She felt beautiful, desirable and reckless.

With a laugh, Rebecca dipped under the surface to let the water, and the freedom, surround her. Who would have believed it?

"Does it always take so little to make you laugh?"

Rebecca ran a hand over her slicked-back hair. Stephen was treading water beside her, smoothly, hardly making a ripple. His skin was dark gold, glistening-wet. His hair was streaked by the sun and dampened by the water, which was almost exactly the color of his eyes. She had to suppress an urge to just reach out and touch.

"A secluded inlet, a beautiful sky, an interesting man." With another sigh, she kicked her legs up so that she could float. "It doesn't seem like so little to me." She studied the vague outline of the mountains, far out of reach. "I promised myself that no matter where I went, what I did, I'd never take anything for granted again."

There was something in the way she said it, some hint of sadness, that pulled at him. The urge to comfort wasn't completely foreign in him, but he hadn't had much practice at it. "Was there a man who hurt you?"

Her lips curved at that, but he couldn't know that she was laughing at herself. Naturally, she'd dated. They had been polite, cautious evenings, usually with little interest on either side. She'd been dull, or at least she had never worked up the nerve to spread her wings.

Once or twice, when she'd felt a tug, she'd been too shy, too much the efficient Rebecca Malone, to do anything about it.

With him, everything was different. Because she loved him. She didn't know how, she didn't know why, but she loved him as much as any woman could love any man.

"No. There's no one." She closed her eyes, trusting the water to carry her. "When my parents died, it hurt. It hurt so badly that I suppose I pulled back from life. I thought it was important that I be a responsible adult, even though I wasn't nearly an adult yet."

Strange that she hadn't thought of it quite that way until she'd stopped being obsessively responsible. Stranger still was how easy it was to tell him what she'd never even acknowledged herself.

"My aunt Jeannie was kind and considerate and loving, but she'd forgotten what it was like to be a young girl. Suddenly I realized I'd missed being young, lazy, foolish, all the things everyone's entitled to be at least once. I decided to make up for it."

Her hair was spread out and drifting on the water. Her eyes were closed, and her face was sheened with water. Not beautiful, Stephen told himself. She was too angular for real beauty. But she was fascinating…in looks, in philosophy…more, in the open-armed way she embraced whatever crossed her path.

He found himself looking around the inlet as he hadn't bothered to look at anything in years. He could see the sun dancing on the surface, could see the ripples spreading and growing from the quiet motion of their bodies. Farther away was the narrow curving strip of white beach, deserted now, but for a few birds fluttering over the sand. It was quiet, almost unnaturally quiet, the only sound the soft, monotonous slap of water against sand. And he was relaxed, totally, mind and body. Perhaps he, too, had forgotten what it was like to be young and foolish.

On impulse he put a hand on her shoulder and pushed her under.

She came up sputtering, dragging wet hair out of her eyes. He grinned at her and calmly continued to tread water. "It was too easy."

She tilted her head, considering him and the distance between them. Challenge leaped into her eyes, sparked with amusement. "It won't be the next time."

His grin only widened. When he moved, he moved fast, streaking under and across the water like an eel. Rebecca had time for a quick squeal. Dragging in a deep breath, she kicked out. He caught her ankle, but she was ready. Unresisting, she let him pull her under. Then, instead of fighting her way back to the surface, she wrapped her arms around him and sent them both rolling in an underwater wrestling match. They were still tangled, her arms around him, her hands hooked over his shoulders, when they surfaced.

"We're even." She gasped for air and shook the water out of her eyes.

"How do you figure?"

"If we'd had a mat I'd have pinned you. Want to go for two out of three?"

"I might." He felt her legs tangle with his as she kicked out lazily. "But for now I prefer this."

He was going to kiss her again. She saw it in his eyes, felt it in the slight tensing of the arm that locked them torso to torso. She wasn't sure she was ready. More, she was afraid she was much too ready.

"Stephen?"

"Hmm?" His lips were a breath away from hers. Then he found himself underwater again, his arms empty. He should have been furious. He nearly was when he pushed to surface. She was shoulder-deep in the water, a few feet away. Her laughter rolled over him, young, delighted, unapologetic.

"It was too easy." She managed a startled "whoops" when he struck out after her. She might have made it— she had enough of a lead—but he swam as though he'd been born in the water. Still, she was agile, and she almost managed to dodge him, but her laughter betrayed her. She gulped in water, choked, then found herself hauled up into his arms in thigh-deep water.

"I like to win." Deciding it was useless to struggle, she pressed a hand to her heart and gasped for air. "It's a personality flaw. Sometimes I cheat at canasta."

"Canasta?" The last thing he could picture the slim, sexy bundle in his arms doing was spending a quiet evening playing cards.

"I can't help myself." Still breathless, she laid her head on his shoulder. "No willpower."

"I find myself having the same problem." With a careless toss, he sent her flying through the air. She hit the water bottom first.

"I guess I deserved that." She struggled to her feet, water raining off her. "I have to sit." Wading through the water, she headed for the gentle slope of beach. She lay, half in and half out of the water, not caring that the sand would cling to her hair and skin. When he dropped down beside her, she reached out a hand for his. "I don't know when I've had a nicer day."

He looked down to where her fingers linked with his. The gesture had been so easy, so natural. He wondered how it could both comfort and arouse. "It's hardly over."

"It seems like it could last forever." She wanted it to go on and on. Blue skies and easy laughter. Cool water and endless hours. There had been a time, not so long before, when the days had dragged into nights and the nights into days. "Did you ever want to run away?"

With her hand still in his, he lay back to watch a few scattered rags of clouds drift. How long had it been, he wondered, since he'd really watched the sky? "To where?"

"Anywhere. Away from the way things are, away from what you're afraid they'll always be." She closed her eyes and could see herself brewing that first cup of coffee at exactly 7:15, opening the first file at precisely 9:01. "To drop out of sight," she murmured, "and pop up somewhere else, anywhere else, as someone completely different."

"You can't change who you are."

"Oh, but you can." Her tone suddenly urgent, she rose on her elbow. "Sometimes you have to."

He reached up to touch the ends of her hair. "What are you running from?"

"Everything. I'm a coward."

He looked into her eyes. They were so clear, so full of enthusiasm. "I don't think so."

"But you don't know me." A flicker of regret, then uncertainty, ran across her face. "I'm not sure I want you to."

"Don't I?" His fingers tightened on her hair, keeping her still. "There are people and circumstances that don't take months or years before they're understood. I look at you and something fits into place, Rebecca. I don't know why, but it is. I know you." He tugged her down for the lightest, the briefest, of kisses. "And I like what I see."

"Do you?" She smiled. "Really?"

"Do you imagine I spend the day with a woman only because I want to sleep with her?" She shrugged, and though her blush was very faint, he noticed it and was amused by it. How many women, he wondered, could kiss a man into oblivion, then blush? "Being with you, Rebecca, is a difficult pleasure."

She chuckled and began to draw circles in the wet sand. What would he say, what would he think, if he knew what she was? Or, more accurately, what she wasn't? It didn't matter, she told herself. She couldn't let it spoil what there was between them.

"I think that's the most wonderful compliment I've ever had."

"Where have you been?" he murmured.

When she moved restlessly, he held her still. "Don't. I'm not going to touch you. Not yet."

"That's not the problem." With her eyes closed, she tilted her chin up and let the sun beat down on her face. "The problem is, I want you to touch me, so much it frightens me." Taking her time, she sat up, gathering her courage. She wanted to be honest, and she hoped she wouldn't sound like a fool. "Stephen, I don't sleep around. I need you to understand, because this is all happening so quickly. But it's not casual."

He lifted a hand to her chin and turned her to face him. His eyes were as blue as the water, and, to her, as unfathomable. "No, it's not." He made the decision quickly, though he had been turning the idea over in his mind all day. "I have to go to Athens tomorrow. Come with me, Rebecca."

"Athens?" she managed, staring at him.

"Business. A day, two at the most. I'd like you with me." And he was afraid, more than he cared to admit, that when he returned she might be gone.

"I…" What should she say? What was right?

"You told me you'd planned to go." He'd push if necessary. Now that the idea had taken root, Stephen had no intention of going anywhere without her.

"Yes, but I wouldn't want to be in the way while you're working."

"You'll be in my way whether you're here or there."

Her head came up at that, and the look she gave him was both shy and stunning. He stifled the need to take her again, to roll until she was beneath him on the sand. He'd said he'd give her time. Perhaps what he'd really meant was that he needed time himself.

"You'll have your own suite. No strings, Rebecca. Just your company."

"A day or two," she murmured.

"It's a simple matter to have your room held for you here for your return."

Her return. Not his. If he left Corfu tomorrow she would probably never see him again. He was offering her another day, perhaps two. Never take anything for granted, she remembered. Never again.

Athens, she thought. It was true that she had planned to see it before she left Greece. But she would have gone alone. A few days before, that had been what she thought she wanted. The adventure of seeing new places, new people, on her own. Now the thought of going with him, of having him beside her when she first caught sight of the Acropolis, of having him want her with him, changed everything.

"I'd love to go with you." She rose quickly and dived into the water. She was in over her head.

Chapter 6

Athens was neither East nor West. It was spitted meat and spices roasting. It was tall buildings and modern shops. It was narrow, unpaved streets and clamorous bazaars. It had been the scene of revolution and brutality. It was ancient and civilized and passionate.

Rebecca quite simply fell in love at first sight.

She'd been seduced by Paris and charmed by London, but in Athens she lost her heart. She wanted to see everything at once, from sunrise to moonlight, and the heat-drenched afternoon between.

All that first morning, while Stephen was immersed in business meetings, she wandered. The hotel he'd chosen was lovely, but she was drawn to the streets and the people. Somehow she didn't feel like a visitor here. She felt like someone who had returned home after a long, long journey. Athens was waiting for her, ready to welcome her back.

Incredible. All her life she had accepted the parameters set for her. Now she was touring Old Athens, with its clicking worry beads and its open-fronted shops, where she could buy cheap plaster copies of monuments or elegant antiques.

She passed tavernas, but she was too excited to be tempted by the rich smells of coffee and baking. She heard the clear notes of a flute as she looked up and saw the Acropolis.

There was only one approach. Though it was still early, other tourists were making their way toward the ruins in twos and in groups. Rebecca let her camera hang by its strap. Despite the chattering around her, she felt alone, but beautifully so.

She would never be able to explain what it felt like to stand in the morning sun and look at something that had been built for the gods—something that had endured war and weather and time. It had been a place of worship. Even now, after centuries had passed, Rebecca felt the spiritual pull. Perhaps the goddess Athena, with her gleaming helmet and spear, still visited there.

Rebecca had been disappointed that Stephen couldn't join her on her first morning in Athens. Now she was glad to be alone—to sit and absorb and imagine without having to explain her thoughts.

How could she, after having seen so much, go back to so little? Sighing, she wandered through the temples. It wasn't just the awe she felt here, or the excitement she had felt in London and Paris, that had changed her. It was Stephen and everything she'd felt, everything she'd wanted, since she'd met him.

Perhaps she would go back to Philadelphia, but she would never be the same person. Once you fell in love, completely, totally in love, nothing was ever the same.

She wished it could be simple, the way she imagined it was simple for so many other women. An attractive man, a physical tug. But with Stephen, as with Athens, she'd lost her heart. However implausible it seemed, she had recognized the man, as well as the city, as being part of her, as being for her. Desire, when tangled up with love, could never be simple.

But how could you be sure you were in love when it had never happened to you before? If she were home, at least she would have a friend to talk to. With a little laugh, Rebecca walked out into the sunlight. How many times had she been on the receiving end of a long, scattered conversation from a friend who had fallen in love—or thought she had. The excitement, the unhappiness, the thrills. Sometimes she'd been envious, and sometimes she'd been grateful not to have the complication in her own life. But always, always, she'd offered calm, practical, even soothing advice.

Oddly enough, she didn't seem to be able to do the same for herself.

All she could think of was the way her heart pounded when he touched her, how excitement, panic and anticipation fluttered through her every time he looked at her. When she was with him, her feelings and fantasies seemed reasonable. When she was with him, she could believe in fate, in the matching of soul to soul.

It wasn't enough. At least that was what she would

have told another woman. Attraction and passion weren't enough. Yet there was no explaining, even to herself, the sense of rightness she experienced whenever she was with him. If she were a fanciful person she would say it was as though she'd been waiting for him, waiting for the time and the place for him to come to her.

It sounded simple—if fate could be considered simple. Yet beneath all the pleasure and that sense of reunion was guilt. She couldn't shake it, and she knew she wouldn't be able to ignore it much longer. She wasn't the woman she had let him believe her to be. She wasn't the well-traveled at-loose-ends free spirit she pretended to be. No matter how many ties she'd cut, she was still Rebecca Malone. How would he feel about her once he knew how limited and dull her life had been?

How and when was she going to tell him?

A few more days, she promised herself as she began the walk back. It was selfish, perhaps it was even dangerous, but she wanted just a few more days.

It was midafternoon before she returned to the hotel. Ignoring the fact that she might be considered overeager, she went straight to Stephen's suite. She couldn't wait to see him, to tell him everything she'd seen, to show him everything she'd bought. Her easy smile faded a bit when his secretary Elana opened the door.

"Miss Malone." Gracious and self-confident, Elana waved her in. "Please sit down. I'll let Stephen know you're here."

"I don't want to interrupt." Rebecca shifted her bags, feeling gauche and foolish.

"Not at all. Have you just come in?"

"Yes, I…" For the first time, Rebecca noticed that her skin was damp and her hair tousled. In contrast, Elana was cool and perfectly groomed. "I really should go."

"Please." Elana urged Rebecca to a chair. "Let me get you a drink." With a half smile, Elana began to pour a tall glass of iced juice. She had expected Stephen's mystery lady to be smooth, controlled and stunning. It pleased her a great deal to find Rebecca wide-eyed, a little unsure, and clearly a great deal in love.

"Did you enjoy your morning?"

"Yes, very much." She accepted the glass and tried to relax. Jealousy, she realized, feeling herself flush at the realization. She couldn't remember ever having experienced the sensation before. Who wouldn't be jealous? she asked herself as she watched Elana walk to the phone. The Greek woman was gorgeous, self-contained, coolly efficient. Above all, she had a relationship with Stephen that Rebecca knew nothing about. How long has she known him? Rebecca wondered. And how well?

"Stephen's just finishing up some business," Elana said as she hung up the phone. With easy, economical moves, she poured herself a drink, then walked to the chair facing Rebecca. "What do you think of Athens?"

"I love it." Rebecca wished she'd taken the time to brush her hair and freshen her makeup. Lecturing herself, she sipped at her juice. "I'm not sure what I expected, but it's everything and more."

"Europeans see it as the East, Orientals see it as the West." Elana crossed her legs and settled back. It surprised her to realize that she was prepared to like Rebecca Malone. "What Athens is is Greek—and, more particularly, Athenian." She paused, studying Rebecca over the rim of her glass. "People often view Stephen in much the same way, and what he is is Stephen."

"How long have you worked for him?"

"Five years."

"You must know him well."

"Better than some. He's a demanding and generous employer and an interesting man. Fortunately, I like to travel and I enjoy my work."

Rebecca rubbed at a spot of dust on her slacks. "It never occurred to me that farming required so much traveling. I never realized how much was involved in growing olives."

Elana's brows rose in obvious surprise, but she continued smoothly when Rebecca glanced back at her. "Whatever Stephen does, he does thoroughly." She smiled to herself, satisfied. She hadn't been certain until now whether the American woman was attracted to Stephen or to his position. "Has Stephen explained to you about the dinner party this evening?"

"He said something about a small party here at the hotel. A business dinner."

"Men take these things more lightly than women." Feeling friendlier, Elena offered her first genuine smile. "It will be small, but quite extravagant." She watched as Rebecca automatically lifted a hand to her hair. "If you need anything—a dress, a salon—the hotel can accommodate you."

Rebecca thought of the casual sportswear she'd tossed into her bag before the impulsive trip to Athens. "I need everything."

With a quick, understanding laugh, Elana rose. "I'll make some calls for you."

"Thank you, but I don't want to interfere with your work."

"Seeing that you're comfortable is part of my work." They both glanced over when the door opened. "Stephen. You see, she hasn't run away." Taking her glass and her pad, she left them alone.

"You were gone a long time." He hated the fact that he'd begun to watch the clock and worry. He'd imagined her hurt or abducted. He'd begun to wonder if she would disappear from his life as quickly as she'd appeared in it. Now she was here, her eyes alive with pleasure, her clothes rumpled and her hair wind-blown.

"I guess I got caught up exploring." She started to rise, but before she could gain her feet he was pulling her out of the chair, seeking, finding her mouth with his.

His desperation whipped through her. His hunger incited her own. Without thought, without hesitation, she clung to him, answering, accepting. Already seduced, she murmured something, an incoherent sound that caught in her throat.

Good God, he thought, it wasn't possible, it wasn't sane, to want like this. Throughout the morning while all the facts and figures and demands of business had been hammering at him, he'd thought of her, of holding her, of tasting her, of being with her. When she had stayed away for so long he'd begun to imagine, then to fear, what his life would be like without her.

It wasn't going to happen. He scraped his teeth over her bottom lip, and she gasped and opened for him. He wouldn't let it happen. Where she came from, where she intended to go, no longer mattered. She belonged to him now. And, though he'd only begun to deal with it, he belonged to her.

But he needed some sanity, some logic. Fighting himself, Stephen drew her away from him. Her eyes remained closed, and her lips remained parted. A soft, sultry sound escaped them as her lashes fluttered upward.

"I…" She took a deep breath and let it out slowly. "I should go sightseeing more often."

Gradually he realized how hard his fingers were pressing into her arms. As if he were afraid she would slip away. Cursing himself, he relaxed. "I would have preferred to go with you."

"I understand you're busy. I'd have bored you silly, poking into every shop and staring at every column."

"No." If there was one thing he was certain of, it was that she would never bore him. "I'd like to have seen your first impression of Athens."

"It was like coming home," she told him, then hurried on because it sounded foolish. "I couldn't get enough." Laughing at herself, she gestured toward her bags. "Obviously. It's so different from anywhere I've ever been. At the Acropolis I couldn't even take any pictures, because I knew they couldn't capture the feeling. Then I walked along the streets and saw old men with *kom— konbou*—" She fumbled over the Greek and finally made a helpless gesture.

"*Kombouloi,*" he murmured. "Worry beads."

"Yes, and I imagined how they might sit in those shadowy doorways watching the tourists go by, day after day, year after year." She sat, pleased to share her impressions with him. "I saw a shop with all these costumes, lots of tinsel, and some really dreadful plaster copies of the monuments."

He grinned and sat beside her. "How many did you buy?"

"Three or four." She bent down to rattle through her bags. "I bought you a present."

"A plaster statue of Athena?"

She glanced up, eyes laughing. "Almost. Then I found this tiny antique shop in the old section. It was all dim and dusty and irresistible. The owner had a handful of English phrases, and I had my phrase book. After we'd confused each other completely, I bought this."

She drew out an S-shaped porcelain pipe decorated with paintings of the wild mountain goats of Greece. Attached to it was a long wooden stem, as smooth as glass, tipped by a tarnished brass mouthpiece.

"I remembered the goats we'd seen on Corfu," she explained as Stephen examined it. "I thought you might like it, though I've never seen you smoke a pipe."

With a quiet laugh, he looked back at her, balancing the gift in both hands. "No, I don't—at least not of this nature."

"Well, it's more ornamental than functional, I suppose. The man couldn't tell me much about it—at least not that I could understand." She reached out to run a finger along the edge of the bowl. "I've never seen anything like it."

"I'm relieved to hear it." When she sent him a puzzled look, he leaned over to brush her lips with his. "*Matia mou,* this is a hashish pipe."

"A hashish pipe?" She stared, first in shock, then in fascination. "Really? I mean, did people actually use it?"

"Undoubtedly. Quite a number, I'd say, since it's at least a hundred and fifty years old."

"Imagine that." She pouted, imagining dark, smoky dens. "I guess it's not a very appropriate souvenir."

"On the contrary, whenever I see it I'll think of you."

She glanced up quickly, unsure, but the amusement in his eyes had her smiling again. "I should have bought you the plaster statue of Athena."

Taking her hands, he drew her to her feet. "I'm flattered that you bought me anything." She felt the subtle change as his fingers tightened on hers. "I want time with you, Rebecca. Hours of it. Days. There's too much I need to know." When she lowered her gaze, he caught her chin. "What are those secrets of yours?"

"Nothing that would interest you."

"You're wrong. Tomorrow I intend to find out all there is to know." He saw the quick flicker of unease in her eyes. Other men, he thought with an uncomfortable surge of jealousy. The hell with them. "No more evasions. I want you, all of you. Do you understand?"

"Yes, but—"

"Tomorrow." He cut her off, suddenly, completely, frustratingly Greek. "I have business that can't be avoided now. I'll come for you at seven."

"All right."

Tomorrow was years away, she told herself. She had time to decide what she would say, how she would say it. Before tomorrow came tonight. She would be everything she'd ever wanted to be, everything he wanted her to be.

"I'd better go." Before he could touch her again, she bent to gather her bags. "Stephen…" She paused at the door and turned to look at him as he stood in the middle of the room, comfortable with the wealth that sur-

rounded him, confident with who and what he was.
"You might be disappointed when you find out."

She left quickly, leaving him frowning after her.

Chapter 7

She was as nervous as a cat. Every time she looked in the mirror Rebecca wondered who the woman was who was staring back at her. It wasn't a stranger, but it was a very, very different Rebecca Malone.

Was it just the different hairstyle, poufed and frizzed and swept around her face? Could it be the dress, the glittery spill of aquamarine that left her arms and shoulders bare? No, it was more than that. More than makeup and clever stylists and glamorous clothes. It was in her eyes. How could she help but see it? How could anyone? The woman who looked back from the mirror was a woman in love.

What was she going to do about it? What could she do? she asked herself. She was still practical enough to accept that some things could never be changed. But was she bold enough, or strong enough, to take what she wanted and live with the consequences?

When she heard the knock on the door, Rebecca took a deep breath and picked up the useless compact-size evening bag she'd bought just that afternoon. It was all happening so fast. When she'd come back from Stephen's suite there had been a detailed message from Elana listing appointments—for a massage, a facial, hairstyling—along with the name of the manager of the hotel's most exclusive boutique. She hadn't had time to think, even for a minute, about her evening with Stephen. Or about any tomorrows.

Perhaps that was best, she decided as she pulled open the door. It was best not to think, not to analyze. It was best to accept and to act.

She looked like a siren, some disciple of Circe, with her windswept hair and a dress the color of seductive seas. Had he told himself she wasn't beautiful? Had he believed it? At that moment he was certain he'd never seen, never would see, a more exciting woman.

"You're amazing, Rebecca." He took her hand and drew her to him so that they stood in the doorway together. On the threshold.

"Why? Because I'm on time?"

"Because you're never what I expect." He brought her hand to his lips. "And always what I want."

Because she was speechless, she was glad when he closed the door at her back and led her to the elevators. He looked different from the man she had first met, the one who dressed with such casual elegance. Tonight there was a formality about him, and the sophistication she had sensed earlier was abundantly apparent in the ease with which he wore the black dinner jacket.

"The way you look," he told her, "it seems a shame to waste the evening on a business dinner."

"I'm looking forward to meeting some of your friends."

"Associates," he said with an odd smile. "When you've been poor—and don't intend to be poor again— you rarely make friends in business."

She frowned. This was a side of him, the business side, that she didn't know. Would he be ruthless? She looked at him, saw it, and accepted it. Yes, a man like Stephen would always be ruthless with what belonged to him. "But enemies?"

"The same rule, in business, applies to friends and enemies. My father taught me more than fishing, Rebecca. He also taught me that to succeed, to attain, you must learn not only how to trust, but how far."

"I've never been poor, but I imagine it's frightening."

"Strengthening." He took her hand again when the elevator doors opened. "We have different backgrounds, Rebecca, but, fortunately, we've come to the same place."

He had no idea *how* different. Trust. He had spoken of trust. She discovered she wanted to tell him, tell him everything. Tell him that she knew nothing of elegant parties and glamorous life-styles. She was a fraud, and when he found out he might laugh at her and brush her aside. But she wanted him to know.

"Stephen, I want to—"

"Stephen. Once more you outdo us all in your choice of women."

"Dimitri."

Rebecca stopped, caught on the brink of confession.

The man who faced her was classically handsome. His silver mane contrasted with bronzed skin lined by a half century of sun. He wore a mustache that swept majestically over gleaming teeth.

"It was kind of you to invite us here this evening, but it would be kinder still to introduce me to your lovely companion."

"Rebecca Malone, Dimitri Petropolis."

A diamond glittered on the hand he lifted to clasp Rebecca's. The hand itself was hard as rock. "A pleasure. Athens is already abuzz with talk of the woman who arrived with Stephen."

Certain he was joking, she smiled. "Then Athens must be in desperate need of news."

His eyes widened for a moment, then creased at the corners when he laughed. "I have no doubt you will provide an abundance of it."

Stephen slipped a hand under Rebecca's elbow. The look he sent Dimitri was very quick and very clear. They had competed over land, but there would be no competition over Rebecca.

"If you'll excuse us a moment, Dimitri, I'd like to get Rebecca some champagne."

"Of course." Amused—and challenged—Dimitri brushed at his mustache as he watched them walk away.

Rebecca had no way of knowing that to Stephen a small dinner party meant a hundred people. She sipped her first glass of wine, hoping she wouldn't embarrass them both by being foolishly shy and tongue-tied. In the past, whenever she had found herself in a crowd, she had always looked for the nearest corner to fade into. Not tonight, she promised herself, straightening her shoulders.

There were dozens of names to remember, but she filed them away as easily as she had always filed numbers. In the hour before dinner, while the guests mixed and mingled, she found herself at ease. The stomach flutters and hot blushes she'd often experienced at parties and functions simply didn't happen.

Perhaps she was the new Rebecca Malone after all.

She heard business discussed here and there. Most of it seemed to be hotel and resort business—talk of remodeling and expansions, mergers and takeovers. She found it odd that so many of the guests were in that trade, rather than prosperous farmers or olive growers.

Stephen came up behind her and murmured in her ear, "You look pleased with yourself."

"I am." He couldn't know that she was pleased to find herself at ease and comfortable in a party of strangers. "So many interesting people."

"Interesting." He brushed a finger over her wispy bangs. "I thought you might find it dull."

"Not at all." She took a last sip of champagne, then set the glass aside. Instantly a waiter was at her side, offering another. Stephen watched her smile her thanks.

"So you enjoy parties?"

"Sometimes. I'm enjoying this one, and having a chance to meet your associates."

Stephen glanced over her shoulder, summing up the looks and quiet murmurs. "They'll be talking about you for weeks to come."

She only laughed, turning in a slow circle. Around her was the flash of jewels and the gleam of gold. The sleek and the prosperous, the rich and the successful. It pleased her that she'd found more to talk about than tax shelters.

"I can't imagine they have so little on their minds. This is such a gorgeous room."

She looked around the huge ballroom, with its cream-and-rose walls, its glittering chandeliers and its gleaming floors. There were alcoves for cozy love seats and tall, thriving ornamental trees in huge copper pots. The tables, arranged to give a sense of intimacy, were already set with ivory cloths and slender tapers.

"It's really a beautiful hotel," she continued. "Everything about it runs so smoothly." She smiled up at him. "I'm torn between the resort in Corfu and this."

"Thank you." When she gave him a blank look, he tipped up her chin with his finger. "They're mine."

"Your what?"

"My hotels," he said simply, then led her to a table.

She spoke all through dinner, though for the first fifteen minutes she had no idea what she said. There were eight at Stephen's table, including Dimitri, who had shifted name cards so that he could sit beside her. She toyed with her seafood appetizer, chatted and wondered if she could have made a bigger fool out of herself.

He wasn't simply prosperous. He wasn't simply well-off. There was enough accountant left in Rebecca to understand that when a man owned what Stephen owned he was far, far more than comfortable.

What would he think of her when he found out what she was? Trust? How could she ever expect him to trust her now? She swallowed without tasting and managed to smile. Would he think she was a gold digger, that she had set herself up to run into him?

No, that was ridiculous.

She forced herself to look over and saw that

Stephen was watching her steadily. She picked up her fork with one hand and balled up the napkin in her lap with the other.

Why couldn't he be ordinary? she wondered. Someone vacationing, someone working at the resort? Why had she fallen in love with someone so far out of her reach?

"Have you left us?"

Rebecca jerked herself back to see Dimitri smiling at her. Flushing, she noticed that the next course had been served while she'd been daydreaming. "I'm sorry." With an effort she began to toy with the *salata Athenas*.

"A beautiful woman need never apologize for being lost in her own thoughts." He patted her hand, then let his fingers linger. He caught Stephen's dark look and smiled. If he didn't like the boy so much, he thought, he wouldn't get nearly so much pleasure from irritating him. "Tell me, how did you meet Stephen?"

"We met in Corfu." She thought of that first meal they had shared…quiet, relaxed, alone.

"Ah, soft nights and sunny days. You are vacationing?"

"Yes." Rebecca put more effort into her smile. If she stared into her salad she would only embarrass herself, and Stephen. "He was kind enough to show me some of the island."

"He knows it well, and many of the other islands of our country. There's something of the gypsy in him."

She had sensed that. Hadn't that been part of the attraction? Hadn't Rebecca just discovered the gypsy in herself? "Have you know him long?"

"We have a long-standing business relationship. Friendly rivals, you might say. When Stephen was hardly more than a boy he accumulated an impressive amount of land." He gestured expansively. "As you can see, he used it wisely. I believe he has two hotels in your country."

"Two? More?" Rebecca picked up her glass and took a long swallow of wine.

"So you see, I had wondered if you had met in America and were old friends."

"No." Rebecca nodded weakly as the waiter removed the salad and replaced it with moussaka. "We only just met a few days ago."

"As always, Stephen moves quickly and stylishly." Dimitri took her hand again, more than a little amused by the frown he saw deepening in Stephen's eyes. "Where is it in America you are from?"

"Philadelphia." Relax, she ordered herself. Relax and enjoy. "That's in the Northeast."

It infuriated Stephen to watch her flirting so easily, so effectively, with another man. She sat through course after course, barely eating, all the while gifting Dimitri with her shy smiles. Not once did she draw away when the older man touched her hand or leaned close. From where he sat, Stephen could catch a trace of her scent, soft, subtle, maddening. He could hear her quiet laugh when Dimitri murmured something in her ear.

Then she was standing with him, her hand caught in his, as he led her to the dance floor.

Stephen sat there, battling back a jealousy he despised, and watched them move together to music made for lovers. Under the lights her dress clung, then swayed, then shifted. Her face was close, too damn close, to Dimitri's. He knew what it was like to hold her like that, to breathe in the scent of her skin and her hair. He knew what it was to feel her body brush against his, to feel the life, the passion, bubbling. He knew what it was to see her eyes blur, her lips part, to hear that quiet sigh.

He had often put his stamp on land, but never on a woman. He didn't believe in it. But only a fool sat idly by and allowed another man to enjoy what was his. With a muttered oath, Stephen rose, strode out onto the dance floor and laid a hand on Dimitri's shoulder.

"Ah, well." The older man gave a regretful sigh and stepped aside. "Until later."

Before she could respond, Rebecca was caught against Stephen. With a sigh of her own, she relaxed and matched her steps to his. Maybe it was like a dream, she told herself as she closed her eyes and let the music fill her head. But she was going to enjoy every moment until it was time to wake up.

She seemed to melt against him. Her fingers moved lightly through his hair as she rested her cheek against his. Was this the way she'd danced with Dimitri? Stephen wondered, then cursed himself. He was being a fool, but he couldn't seem to stop himself. Then again, he'd had to fight for everything else in his life. Why should his woman be any different?

He wanted to drag her off then and there, away from everyone, and find some dark, quiet place to love her.

"You're enjoying yourself?"

"Yes." She wouldn't think about what he was, not now. Soon enough the night would be over and tomorrow would have to be faced. While the music played and he held her, she would only think of what he meant to her. "Very much."

The dreamy tone of her voice almost undid him. "Apparently Dimitri entertained you well."

"Mmm. He's a very nice man."

"You moved easily from his arms to mine."

Something in his tone pried through the pleasure she felt. Carefully she drew back so that she could see his face. "I don't think I know what you mean."

"I believe you do."

She was tempted to laugh, but there was no humor in Stephen's eyes. Rebecca felt her stomach knot as it always did when she was faced with a confrontation. "If I do, then I'd have to think you ridiculous. Maybe we'd better go back to the table."

"So you can be with him?" Even as the words came out he realized the unfairness, even the foolishness, of them.

She stiffened, retreating as far as she could from anger. "I don't think this is the place for this kind of discussion."

"You're quite right." As furious with himself as he was with her, he pulled her from the dance floor.

Chapter 8

"Stop it." By the time he'd dragged her to the elevators, Rebecca had gotten over her first shock. "What's gotten into you?"

"I'm simply taking you to a more suitable place for our discussion." He pulled her into the elevator, then punched the button for their floor.

"You have guests," she began, but he sent her a look than made her feel like a fool. Falling back on dignity, she straightened her shoulders. "I prefer to be asked if I want to leave, not dragged around as though I were a pack mule."

Though her heart was pounding, she sailed past him when the doors opened, intending to breeze into her own rooms and slam the door in his face. In two steps he had her arm again. Rebecca found herself guided, none too gently, into Stephen's suite.

"I don't want to talk to you," she said, because she was certain her teeth would begin to chatter at any moment. She didn't argue well in the best of circumstances. Faced with Stephen's anger, she was certain she would lose.

He said nothing as he loosened his tie and the first two buttons of his shirt. He went to the bar and poured two brandies. He was being irrational and he knew it, but he seemed unable to control it. That was new, he decided. But there had been many new emotions in him since Rebecca.

Walking back to Rebecca, he set one snifter by her elbow. When he looked at her…he wanted to shout, to beg, to demand, to plead. As a result, his voice was clipped and hard.

"You came to Athens with me, not with Dimitri or any other man."

She didn't touch the snifter. She was certain her hands would shake so hard that it would slip out of her grip. "Is that a Greek custom?" It amazed her—and bolstered her confidence—to hear how calm her voice was. "Forbidding a woman to speak to another man?"

"Speak?" He could still see the way Dimitri had bent his head close to hers. Dimitri, who was smooth and practiced. Dimitri, whose background would very likely mirror Rebecca's. Old money, privileged childhoods, quiet society. "Do you allow every man who speaks to you to hold you, to touch you?"

She didn't blush. Instead, the color faded from her cheeks. She shook, not with fear but with fury. "What I do, and with whom I do it, is my business. Mine."

Very deliberately he lifted his snifter and drank. "No."

"If you think that because I came here with you you have the right to dictate to me you're wrong. I'm my own person, Stephen." It struck her even as she said it that it was true. She was her own person. Each decision she made was her own. Filled with a new sense of power, she stepped forward. "No one owns me, not you, not anyone. I won't be ordered, I won't be forced, I won't be pressured." With a flick of her skirts, she turned. He had her again quickly, his hands on both of her arms, his face close.

"You won't go back to him."

"You couldn't stop me if that was what I wanted." She tossed her head back challengingly. "But I have no intention of going back downstairs to Dimitri, or anyone else." She jerked her arms free. "You idiot. Why should I want to be with him when I'm in love with you?"

She stopped, her eyes wide with shock, her lips parted in surprise. Overwhelmed by a combination of humiliation and fury, she spun around. Then she was struggling against him. "Leave me alone! Oh, God, just leave me alone!"

"Do you think I could let you go now?" He caught her hair in his hand, dragging it back until her eyes met his. In them she saw triumph and desire. "I feel as though I've waited all my life to hear you say those words." He rained kisses over her face until her struggles ceased. "You drive me mad," he murmured. "Being with you, being without you."

"Please." Colors, shapes, lights were whirling in her head. "I need to think."

"No. Ask me for anything else, but not more time." Gathering her close, he buried his face in her hair. "Do you think I make a fool of myself over every woman?"

"I don't know." She moaned when his lips trailed down her throat. Something wild and terrifying was happening inside her body. "I don't know you. You don't know me."

"Yes, I do." He pulled away just far enough to look down at her. "From the first moment I saw you, I knew you. Needed you. Wanted you."

It was true. She knew it, felt it, but she shook her head in denial. "It's not possible."

"I've loved you before, Rebecca, almost as much as I do now." He felt her go still. The color fled from her face again, but her eyes stayed steady on his.

"I don't want you to say what isn't real, what you're not sure of."

"Didn't you feel it, the first time I kissed you?" When he saw the acknowledgment in her eyes, his grip tightened. He could feel her heart thundering, racing to match the rhythm of his own. "Somehow you've come back to me, and I to you. No more questions," he said, before she could speak. "I need you tonight."

It was real. She felt the truth and the knowledge when his mouth found hers. If it was wrong to go blindly into need, then she would pay whatever price was asked. She could no longer deny him…or herself.

There was no gentleness in the embrace. It was as it had been the first time, lovers reunited, a hunger finally quenched. All heat and light. She gave more than she'd known she had. Her mouth was as avid as his, as seeking. Her murmurs were as desperate. Her hands didn't shake as they moved over him. They pressed, gripped, demanded. Greedy, she tugged the jacket from his shoulders.

Yes, he'd come back to her. If it was madness to believe it, then for tonight she'd be mad.

The taste of her, just the taste of her, was making his head swim and his blood boil. He nipped at her lip, then sucked until he heard her helpless whimper. He wanted her helpless. Something fierce and uncivilized inside him wanted her weak and pliant and defenseless. When she went limp in his arms he dived into her mouth and plundered. Her response tore at him, so sweet, so vulnerable, then suddenly so ardent.

Her hands, which had fluttered helplessly to her side, rose up again to pull at his shirt, to race under it to warmed flesh. She could only think of how right it felt to touch him, to press against him and wait for him to light new fires inside her.

With an oath, he swept her up into his arms and carried her to the bedroom.

The moon was waning and offered only the most delicate light. It fell in slants and shadows on the bed, dreamlike. But the vibrating of Rebecca's pulse told her this was no dream. There was the scent of jasmine from the sprigs in the vase beside the bed. It was a scent she would always remember, just as she would remember how dark and deep were the color of his eyes.

Needful, desperate, they tumbled onto the bed.

He wanted to take care with her. She seemed so small, so fragile. He wanted to show her how completely she filled his heart. But his body was on fire, and she was already moving like a whirlwind beneath him.

His mouth was everywhere, making her shudder and arch and ache. Desires she'd never known sprang to life inside her and took control. Delirious, she obeyed them, reveled in them, then searched for more.

They rolled across the bed in a passionate war that would have two victors, touching, taking, discovering. Impatient, he peeled the dress from her, moaning as he found her breasts with his hands, his lips, his teeth. Unreasoning desire catapulted through him when he felt her soar.

Her body felt like a furnace, impossibly hot, impossibly strong. Sensations rammed into her, stealing her breath. Mindless and moaning, she writhed under him, open for any demand he might make, pulsing for any new knowledge he might offer.

Finally, finally, she knew what it was to love, to be loved, to be wanted beyond reason. Naked, she clung to him, awash in the power and the weakness, the glory and the terror.

He raced over her as if he already knew what would make her tremble, what would make her yearn. Never before had she been so aware, so in tune with another.

She made him feel like a god. He touched, and her skin vibrated under his hand. He tasted, and her flavor was like no other. She was moist, heated, and utterly willing. She seemed to explode beneath him, lost in pleasure, drugged by passion. No other woman had ever driven him so close to madness. Her head was thrown back, and one hand was flung out as her fingers dug into the sheets. Wanton, waiting, wild.

With her name on his lips, he drove into her. His breath caught. His mind spun. Her cry of pain and release echoed in his head, bringing him both triumph and guilt. His body went rigid as he fought to claw his way back. Then she seemed to close around him, body, heart, soul. As helpless as she, he crossed the line into madness and took her with him.

Chapter 9

Aftershocks of passion racked her. Stunned and confused, she lay in the shadowed light. Nothing had prepared her for this. No one had ever warned her that pleasure could be so huge or that need could be so jagged. If she had known... Rebecca closed her eyes and nearly laughed out loud. If she had known, she would have left everything behind years ago and searched the world for him.

Only him. She let out a quiet, calming sigh. Only him.

He was cursing himself, slowly, steadily, viciously. Innocent. Dear God. She'd been innocent, as fresh and untouched as spring, and he'd used her, hurt her, taken her.

Disgusted with himself, he sat up and reached for a cigar. He needed more than tobacco. He needed a drink, but he didn't trust his legs to carry him.

The flick of his lighter sounded like a gunshot. For

an instant his face, hardened by anger and self-loathing, was illuminated.

"Why didn't you tell me?"

Still floating on an ocean of pleasure, she blinked her eyes open. "What?"

"Damn it, Rebecca, why didn't you tell me you hadn't been with a man before? That this—that I was your first?"

There was an edge of accusation in his voice. For the first time, she realized she was naked. Her cheeks grew hot as she fumbled for the sheet. One moment there was glory; the next, shame. "I didn't think of it."

"Didn't think of it?" His head whipped around. "Don't you think I had a right to know? Do you think this would have happened if I had known?"

She shook her head. It was true that she hadn't thought of it. It hadn't mattered. He was the first, the last, the only. But now it occurred to her that a man like him might not want to make love with an inexperienced woman. "I'm sorry." Her heart seemed to shrivel in her breast. "You said that you loved me, that you wanted me. The rest didn't seem to matter."

She'd cried out. He'd heard the shock and pain in her voice. And he hadn't been able to stop himself. Yes, he needed a drink. "It mattered," he tossed back as he rose and strode into the other room.

Alone, she let out a shuddering breath. Of course it mattered. Only a fool would have thought otherwise. He'd thought he was dealing with an experienced, emotionally mature woman who knew how to play the game. Words like *love* and *need* and *want* were interchangeable. Yes, he'd said he loved her, but to many love was physical and physical only.

She'd made a fool of herself and she'd infuriated him, and all because she'd begun a relationship built on illusions.

She'd knowingly taken the risk, Rebecca reminded herself as she climbed out of bed. Now she'd pay the price.

He was calmer when he started back to the bedroom. Calmer, though anger still bubbled inside him. First he would show her how it should have been, how it could be. Then they had to talk, rationally, coherently.

"Rebecca…" But when he looked at the bed it was empty.

She was wrapped in a robe and was hurling clothing into her suitcase when she heard him knock. With a shake of her head, she rubbed the tears from her cheeks and continued her frenzied packing. She wouldn't answer…. She wouldn't answer and be humiliated again.

"Rebecca." The moment of calm he'd achieved had vanished. Swearing through gritted teeth, he pounded on the door. "Rebecca, this is ridiculous. Open this door."

Ignoring him, she swept bottles and tubes of toiletries off the bureau and into her bag. He'd go away, she told herself, hardly aware that she'd begun to sob. He'd go away and then she'd leave, take a cab to the airport and catch the first plane to anywhere.

The sound of splintering wood had her rushing into the parlor in time to see the door give way.

She'd thought she'd seen fury before, but she'd been wrong. She saw it now as she stared into Stephen's face. Speechless, she looked from him to the broken door and back again.

Elana, tying the belt of her robe, rushed down the hall. "Stephen, what's happened? Is there a—"

He turned on her, hurling one short sentence in clipped Greek at her. Her eyes widened and she backed away, sending Rebecca a look that combined sympathy and envy.

"Do you think you have only to walk away from me?" He pushed the door back until it scraped against the battered jamb.

"I want—" Rebecca lifted a hand to her throat as if to push the words out. "I want to be alone."

"The hell with what you want." He started toward her, only to stop dead when she cringed and turned away. He'd forgotten what it was like to hurt, truly hurt, until that moment. "I asked you once if you were afraid of me. Now I see that you are." Searching for control, he dipped his hands into the pockets of the slacks he'd thrown on. She looked defenseless, terrified, and tears still streaked her cheeks. "I won't hurt you again. Will you sit?" When she shook her head, he bit off an oath. "I will."

"I know you're angry with me," she began when he'd settled into a chair. "I'll apologize if it'll do any good, but I do want to be alone."

His eyes had narrowed and focused. "You'll apologize? For what?"

"For…" What did he expect her to say? Humiliated, she crossed her arms and hugged her elbows. "For what happened…for not…explaining," she finished lamely. "For whatever you like," she continued as the tears started again. "Just leave me alone."

"Sweet God." He rubbed a weary hand over his face. "I can think of nothing in my life I've handled as badly as this." He rose, but stopped again when she automatically retreated. "You don't want me to touch you." His voice had roughened. He had to swallow to clear his throat. "I won't, but I hope you'll listen."

"There's nothing more to say. I understand how you feel and why you feel it. I'd rather we just left it at that."

"I treated you inexcusably."

"I don't want an apology."

"Rebecca—"

"I don't." Her voice rose, stopping his words, stopping her tears. "It's my fault. It's been my fault all along. No, no, no!" she shouted when he took another step. "I don't want you to touch me. I couldn't bear it."

He sucked in his breath, then let it out slowly. "You twist the knife well."

But she was shaking her head and pacing the room now. "It didn't matter at first—at least I didn't think it would matter. I didn't know who you were or that I would fall in love with you. Now I've waited too long and ruined everything."

"What are you talking about?"

Perhaps it was best, best for both of them, to lay out the truth. "You said you knew me, but you don't, because I've done nothing but lie to you, right from the first moment."

Slowly, carefully, he lowered himself to the arm of a chair. "What have you lied to me about?"

"Everything." Her eyes were drenched with regret when she looked at him. "Then, tonight… First I found out that you own hotels. *Own* them."

"It was hardly a secret. Why should it matter?"

"It wouldn't." She dropped her hands to her sides. "If I was what I'd pretended to be. After we'd made love and you—I realized that by pretending I'd let you have feelings for someone who didn't even exist."

"You're standing in front of me, Rebecca. You exist."

"No. Not the way you think, not the way I've let you think."

He prepared himself for the worst. "What have you done? Were you running away from America?"

"No. Yes." She had to laugh at that. "Yes, I was running." She gathered what composure she had left and folded her hands. "I did come from Philadelphia, as I told you. I've lived there all my life. Lived there, went to school there, worked there." She found a tissue in the pocket of her robe. "I'm an accountant."

He stared at her, one brow lifting, as she blew her nose. "I beg your pardon?"

"I said, I'm an accountant." She hurled the words at him, then whirled away to face the window. Stephen started to rise, then thought better of it.

"I find it difficult to imagine you tallying ledgers, Rebecca. If you'd sit down, maybe we could talk this through."

"Damn it, I said I'm an accountant. A CPA, specializing in corporate taxes. Up until a few weeks ago I worked for McDowell, Jableki and Kline in Philadelphia."

He spread his hands, taking it all in. "All right. What did you do? Embezzle?"

She tossed back her head and nearly exploded with laughter. If she said yes he'd probably be intrigued. But the time for intrigue was over. The time for the truth was now. "No. I've never done anything illegal in my life. I've never even had a parking ticket. I've never done anything at all out of the ordinary until a few weeks ago."

She began to pace again, too agitated to keep still. "I'd never traveled, never had a man send a bottle of champagne to my table, never walked along the beach in the moonlight, never had a lover."

He said nothing, not because he was angry or bored but because he was fascinated.

"I had a good job, my car was paid for, I had good, conservative investments that would have ensured me a comfortable retirement. In my circle of friends I'm known as dependable. If someone needs a sitter they know they can call Rebecca. If they need advice or someone to feed their fish while they're on vacation they don't have to worry. I was never late for work, never took five minutes extra for lunch."

"Commendable," he said, and earned a glare.

"Just the type of employee I imagine you'd like to hire."

He swallowed a chuckle. He'd been prepared for her to confess she had a husband, five husbands, a prison record. Instead she was telling him she was an accountant with an excellent work record. "I have no desire to hire you, Rebecca."

"Just as well." She turned away and started to prowl the room again. "You'd undoubtedly change your mind after I tell you the rest."

Stephen crossed his ankles and settled back. God, what a woman she was. "I'm anxious to hear it."

"My aunt died about three months ago, suddenly."

"I'm sorry." He would have gone to her then, but he could see she was far from ready. "I know how difficult it is to lose family."

"She was all I had left." Because she needed something to do, she pushed open the balcony doors. Warm, fragrant night air rushed in. "I couldn't believe she was gone. Just like that. No warning. Of course, I handled the funeral arrangements. No fuss, no frills. Just the way Aunt Jeannie would have wanted. She was a very economical woman, not only in finances but in dress, in speech, in manner. As long as I can remember, people compared me to her."

Stephen's brow lifted again as he studied the woman being buffeted by the breeze—the short red silk robe, the tousled hair.

"Soon after her death—I don't know if it was days or a week—something just snapped. I looked at myself, at my life, and I hated it." She dragged her hair back, only to have the wind catch it again. "I was a good employee, just like my aunt, a good credit risk, a dependable friend. Law-abiding, conservative and boring. Suddenly I could see myself ten, twenty, thirty years down the road, with nothing more than I had at that moment. I couldn't stand it."

She turned around. The breeze caught at the hem of her robe and sent it dancing around her legs. "I quit my job, and I sold everything."

"Sold?"

"Everything I owned—car, apartment, furniture, books, absolutely everything. I turned all the cash into traveler's checks, even the small inheritance from my aunt. Thousands of dollars. I know it might not sound like a lot to you, but it was more than I'd ever imagined having at once."

"Wait." He held up a hand, wanting to be certain he understood everything. "You're telling me that you sold your possessions, *all* your possessions?"

She couldn't remember ever having felt more foolish, and she straightened her shoulders defensively. "Right down to my coffeepot."

"Amazing," he murmured.

"I bought new clothes, new luggage, and flew to London. First-class. I'd never been on a plane before in my life."

"You'd never flown, but took your first trip across the Atlantic."

She didn't hear the admiration in his voice, only the amusement. "I wanted to see something different. To *be* something different. I stayed at the Ritz and took pictures of the changing of the guard. I flew to Paris and had my hair cut." Self-consciously she lifted a hand to it.

Because he could see that she was overwrought, he was careful not to smile. "You flew to Paris for a haircut."

"I'd heard some women discussing this stylist, and I— Never mind." It was no use trying to explain that she'd gone to the same hairdresser, to the same shops, for years. The same everything. "Right after Paris, I came here," she went on. "I met you. Things happened. I let them happen." Tears threatened. She could only pray he didn't see them. "You were exciting, and attracted to me. Or attracted to who you thought I was. I'd never had a romance. No one had ever looked at me the way you did."

Once more he chose his words carefully. "Are you saying that being with me was different? An adventure, like flying to a Paris salon?"

She would never be able to explain what being with him had meant to her. "Apologies and explanations really don't make any difference now. But I am sorry, Stephen. I'm sorry for everything."

He didn't see the tears, but he heard the regret in her voice. His eyes narrowed. His muscles tensed. "Are you apologizing for making love with me, Rebecca?"

"I'm apologizing for whatever you like. I'd make it up to you if I could, but I don't know how, unless I jump out the window."

He paused, as if he were considering it. "I don't think this requires anything quite that drastic. Perhaps if you'd sit down calmly?"

She shook her head and stayed where she was. "I can't handle any more of this tonight, Stephen. I'm sorry. You've every right to be angry."

He rose, the familiar impatience building. But she was so pale, looked so fragile, sounded so weary. He hadn't treated her gently before. At least he could do so now.

"All right. Tomorrow, then, after you've rested." He started to go to her, then checked himself. It would take time to show her that there were other ways to love. Time to convince her that love was more, much more than an adventure. "I want you to know that I regret what happened tonight. But that, too, will wait until tomorrow." Though he wanted to touch a hand to her cheek, he kept it fisted in his pocket. "Get some rest."

She had thought her heart was already broken. Now it shattered. Not trusting her voice, she nodded.

He left her alone. The door scraped against the splintered jamb as he secured it. She supposed there might have been a woman somewhere who'd made a bigger fool of herself. At the moment, it didn't seem to matter.

At least there was something she could do for both of them. Disappear.

Chapter 10

It was her own fault, she supposed. There were at least half a dozen promising accounting positions in the want ads. Not one of them interested her. Rebecca circled them moodily. How could she be interested in dental plans and profit sharing? All she could think about, all she'd been able to think about for two weeks, was Stephen.

What had he thought when he'd found her gone? Relief? Perhaps a vague annoyance at business left unfinished? Pen in hand, Rebecca stared out of the window of the garden apartment she'd rented. In her fantasies she imagined him searching furiously for her, determined to find her, whatever the cost. Reality, she thought with a sigh, wasn't quite so romantic. He would have been relieved. Perhaps she wasn't sophisticated, but at least she'd stepped out of his life with no fuss.

Now it was time to get her own life in order.

First things first. She had an apartment, and the little square of lawn outside the glass doors was going to make her happy. That in itself was a challenge. Her old condo had been centrally located on the fifth floor of a fully maintained modern building.

This charming and older development was a good thirty miles from downtown, but she could hear the birds in the morning. She would be able to look out at old oaks and sweeping maples and flowers she would plant herself. Perhaps it wasn't as big a change as a flight to Paris, but for Rebecca it was a statement.

She'd bought some furniture. *Some* was the operative word. Thus far she'd picked out a bed, one antique table and a single chair.

Not logical, Rebecca thought with a faint smile. No proper and economical living room suite, no tidy curtains. Even the single set of towels she'd bought was frivolous. And exactly what she'd wanted. She would do what she'd secretly wanted to do for years—buy a piece here, a piece there. Not because it was a good buy or durable, but because she wanted it.

She wondered how many people would really understand the satisfaction of making decisions not because they were sensible but because they were desirable. She'd done it with her home, her wardrobe. Even with her hair, she thought, running a hand through it. Outward changes had led to inner changes. Or vice versa. Either way, she would never again be the woman she'd been before.

Or perhaps she would be the woman she'd always been but had refused to acknowledge.

Then why was she circling ads in the classifieds?

Rebecca asked herself. Why was she sitting here on a beautiful morning planning a future she had no interest in? Perhaps it was true that she would never have the one thing, the one person, she really wanted. There would be no more picnics or walks in the moonlight or frantic nights in bed. Still, she had the memories, she had the moments, she had the dreams. There would be no regrets where Stephen was concerned. Not now, and not ever. And if she was now more the woman she had been with him, it had taken more than a change in hairstyle.

She was stronger. She was surer. She was freer. And she'd done it herself.

She could think of nothing she wanted less than to go back into someone else's firm, tallying figures, calculating profit and loss. So she wouldn't. Rebecca sank into the chair as the thought struck home.

She wouldn't. She wouldn't go job hunting, carrying her résumé, rinsing sweaty palms in the rest room, putting her career and life in someone else's hands again. She'd open her own firm. A small one, certainly. Personalized. Exclusive, she decided, savoring the word. Why not? She had the skill, the experience, and— finally—she had the courage.

It wouldn't be easy. In fact, it would be risky. The money she had left would have to go toward renting office space, equipment, a phone system, advertising. With a bubbling laugh, she sprang up and searched for a legal pad and a pencil. She had to make lists—not only of things to do but of people to call. She had enough contacts from her McDowell, Jableki and Kline days. Maybe, just maybe, she could persuade some of her former clients to give her a try.

"Just a minute," she called out when she heard the knock on the door. She scribbled a reminder to look for file cabinets as she went to answer. She'd much rather have some good solid oak file cabinets than a living room sofa.

She knew better than to open the door without checking the security peephole, but she was much too involved with her plans to think about such things. When she opened the door, she found herself face-to-face with Stephen.

Even if she could have spoken, he wasn't in the mood to let her. "What in the hell do you think you're doing?" he demanded as he slammed the door behind him. "Do you deliberately try to drive me mad, or does it come naturally to you?"

"I—I don't—" But he was already yanking her against him. Whatever words she might have spoken dissolved into a moan against his lips. Her pad fell to the floor with a slap. Even as her arms came up around him he was thrusting her away.

"What kind of game are you playing, Rebecca?" When she just shook her head, he dug his hands into his pockets and paced the wide, nearly empty room. He was unshaven, disheveled and absolutely gorgeous. "It's taken me two weeks and a great deal of trouble to find you. I believe we'd agreed to talk again. I was surprised to discover you'd not only left Athens, but Europe." He swung back and pinned her with a look. "Why?"

Still reeling from his entrance, she struggled not to babble. "I thought it best that I leave."

"You thought?" He took a step toward her, his fury so palatable that she braced herself. "You thought it best," he repeated. "For whom?"

"For you. For both of us." She caught herself fiddling with the lapels of her robe and dropped her hands. "I knew you were angry with me for lying to you and that you regretted what had happened between us. I felt it would be better for both of us if I—"

"Ran away?"

Her chin came up fractionally. "Went away."

"You said you loved me."

She swallowed. "I know."

"Was that another lie?"

"Please don't." She turned away, but there was nowhere to go. "Stephen, I never expected to see you again. I'm trying to make some sense out of my life, to do things in a way that's not only right but makes me happy. In Greece, I guess, I did what made me happy, but I didn't think about what was right. The time with you was…"

"Was what?"

Dragging both hands through her hair, she turned to him again. It was as if the two weeks had never been. She was facing him again, trying to explain what she feared she could never explain. "It was the best thing that ever happened to me, the most important, the most unforgettable, the most precious. I'll always be grateful for those few days."

"Grateful." He wasn't sure whether to laugh or murder her. Stepping forward, he surprised them both by slipping his hands lightly around her throat. "For what? For my giving you your first fling? A fast, anonymous romance with no consequences?"

"No." She lifted a hand to his wrist but made no attempt to struggle. "Did you come all this way to make me feel more guilty?"

"I came all this way because I finish what I begin. We'd far from finished, Rebecca."

"All right." Be calm, she told herself. When a man was this close to the edge, a woman's best defense was serenity. "If you'll let me go, we'll talk. Would you like some coffee?"

His fingers tightened reflexively, then slowly relaxed. "You've bought a new pot."

"Yes." Was that humor in his eyes? she wondered. "There's only one chair. Why don't you use it while I go into the kitchen?"

He took her arm. "I don't want coffee, or a chair, or a pleasant conversation."

It seemed serenity wouldn't work. "All right, Stephen. What do you want?"

"You. I'd thought I'd made that fairly obvious." When she frowned, he glanced around the apartment. "Now tell me, Rebecca, is this what you want? A handful of rooms to be alone in?"

"I want to make the best of the rest of my life. I've already apologized for deceiving you. I realize that—"

"Deceiving me." He held up a finger to stop her. "I've wanted to clear that point up myself. How did you deceive me?"

"By letting you think that I was something I'm not."

"You're not a beautiful, interesting woman? A passionate woman?" He lifted a brow as he studied her. "Rebecca, I have too much pride to ever believe you could deceive me that completely."

He was confusing her—deliberately, she was sure. "I told you what I'd done."

"What you'd done," he agreed. "And how you'd done

it." He brought his hand to her throat again, this time in a caress. His anger hadn't made her knees weak. She felt them tremble now at his tenderness. "Selling your possessions and flying to Paris for a new hairstyle. Quitting your job and grabbing life with both hands. You fascinate me." Her eyes stayed open wide when he brushed his lips over hers. "I think the time is nearly over when you'll be so easily flattered. It's almost a pity." He drew her closer, slowly, while his mouth touched hers. Relief coursed through him as he felt her melt and give. "Do you think it was your background that attracted me?"

"You were angry," she managed.

"Yes, angry at the idea that I had been part of your experiment. Furious," he added before he deepened the kiss. "Furious that I had been of only passing interest." She was heating in his arms, just as he remembered, just as he needed, softening, strengthening. "Shall I tell you how angry? Shall I tell you that for two weeks I couldn't work, couldn't think, couldn't function, because you were everywhere I looked and nowhere to be found?"

"I had to go." She was already tugging at his shirt to find the flesh beneath. To touch him again, just for a moment. To be touched by him. "When you said you regretted making love…" Her own words brought her back. Quickly she dropped her hands and stepped away.

He stared at her for a moment, then abruptly swore and began to pace. "I've never thought myself this big a fool. I hurt you that night in a much different way than I'd believed. Then I handled it with less finesse than I might the most unimportant business transaction." He paused, sighing. For the first time she saw clearly how incredibly weary he was.

"You're tired. Please, sit down. Let me fix you something."

He took a moment to press his fingers to his eyes. Again he wanted to laugh—while he strangled her. She was exactly what he needed, what he understood. Yet at the same time she baffled him.

"You weaken me, Rebecca, and bring out the fool I'd forgotten I could be. I'm surprised you allowed me to set foot into your home. You should have—" As quickly as the anger had come, it faded. As quickly as the tension had formed, it eased. Everything he'd needed to see was in her eyes. Carefully now, he drew a deep breath. A man wasn't always handed so many chances at happiness.

"Rebecca, I never regretted making love with you." He stopped her from turning with the lightest of touches on her shoulder. "I regretted only the way it happened. Too much need and too little care. I regret, I'll always regret, that for your first time there was fire but no warmth." He took her hands in his and brought them to his lips.

"It was beautiful."

"In its way." His fingers tightened on hers. Still so innocent, he thought. Still so generous. "It was not kind or patient or tender, as love should be the first time."

She felt hope rise in her heart again. "None of that mattered."

"It mattered, more than I can ever tell you. After, when you told me everything, it only mattered more. If I had done what my instincts told me to do that night you would never have left me. But I thought you needed time before you could bear to have me touch you again." Slowly, gently, he drew the tip of her finger into his mouth and watched her eyes cloud over. "Let me show you what I should have shown you then." With her hands locked in his, he looked into her eyes. "Do you want me?"

It was time for the truth. "Yes."

He lifted her into his arms and heard her breath catch. "Do you trust me?"

"Yes."

When he smiled, her heart turned over. "Rebecca, I must ask you one more thing."

"What is it?"

"Do you have a bed?"

She felt her cheeks heat even as she laughed. "In there."

She was trembling. It reminded him how careful he had to be, how precious this moment was to both of them. The sun washed over the bed, over them, as he lay beside her. And kissed her—only kissed her, softly, deeply, thoroughly, until her arms slipped from around him to fall bonelessly to her sides. She trembled still as he murmured to her, as his lips brushed over her cheeks, her throat.

He had shown her the desperation love could cause, the sharp-edged pleasure, the speed and the fury. Now he showed her that love could mean serenity and sweetness.

And she showed him.

He had thought to teach her, not to learn, to reassure her but not to be comforted. But he learned, and he was comforted. The need was there, as strong as it had been the first time. But strength was tempered with patience. As he slipped his hands down her robe to part it, to slide it away from her skin, he felt no need to hurry. He could delight in the way the sun slanted across her body, in the way her flesh warmed to his touch.

Her breath was as unsteady as her hands as she undressed him. But not from nerves. She understood that now. She felt strong and capable and certain. Anticipation made her tremble. Pleasure made her shudder. She gave a sigh that purred out of her lips as she arched against his seeking hands. Then he nipped lightly at her breast and she bounded from serenity to passion in one breathless leap.

Still he moved slowly, guiding her into a kind of heated torment she'd never experienced. Desire boiled in her, and his name sprang to her lips and her body coiled like a spring. Chaining down his own need, he set hers free and watched as she flew over the first peak.

"Only for me," he murmured as she went limp in his arms. "Only for me, Rebecca." With his own passions strapped, he slipped into her, determined to watch her build again. "Tell me you love me. Look at me and tell me."

She opened her eyes. She could barely breathe. Somehow the strength was pouring back into her, but so fast, so powerfully. Sensation rolled over sensation, impossibly. She moved with him, pressed center to center, heart to heart, but all she could see were his eyes, so dark, so blue, so intense. Perhaps she was drowning in them.

"I love you, Stephen."

Then she was falling, fathoms deep, into his eyes, into the sea. With her arms locked around him, she dragged him under with her.

He pulled her against him so that he could stroke her hair and wait for his pulse to level. She'd been innocent. But the surprise, the one he'd been dealing with for weeks, was that until Rebecca he'd been just as innocent. He'd known passion, but he'd never known intimacy, not the kind that reached the heart as fully as the body. And yet...

"We've been here before," he murmured. "Do you feel it, too?"

She linked her fingers with his. "I never believed in things like that until you. When I'm with you it's like remembering." She lifted her head to look at him. "I can't explain it."

"I love you, Rebecca, only more knowing who you are, why you are."

She touched a hand to his cheek. "I don't want you to say anything you don't really feel."

"How can a woman be so intelligent and still so stupid?" With a shake of his head, Stephen rolled on top of her. "A man doesn't travel thousands of miles for this, however delightful it may be. I love you, and though it annoyed me for quite some time I'm accustomed to it now."

"Annoyed you."

"Infuriated." He kissed her to cut off whatever retort she might make. "I'd seen myself remaining free for years to come. Then I met a woman who sold her coffeepot so she could take pictures of goats."

"I certainly have no intention of interfering with your plans."

"You already have." He smiled, holding her still when she tried to struggle away. "Marriage blocks off certain freedoms and opens others."

"Marriage?" She stopped struggling but turned her head to avoid another kiss.

"Soon." He nuzzled her neck. "Immediately."

"I never said I'd marry you."

"No, but you will." With his fingertips only, he began to arouse her. "I'm a very persuasive man."

"I need to think." But she was trembling again. "Stephen, marriage is very serious."

"Deadly. And I should warn you that I've already decided to murder any man you look at for more than twenty seconds."

"Really?" She turned her head back, prepared to be angry. But he was smiling. No one else had ever smiled at her in quite that way. "Really?"

"I can't let you go, Rebecca. Can't and won't. Come back with me. Marry me. Have children with me."

"Stephen—"

He laid a finger to her lips. "I know what I'm asking you. You've already started a new life, made new plans. We've had only days together, but I can make you happy. I can promise to love you for a lifetime, or however many lifetimes we have. You once dived into the sea on impulse. Dive with me now, Rebecca. I swear you won't regret it."

Gently she pressed her lips to his fingertip, then drew his hand away. "All my life I've wondered what I might find if I had the courage to look. I found you, Stephen." With a laugh she threw her arms around him. "When do you want to leave?"

* * * * *

TEMPTATION

This book is dedicated with gratitude
and affection to Nancy Jackson.

Chapter 1

"If there's one thing I hate," Eden mumbled, "it's six o'clock in the morning."

Sunlight poured through the thinly screened windows of the cabin and fell on the wooden floor, the metal bars of her bunk, and her face. The sound of the morning bell echoed dully in her head. Though she'd known that long, clanging ring for only three days, Eden already hated it.

For one fanciful moment, she buried her face under the pillow, imagining herself cuddled in her big four-poster. The Irish-linen sheets would smell ever-so-slightly of lemon. In her airy pastel bedroom, the curtains would be drawn against the morning, the scent of fresh flowers sweetening the air.

The pillowcase smelled of feathers and detergent.

With a grunt, Eden tossed the pillow to the floor, then

struggled to sit up. Now that the morning bell had stopped, she could hear the cries of a couple of excited crows. From the cabin directly across the compound came a happy blast of rock music. With glazed eyes, she watched Candice Bartholomew bound out of the adjoining bunk. Her sharp-featured pixie's face was split by a grin.

"Morning." Candy's long, clever fingers ran through her thatch of red hair like scoops, causing it to bounce into further disarray. Candy was, Eden had always thought, all bounce. "It's a beautiful day," she announced, in a voice as cheerful as the rest of her. Watching her friend stretch in frilly baby-doll pajamas, Eden gave another noncommittal grunt. She swung her bare legs off the mattress and contemplated the accomplishment of putting her feet on the floor.

"I could grow to hate you." Eden's voice, still husky with sleep, carried the rounded tones of her finishing-school education. Eyes shut, she pushed her own tousled blond hair away from her face.

Grinning, Candy tossed open the cabin door so that she could breathe in the fresh morning air while she studied her friend. The strong summer sunlight shot through Eden's pale hair, making it look fragile where it lay against her forehead and cheeks. Her eyes remained shut. Her slender shoulders slumped, she let out an enormous yawn. Candy wisely said nothing, knowing Eden didn't share her enthusiasm for sunrise.

"It can't be morning," Eden grumbled. "I swear I only lay down five minutes ago." Resting her elbows on her knees, she dropped her face into her hands. Her complexion was creamy, with just a suggestion of rose on the crest of her cheekbones. Her nose was small, with a hint of an upward tilt at the tip. What might have been a coolly aristocratic face was gentled by a full, generous mouth.

Candy took in one last breath of air, then shut the door. "All you need is a shower and some coffee. The first week of camp's the toughest, remember?"

Eden opened wide, lake-blue eyes. "Easy for you to say. You're not the one who fell in the poison ivy."

"Still itching?"

"A little." Because her own foul mood was making her feel guilty, Eden managed a smile. Everything softened, eyes, mouth, voice. "In any case, this is the first time we're the campees instead of the campers." Letting out another fierce yawn, she rose and tugged on a robe. The air coming through the screens was fresh as a daisy, and chilly enough to make Eden's toes curl. She wished she could remember what she'd done with her slippers.

"Try under the bunk," Candy suggested.

Eden bent down and found them. They were embroidered pink silk, hardly practical, but it hadn't seemed worthwhile to invest in another pair. Putting them on gave her an excuse to sit down again. "Do you really think five consecutive summers at Camp Forden for Girls prepared us for this?"

Haunted by her own doubts, Candy clasped her hands together. "Eden, are you having second thoughts?"

Because she recognized distress in the bubbly voice, Eden buried her own doubts. She had both a financial and emotional interest in the newly formed Camp Liberty. Complaining wasn't going to put her on the road to success. With a shake of her head, she walked over to squeeze Candy's shoulder. "What I have is a terminal case of morning crankiness. Let me get that shower, then I'll be ready to face our twenty-seven tenants."

"Eden." Candy stopped her before she closed the bathroom door. "It's going to work, for both of us. I know it."

"I know it, too." Eden closed the bathroom door and leaned against it. She could admit it now, while she was alone. She was scared to death. Her last dime, and her last ray of hope, were tied up in the six cabins, the stables and the cafeteria that were Camp Liberty. What did Eden Carlbough, former Philadelphia socialite, know about managing a girls' summer camp? Just enough to terrify her.

If she failed now, with this, could she pick up the pieces and go on? Would there be any pieces left? Confidence was what was needed, she told herself as she turned the taps on. Once inside the narrow shower stall, she gave the tap optimistically marked HOT another twist. Water, lukewarm, dripped out halfheartedly. Confidence, Eden thought again as she shivered under the miserly spray. Plus some cold hard cash and a whole barrel of luck.

She found the soap and began to lather with the soft-scented French milled she still allowed herself to indulge in. A year ago she would never have considered something as lowly as soap an indulgence.

A year ago.

Eden turned so that the rapidly cooling water hit her back. A year ago she would have risen at eight, had a leisurely, steaming shower, then breakfasted on toast and coffee, perhaps some shirred eggs. Sometime before ten, she would have driven to the library for her volunteer morning. There would have been lunch with Eric, perhaps at the Deux Cheminées before she gave her afternoon to the museum or one of Aunt Dottie's charities.

The biggest decision she might have made was whether to wear her rose silk suit or her ivory linen. Her evening might have been spent quietly at home, or at one of Philadelphia's elegant dinner parties.

No pressure. No problems. But then, Papa had been alive.

Eden sighed as she rinsed away the last of the lather. The light French scent clung to her even as she dried her skin with the serviceable camp-issue towel. When her father had been alive, she had thought that money was simply something to spend and that time was forever. She had been raised to plan a menu, but not to cook; to run a home, but not to clean it.

Throughout her childhood, she had been carelessly happy with her widowed father in the ageless elegance of their Philadelphia home. There had always been party dresses and cotillions, afternoon teas and riding lessons. The Carlbough name was an old and respected one. The Carlbough money had been a simple fact of life.

How quickly and finally things could change.

Now she was giving riding instructions and juggling columns in a ledger with the vain hope that one and one didn't always make two.

Because the tiny mirror over the tiny sink was dripping with condensation, Eden rubbed it with the towel. She took a miserly dab of the half pot of imported face cream she had left. She was going to make it last through the summer. If *she* lasted through the summer herself, another pot would be her reward.

Eden found the cabin empty when she opened the bathroom door. If she knew Candy, and after twenty years she certainly did, the redhead would be down with the girls already. How easily she became acclimatized, Eden thought; then she reminded herself it was time she did the same. She took her jeans and her red T-shirt with CAMP LIBERTY emblazoned on the chest, and began to dress. Even as a teenager, Eden had rarely dressed so casually.

She had enjoyed her social life—the parties, the well-chaperoned ski trips to Vermont, the trips to New York for shopping or the theater, the vacations in Europe. The prospect of earning a living had never been considered, by her, or her father. Carlbough women didn't work, they chaired committees.

College years had been spent with the idea of rounding out her education rather than focusing on a career. At twenty-three, Eden was forced to admit she was qualified to do absolutely nothing.

She could have blamed her father. But how could she blame a man who had been so indulgent and loving? She had adored him. She could blame herself for being naive and shortsighted, but she could never blame her father. Even now, a year after his sudden death, she still felt pangs of grief.

She could deal with that. The one thing she had been taught to do, the one thing she felt herself fully qualified to accomplish, was to cover emotion with poise, with control, or with disdain. She could go day after day, week after week through the summer, surrounded by the girls at camp and the counselors Candy had hired, and none of them would know she still mourned her father. Or that her pride had been shattered by Eric Keeton.

Eric, the promising young banker with her father's firm. Eric, always so charming, so attentive, so suitable. It had been during her last year of college that she had accepted his ring and made her promises to him. And he had made promises to her.

When she discovered the hurt was still there, Eden coated it, layer by layer, with anger. Facing the mirror, she tugged her hair back in a short ponytail, a style her hairdresser would have shuddered at.

It was more practical, Eden told her reflection. She was a practical woman now, and hair waving softly to the shoulders would just have got in the way during the riding lessons she was to give that morning.

For a moment, she pressed her fingers against her eyes. Why were the mornings always the worst? She would wake, expecting to come out of some bad dream and find herself at home again. But it wasn't her home any longer. There were strangers living in it now. Brian Carlbough's death had not been a bad dream, but a horrible, horrible reality.

A sudden heart attack had taken him overnight, leaving Eden stunned with shock and grief. Even before the grief could fade, Eden had been struck with another shock.

There had been lawyers, black-vested lawyers with long, technical monologues. They had had offices that had smelled of old leather and fresh polish. With solemn faces and politely folded hands, they had shattered her world.

Poor investments, she had been told, bad market trends, mortgages, second mortgages, short-term loans. The simple fact had been, once the details had been sifted through, there had been no money.

Brian Carlbough had been a gambler. At the time of

his death, his luck had turned, and he hadn't had time to recoup his losses. His daughter had been forced to liquidate his assets in order to pay off the debts. The house she had grown up in and loved was gone. She had still been numbed by grief when she had found herself without a home or an income. Crashing down on top of that had been Eric's betrayal.

Eden yanked open the cabin door and was met by the balmy morning air of the mountains. The breathtaking view of greening hills and blue sky didn't affect her. She was back in Philadelphia, hearing Eric's calm, reasonable voice.

The scandal, she remembered and began marching toward the big cabin where mess would be served. *His* reputation. *His* career. Everything she had loved had been taken away, but he had only been concerned with how he might be affected.

He had never loved her. Eden jammed her hands into her pockets and kept walking. She'd been a fool not to see it from the beginning. But she'd learned, Eden reminded herself. How she'd learned. It had simply been a merger to Eric, the Carlbough name, the Carlbough money and reputation. When they had been destroyed, he had cut his losses.

Eden slowed her quick pace, realizing she was out of breath, not from exertion but from temper. It would never do to walk into breakfast with her face flushed and her eyes gleaming. Giving herself a moment, she took a few deep breaths and looked around her.

The air was still cool, but by midmorning the sun would be warm and strong. Summer had barely begun.

And it was beautiful. Lining the compound were a

half-dozen small cabins with their window flaps open to the morning. The sound of girlish laughter floated through the windows. Along the pathway between cabins four and five was a scattering of anemones. A dogwood, with a few stubborn blooms clinging to it, stood nearby. Above cabin two, a mockingbird chattered.

Beyond the main camp to the west were rolling hills, deeply green. Grazing horses and trees dotted them. There was an openness here, a sense of space which Eden found incredible. Her life had always been focused on the city. Streets, buildings, traffic, people, those had been the familiar. There were times when she felt a quick pang of need for what had been. It was still possible for her to have all that. Aunt Dottie had offered her home and her love. No one would ever know how long and hard Eden had wrestled with the temptation to accept the invitation and let her life drift.

Perhaps gambling was in Eden's blood, too. Why else would she have sunk what ready cash she had had left into a fledgling camp for girls in the hills?

Because she had had to try, Eden reminded herself. She had had to take the risk on her own. She could never go back into the shell of the fragile porcelain doll she had been. Here, centered in such open space, she would take the time to learn about herself. What was inside Eden Carlbough? Maybe, just maybe, by expanding her horizons, she would find her place.

Candy was right. Eden took a long last breath. It was going to work. They were going to make it work.

"Hungry?" Her hair damp from whatever shower she'd popped into, Candy cut across Eden's path.

"Starved." Content, Eden swung a friendly arm around Candy's shoulder. "Where did you run off to?"

"You know me, I can't let any part of this place run by itself." Like Eden, Candy swept her gaze over the camp. Her expression reflected everything inside her—the love, the fear, the fierce pride. "I was worried about you."

"Candy, I told you, I was just cranky this morning." Eden watched a group of girls rush out of a cabin and head for breakfast.

"Eden, we've been friends since we were six months old. No one knows better than I what you're going through."

No, no one did, and since Candy was the person she loved best, Eden determined to do a better job of concealing the wounds that were still open. "I've put it behind me, Candy."

"Maybe. But I know that the camp was initially my venture, and that I roped you in."

"You didn't rope me in. I wanted to invest. We both know it was a pitifully small amount."

"Not to me. The extra money made it possible for me to include the equestrian program. Then, when you agreed to come in and give riding lessons…"

"Just keeping a close eye on my investment," Eden said lightly. "Next year I won't be a part-time riding instructor and bookkeeper. I'll be a full-fledged counselor. No regrets, Candy." This time she meant it. "It's ours."

"And the bank's."

Eden shrugged that away. "We need this place. You, because it's what you've always wanted to do, always worked and studied toward. Me…" She hesitated, then sighed. "Let's face it, I haven't got anything else. The camp's putting a roof over my head, giving me three meals a day and a goal. I need to prove I can make it."

"People think we're crazy."

The pride came back, with a feeling of recklessness Eden was just learning to savor. "Let them."

With a laugh, Candy tugged at Eden's hair. "Let's eat."

Two hours later, Eden was winding up the day's first riding lesson. This was her specialty, her contribution to the partnership she and Candy had made. It had also been decided to trust Eden with the books, mainly because no one could have been more inept with figures than Candice Bartholomew.

Candy had interviewed and hired a staff of counselors, a nutritionist and a nurse. They hoped to have a pool and a swimming instructor one day, but for now there was supervised swimming and rowing on the lake, arts and crafts, hiking and archery. Candy had spent months refining a program for the summer, while Eden had juggled the profit-and-loss statements. She prayed the money would hold out while Candy ordered supplies.

Unlike Candy, Eden wasn't certain the first week of camp would be the toughest. Her partner had all the training, all the qualifications for running the camp, but Candy also had an optimist's flair for overlooking details like red ink on the books.

Pushing those thoughts aside, Eden signaled from the center of the corral. "That's all for today." She scanned the six young faces under their black riding hats. "You're doing very well."

"When can we gallop, Miss Carlbough?"

"After you learn to trot." She patted one of the horses' flanks. Wouldn't it be lovely, she thought, to gallop off into the hills, riding so fast even memories couldn't follow? Foolish, Eden told herself; she gave her attention back to the girls. "Dismount, then cool down your horses. Remember, they depend on you." The breeze tossed her bangs, and she brushed at them absently. "Remember to put all the tack in its proper place for the next class."

This caused the groans she expected. Riding and playing with the horses was one thing, tidying up afterward was another. Eden considered exerting discipline without causing resentment another accomplishment. Over the past week, she'd learned to link the girls' faces and names. The eleven- and twelve-year-olds in her group had an enthusiasm that kept her on her toes. She'd already separated in her mind the two or three she instructed who had the kind of horse fever she recognized from her own adolescence. It was rewarding, after an hour on her feet in the sun, to answer the rapid-fire questions. Ultimately, one by one, she nudged them toward the stables.

"Eden!" Turning, she spotted Candy hustling toward her. Even from a distance, Eden recognized concern.

"What's happened?"

"We're missing three kids."

"What?" Panic came first, and quickly. Years of training had her pulling it back. "What do you mean, missing?"

"I mean they're nowhere in camp. Roberta Snow, Linda Hopkins and Marcie Jamison." Candy dragged a hand through her hair, a habitual gesture of tension. "Barbara was lining up her group for rowing, and they didn't show. We've looked everywhere."

"We can't panic," Eden said, as much to warn herself

as Candy. "Roberta Snow? Isn't she the little brunette who stuck a lizard down one of the other girls' shirts? And the one who set off the morning bell at 3:00 a.m.?"

"Yes, that's her." Candy set her teeth. "The little darling. Judge Harper Snow's granddaughter. If she's skinned her knee, we'll probably face a lawsuit." With a shake of her head, Candy switched to an undertone. "The last anyone saw of her this morning, she was walking east." She pointed a finger, paint-spattered from her early art class. "No one noticed the other girls, but my bet is that they're with her. Darling Roberta is an inveterate leader."

"If she's walking that way, wouldn't she run into that apple orchard?"

"Yeah." Candy shut her eyes. "Oh, yeah. I'm going to have six girls up to their wrists in modeling clay in ten minutes, or I'd go off myself. Eden, I'm almost sure they headed for the orchard. One of the other girls admitted she heard Roberta planning to sneak over there for a few samples. We don't want any trouble with the owner. He's letting us use his lake only because I begged, shamelessly. He wasn't thrilled about having a girls' summer camp for a neighbor."

"Well, he has one," Eden pointed out. "So we'll all have to deal with it. I'm the one most easily spared around here, so I'll go after them."

"I was hoping you'd say that. Seriously, Eden, if they've snuck into that orchard, which I'd bet my last dime they have, we could be in for it. The man made no bones about how he feels about his land and his privacy."

"Three little girls are hardly going to do any damage to a bunch of apple trees." Eden began to walk, with Candy scurrying to keep pace.

"He's Chase Elliot. You know, Elliot Apples? Juice, cider, sauce, jelly, chocolate-covered apple seeds, whatever can be made from an apple, they do it. He made it abundantly clear that he didn't want to find any little girls climbing his trees."

"He won't find them, I will." Leaving Candy behind, Eden swung over a fence.

"Put Roberta on a leash when you catch up to her." Candy watched her disappear through the trees.

Eden followed the path from the camp, pleased when she found a crumpled candy wrapper. Roberta. With a grim smile, Eden picked it up and stuffed it in her pocket. Judge Snow's granddaughter had already earned a reputation for her stash of sweets.

It was warm now, but the path veered through a cool grove of aspens. Sunlight dappled the ground, making the walk, if not her errand, pleasant. Squirrels dashed here and there, confident enough in their own speed not to be alarmed at Eden's intrusion. Once a rabbit darted across her path, and disappeared into the brush with a frantic rustle. Overhead a woodpecker drummed, sending out an echo.

It occurred to Eden that she was more completely alone than she had ever been before. No civilization here. She bent down for another candy wrapper. Well, very little of it.

There were new scents here, earth, animal, vegetation, to be discovered. Wildflowers sprang up, tougher and more resilient than hothouse roses. It pleased her that she was even beginning to be able to recognize a few. They came back, year after year, without pampering, taking what came and thriving on it. They gave her hope. She could find a place here. Had found a place, she corrected herself. Her friends in Philadelphia might think her mad, but she was beginning to enjoy it.

The grove of aspens thinned abruptly, and the sunlight was strong again. She blinked against it, then shielded her eyes as she scanned the Elliot orchards.

Apple trees stretched ahead of her as far as she could see, to the north, south and east. Row after row after row of trees lined the slopes. Some of them were old and gnarled, some young and straight. Instantly she thought of early spring and the overwhelming scent of apple blossoms.

It would be magnificent, she thought as she stepped up to the fence that separated the properties. The fragrance, the pretty white-and-pink blossoms, the freshly green leaves, would be a marvelous sight. Now the leaves were dark and thick, and instead of blossoms, she could see fruit in the trees closest to her. Small, shiny, and green they hung, waiting for the sun to ripen them.

How many times had she eaten applesauce that had begun right here? The idea made her smile as she began to climb the fence. Her vision of an orchard had been a lazy little grove guarded by an old man in overalls. A quaint picture, but nothing as huge and impressive as the reality.

The sound of giggling took her by surprise. Shifting toward the direction of the sound, Eden watched an apple fall from a tree and roll toward her feet. Bending, she picked it up, tossing it away as she walked closer. When she looked up, she spotted three pairs of sneakers beneath the cover of leaves and branches.

"Ladies." Eden spoke coolly and was rewarded by

three startled gasps. "Apparently you took a wrong turn on your way to the lake."

Roberta's triangular, freckled face appeared through the leaves. "Hi, Miss Carlbough. Would you like an apple?"

The devil. But even as she thought it, Eden had to tighten her lips against a smile. "Down," she said simply, then stepped closer to the trunk to assist.

They didn't need her. Three agile little bodies scrambled down and dropped lightly onto the ground. In a gesture she knew could be intimidating, Eden lifted her left eyebrow.

"I'm sure you're aware that leaving camp property unsupervised and without permission is against the rules."

"Yes, Miss Carlbough." The response would have been humble if it hadn't been for the gleam in Roberta's eye.

"Since none of you seem interested in rowing today, Mrs. Petrie has a great deal of washing up to be done in the kitchen." Pleased by her own inspiration, Eden decided Candy would approve. "You're to report to Miss Bartholomew, then to Mrs. Petrie for kitchen detail."

Only two of the girls dropped their heads and looked down at the ground.

"Miss Carlbough, do you think it's fair to give us extra kitchen detail?" Roberta, one half-eaten apple still in hand, tilted her pointed chin. "After all, our parents are paying for the camp."

Eden felt her palms grow damp. Judge Snow was a wealthy and powerful man with a reputation for indulging his granddaughter. If the little monster complained… No. Eden took a deep breath and not by a flicker showed her anxiety. She wouldn't be intimidated or blackmailed by a pint-size con artist with apple juice on her chin.

"Yes, your parents are paying for you to be entertained, instructed and disciplined. When they signed you up for Camp Liberty, it was with the understanding that you would obey the rules. But if you prefer, I'd be glad to call your parents and discuss this incident with them."

"No, ma'am." Knowing when to retreat, Roberta smiled charmingly. "We'll be glad to help Mrs. Petrie, and we're sorry for breaking the rules."

And I'm sure you have a bridge I could buy, Eden thought, but she kept her face impassive. "Fine. It's time to start back."

"My hat!" Roberta would have darted back up the tree if Eden hadn't made a lucky grab for her. "I left my hat up there. Please, Miss Carlbough, it's my Phillies cap, and it's autographed and everything."

"You start back. I'll get it. I don't want Miss Bartholomew to worry any longer than necessary."

"We'll apologize."

"See that you do." Eden watched them scramble over the fence. "And no detours," she called out. "Or I keep the cap." One look at Roberta assured her that that bit of blackmail was all that was needed. "Monsters," she murmured as they jogged back into the grove, but the smile finally escaped. Turning back, she studied the tree.

All she had to do was climb up. It had looked simple enough when Roberta and her partners-in-crime had done it. Somehow, it didn't look as simple now. Squaring her shoulders, Eden stepped forward to grab a low-hanging branch. She'd done a little mountain-climbing in Switzerland; how much harder could this be? Pulling herself up, she hooked her foot in the first

vee she found. The bark was rough against her palm.
Concentrating on her goal, she ignored the scrapes. With
both feet secured, she reached for the next branch and
began to work her way up. Leaves brushed her cheeks.

She spotted the cap hanging on a short branch, two
arms' lengths out of reach. When she made the mistake
of looking down, her stomach clenched. So don't look,
Eden ordered herself. What you can't see can't hurt
you. She hoped.

Eden cautiously inched her way out to the cap. When
her fingers made contact with it, she let out a low breath
of relief. After setting it on her own head, she found
herself looking out, beyond the tree, over the orchard.

Now it was the symmetry that caught her admiration.
From her bird's height, she could see the order as well
as the beauty. She could just barely glimpse a slice of
the lake beyond the aspens. It winked blue in the
distance. There were barnlike buildings, and what
appeared to be a greenhouse, far off to the right. About
a quarter of a mile away, there was a truck, apparently
abandoned, on a wide dirt path. In the quiet, birds began
to sing again. Turning her head, she saw the bright
yellow flash of a butterfly.

The scent of leaves and fruit and earth was tangy,
basic. Unable to resist, Eden reached out and plucked a
sun-warmed apple.

He'd never miss it, she decided as she bit into the
skin. The tart flavor, not quite ripe, shot into her mouth.
She shivered at the shock of it, the sensual appeal, then
bit again. Delicious, she thought. Exciting. Forbidden
fruit usually was, she remembered, but she grinned as
she took a third bite.

"What in the devil are you doing?"

She started, almost unseating herself, as the voice boomed up from below. She swallowed the bite of apple quickly before peering down through the leaves.

He stood with his hands on his hips, narrow, lean, spare. A faded denim workshirt was rolled up past the elbows to show tan and muscle. Warily, Eden brought her eyes to his face. It was tanned like his arms, with the skin drawn tight over bone. His nose was long and not quite straight, his mouth full and firm and frowning. Jet-black and unruly, his hair fell over his brow and curled just beyond the collar of his shirt. Pale, almost translucent green eyes scowled up at her.

An apple, Eden, and now the serpent. The idea ran through her head before she drew herself back.

Wonderful, she thought. She'd been caught pinching apples by the foreman. Since disappearing wasn't an option, she opened her mouth to start a plausible explanation.

"Young lady, do you belong at the camp next door?"

The tone brought on a frown. She might be penniless, she might be scrambling to make a living, but she was still a Carlbough. And a Carlbough could certainly handle an apple foreman. "Yes, that's right. I'd like to—"

"Are you aware that this is private property, and that you're trespassing?"

The color of her eyes deepened, the only outward sign of her embarrassed fury. "Yes, but I—"

"These trees weren't planted for little girls to climb."

"I hardly think—"

"Come down." There was absolute command in his tone. "I'll have to take you back to the camp director."

The temper she had always gently controlled bubbled up until she gave serious consideration to throwing what was left of the apple down on his head. No one, absolutely no one, gave her orders. "That won't be necessary."

"I'll decide what's necessary. Come down here."

She'd come down all right, Eden thought. Then, with a few well-chosen words, he'd be put precisely in his place. Annoyance carried her from branch to branch, leaving no room for thoughts of height or inexperience. The two scrapes she picked up on the trip were hardly felt. Her back was to him as she lowered herself into a vee of the trunk. The pleasure of demolishing him with icy manners would be well worth the embarrassment of having been caught in the wrong place at the wrong time. She imagined him cringing and babbling an incoherent apology.

Then her foot slipped, and her frantic grab for a limb was an inch short of the mark. With a shriek that was equal parts surprise and dismay, she fell backward into space.

The breath whooshed back out of her as she connected with something solid. The tanned, muscled arms she'd seen from above wrapped around her. Momentum carried them both to the ground and, like the apple, they rolled. When the world stopped spinning, Eden found herself beneath a very firm, very long body.

Roberta's cap had flown off and Eden's face, no longer shadowed by the brim, was left unguarded in the sunlight. Chase stared down at her and felt soft breasts yield under him.

"You're not twelve years old," he murmured.

"Certainly not."

Amused now, he shifted his weight, but didn't

remove it. "I didn't get a good look at you when you were in the tree." He had time to make up for that now, he decided, and he looked his fill. "You're quite a windfall." Carelessly, he brushed stray strands of hair away from her face. His fingertips were as rough against her skin as the bark had been to her palms. "What are you doing in a girls' summer camp?"

"Running it," she said coldly. It wasn't a complete lie. Because it would have bruised her dignity even more to squirm, she settled on sending him an icy look. "Would you mind?"

"Running it?" Since she had dropped out of one of his trees, he had no qualms about ignoring her request. "I met someone. Bartholomew—red hair, appealing face." He scanned Eden's classic features. "You're not her."

"Obviously not." Because his body was too warm, too male, and too close, she sacrificed some dignity by putting her hands to his shoulders. He didn't budge. "I'm her partner. Eden Carlbough."

"Ah, of the Philadelphia Carlboughs."

The humor in his voice was another blow to her pride. Eden combated it with a withering stare. "That's correct."

Intriguing little package, he thought. All manners and breeding. "A pleasure, Miss Carlbough. I'm Chase Elliot of the South Mountain Elliots."

Chapter 2

Perfect, just perfect, Eden thought as she stared up at him. Not the foreman, but the bloody owner. Caught stealing apples by, falling out of trees on and pinned to the ground under, the owner. She took a deep breath.

"How do you do, Mr. Elliot."

She might have been in the front parlor pouring tea, Chase thought; he had to admire her. Then he burst out laughing. "I do just fine, Miss Carlbough. And you?"

He was laughing at her. Even after the scandal and shame she had faced, no one had dared laugh at her. Not to her face. Her lips trembled once before she managed to control them. She wouldn't give the oaf the pleasure of knowing how much he infuriated her.

"I'm quite well, thank you, or will be when you let me up."

City manners, he thought. Socially correct and absolutely meaningless. His own were a bit cruder, but more honest. "In a minute. I'm finding this conversation fascinating."

"Then perhaps we could continue it standing up."

"I'm very comfortable." That wasn't precisely true. The soft, slender lines of her body were causing him some problems. Rather than alleviate them, Chase decided to enjoy them. And her. "So, how are you finding life in the rough?"

He was still laughing at her, without troubling to pretend otherwise. Eden tasted the fury bubbling up in her throat. She swallowed it. "Mr. Elliot—"

"Chase," he interrupted. "I think, under the circumstances, we should dispense with formalities."

Control teetered long enough for her to shove against his shoulders again. It was like pushing rock. "This is ridiculous. You *have* to let me up."

"I rarely have to do anything." His voice was a drawl now, and insolent, but no less imposing than the bellow that had first greeted her. "I've heard a lot about you, Eden Carlbough." And he'd seen the newspaper pictures that he now realized had been just shy of the mark. It was difficult to capture that cool sexuality in two dimensions. "I never expected a Carlbough of Philadelphia to fall out of one of my trees."

Her breathing became unsteady. All the training, the years she'd spent being taught how to coat every emotion with politeness, began to crack. "It was hardly my intention to fall out of one of your trees."

"Wouldn't have fallen out if you hadn't climbed up." He smiled, realizing how glad he was that he'd decided to check this section of the orchard himself.

This couldn't be happening. Eden closed her eyes a moment and waited for things to fall back into their proper places. She couldn't be lying flat on her back under a stranger. "Mr. Elliot." Her voice was calm and reasonable when she tried it again. "I'd be more than happy to give you a complete explanation if you'd let me up."

"Explanation first."

Her mouth quite simply fell open. "You are the most unbelievably rude and boorish man I have ever met."

"My property," he said simply. "My rules. Let's hear your explanation."

She almost shuddered with the effort to hold back the torrent of abuse that leaped to her tongue. Because of her position, she had to squint up at him. Already a headache was collecting behind her eyes. "Three of my girls wandered away from camp. Unfortunately, they climbed over the fence and onto your property. I found them, ordered them down and sent them back to the camp, where they are being properly disciplined."

"Tar and feathers?"

"I'm sure you'd prefer that, but we settled on extra kitchen detail."

"Seems fair. But that doesn't explain you falling out of my tree and into my arms. Though I've about decided not to complain about that. You smell like Paris." To Eden's amazement, he leaned down and buried his face in her hair. "Wicked nights in Paris."

"Stop it." Now her voice wasn't calm, wasn't disciplined.

Chase felt her heart begin to thud against his own. It ran through his mind that he wanted to do more than sample her scent. But when he lifted his head, her eyes were wide. Along with the awareness in them was a trace of fear.

"Explanation," he said lightly. "That's all I intend to take at the moment."

She could hear her own pulse hammering in her throat. Of its own accord, her gaze fell upon his mouth. Was she mad, or could she almost taste the surge of masculine flavor that would certainly be on his lips? She felt her muscles softening, then instantly stiffened. She might very well be mad. If an explanation was what it took, she'd give it to him and get away. Far away.

"One of the girls…" Her mind veered vengefully to Roberta. "One of them left her cap in the tree."

"So you went up after it." He nodded, accepting her explanation. "That doesn't explain why you were helping yourself to one of my apples."

"It was mealy."

Grinning again, he ran a hand along her jawline. "I doubt that. I'd imagine it was hard and tart and delicious. I had my share of stomachaches from green apples years ago. The pleasure's usually worth the pain."

Something uncomfortably like need was spreading through her. The fear of it chilled both her eyes and voice. "You have your explanation, and your apology."

"I never heard an apology."

She'd be damned, she'd be twice damned if she'd give him one now. Glaring at him, she nearly managed to look regal. "I want you to let me up this instant. You're perfectly free to prosecute if you feel the need for compensation for a couple of worm-filled apples, but for now, I'm tired of your ridiculous backwoods arrogance."

His apples were the best in the state, the best in the

country. But at the moment, he relished the idea of her sinking her pretty white teeth into a worm. "You haven't had a taste of backwoods arrogance yet. Maybe you should."

"You wouldn't dare," she began, only to have the last word muffled by his mouth.

The kiss caught her completely off guard. It was rough and demanding and as tart as the apple had been. Forbidden fruit. To a woman accustomed to coaxing, to requesting, the hard demand left her limp, unable to respond or protest. Then his hands were on her face, his thumbs tracing her jawline. Like the kiss, his palms were hard and thrilling.

He didn't regret it. Though he wasn't a man used to taking from a woman what wasn't offered, he didn't regret it. Not when the fruit was this sweet. Even though she lay very still, he could taste the panicked excitement on her lips. Yes, very sweet, he thought. Very innocent. Very dangerous. He lifted his head the moment she began to struggle.

"Easy," he murmured, still stroking her chin with his thumb. Her eyes were more frantic than furious. "It seems you're not the woman of the world you're reputed to be."

"Let me up." Her voice was shaking now, but she was beyond caring.

Getting to his feet, Chase brought her with him. "Want some help brushing off?"

"You are the most offensive man I've ever met."

"I can believe it. A pity you've been spoiled and pampered for so long." She started to turn away, but he caught her shoulders for one last look. "It should be interesting to see how long you last here without the basics—like hairdressers and butlers."

He's just like everyone else, she thought; she coated her hurt and doubt with disdain. "I'm very late for my next class, Mr. Elliot. If you'll excuse me?"

He lifted his hands from her shoulders, holding the palms out a moment before dropping them. "Try to keep the kids out of the trees," he warned. "A fall can be dangerous."

His smile had insults trembling on her lips. Clamping her tongue between her teeth, Eden scrambled over the fence.

He watched her, enjoying the view until she was swallowed up by the aspens. Glimpsing the cap at his feet, he bent down for it. As good as a calling card, he decided, tucking it into his back pocket.

Eden went through the rest of the day struggling not to think. About anything. She had deliberately avoided telling Candy about her meeting with Chase. In telling of it, she would have to think about it.

The humiliation of being caught up a tree was hard enough to swallow. Still, under other circumstances, she and Candy might have shared a laugh over it. Under any other circumstances.

But more than the humiliation, even more than the anger, were the sensations. She wasn't sure what they were, but each separate sensation she had experienced in the orchard remained fresh and vibrant throughout the day. She couldn't shake them off or cover them over, and she certainly couldn't ignore them. If she understood anything, she understood how important

it was for her to close off her feelings before they
could grow.

Ridiculous. Eden interrupted her own thoughts. She
didn't know Chase Elliot. Moreover, she didn't want to
know him. It was true that she couldn't block out what
had happened, but she could certainly see that it never
happened again.

Over the past year, she had taken control of the reins
for the first time in her life. She knew what it was to
fumble, what it was to fail, but she also knew she would
never fully release those reins again. Disillusionment
had toughened her. Perhaps that was the one snatch of
silver lining in the cloud.

Because of it, she recognized Chase Elliot as a
man who held his own reins, and tightly. She had
found him rude and overbearing, but she had also
seen his power and authority. She'd had her fill of
dominating men. Rough-edged or polished, they were
all the same underneath. Since her experience with
Eric, Eden's opinion of men in general had reached a
low ebb. Her encounter with Chase had done nothing
to raise it.

It was annoying that she had to remind herself con-
tinually to forget about him.

Learning the camp's routine was enough to occupy
her mind. Since she didn't have Candy's years of training
and experience in counseling, her responsibilities were
relatively few and often mundane, but at least she had the
satisfaction of knowing she was more than a spectator.
Ambition had become a new vice. If her role as appren-
tice meant she mucked out stalls and groomed horses,
then Eden was determined to have the cleanest stables

and the glossiest horses in Pennsylvania. She considered her first blister a badge of accomplishment.

The rush after the dinner bell still intimidated Eden. Twenty-seven girls aged ten to fourteen swarmed the cafeteria. It was one of Eden's new duties to help keep order. Voices were raised on topics that usually ranged from boys to rock stars, then back to boys. With a little luck, there was no jostling or shoving in line. But luck usually required an eagle eye.

Camp Liberty's glossy brochures had promised wholesome food. Tonight's menu included crispy chicken, whipped potatoes and steamed broccoli. Flatware rattled on trays as the girls shuffled, cafeteria-style, down the serving line.

"It's been a good day." Candy stood beside Eden, her eyes shifting back and forth as she managed to watch the entire room at once.

"And nearly over." Even as she said it, Eden realized her back didn't ache quite as much as it had the first couple of days. "I've got two girls in the morning riding session who show real promise. I was hoping I could give them a little extra time a couple of days a week."

"Great, we'll check the schedule." Candy watched one of the counselors convince a camper to put a stem of broccoli on her plate. "I wanted to tell you that you handled Roberta and company beautifully. Kitchen detail was an inspiration."

"Thanks." Eden realized how low her pride had fallen when such a small thing made her glow. "I did have a twinge of guilt about dumping them on Mrs. Petrie."

"The report is they behaved like troopers."

"Roberta?"

"I know." Candy's smile was wry. Both women turned to see the girl in question, already seated and eating daintily. "It's like waiting for the other shoe to drop. Eden, do you remember Marcia Delacroix from Camp Forden?"

"How could I forget?" With the bulk of the campers seated, Eden and Candy joined the line. "She was the one who put the garter snake in Miss Forden's lingerie drawer."

"Yeah." She turned to give Roberta another look. "Do you believe in reincarnation?"

With a laugh, Eden accepted a scoop of potatoes. "Let's just say I'll be checking my underwear." Hefting the tray, she started forward. "You know, Candy, I—" She saw it as if in slow motion. Roberta, the devil's own gleam in her eyes, held her fork vertically, a thick blob of potatoes clinging to the tines. Aim was taken as Roberta pulled back the business end of the fork with an expert flick. Even as Eden opened her mouth, Roberta sent the blob sailing into the hair of the girl across from her. Pandemonium.

Globs of potatoes flew. Girls screamed. More retaliated. In a matter of seconds, floors, tables, chairs and adolescents were coated in a messy layer of white. Like a general leading the way into battle, Candy stepped into the chaos and lifted her whistle. Before she had the chance to blow it, she was hit, right between the eyes.

A shocked silence fell.

With her tray still in her hands, Eden stood, afraid to breathe. One breath, one little breath, she thought, and she would dissolve into helpless laughter. She felt the pressure of a giggle in her lungs as Candy slowly wiped the dollop of potato from the bridge of her nose.

"Young ladies." The two words, delivered in Candy's most ferocious voice, had Eden's breath catching in her throat. "You will finish your meal in silence. Absolute silence. As you finish, you will line up against this wall. When the dinner hour is over, you will be issued rags, mops and buckets. The mess area will shine tonight."

"Yes, Miss Bartholomew." The acknowledgment came in murmured unison. Only Roberta, her hands folded neatly, her face a picture of innocence, responded in clear tones.

After a long ten seconds of silent staring, Candy walked back to Eden and picked up her tray. "If you laugh," she said in an undertone, "I'll tie your tongue into a square knot."

"Who's laughing?" Eden desperately cleared her throat. "I'm not laughing."

"Yes, you are." Candy sailed, like a steamship, to the head table. "You're just clever enough to do it discreetly."

Eden sat, then carefully smoothed her napkin on her lap. "You've got mashed potatoes in your eyebrows." Candy glared at her, and she lifted her coffee cup to hide a grin behind it. "Actually, it's very becoming. You may have found an alternative to hair gel."

Candy glanced down at the cooling potatoes on her own plate. "Would you like to try some?"

"Now, darling, you're the one who's always telling me we have to set an example." Eden took a satisfying bite of her chicken. "Mrs. Petrie's a gem, isn't she?"

It took the better part of two hours to clean the mess area and to mop up the puddles of water spilled by the inexperienced janitorial crew. By lights-out most of the girls were too tired to loiter. A pleasant late-evening hush covered the camp.

If the mornings were the worst for Eden, the evenings were invariably the best. A long day of physical activity left her comfortably tired and relaxed. The sounds of night birds and insects were becoming familiar. More and more, she looked forward to an hour of solitude with a sky full of stars. There was no theater to dress for, no party to attend. The longer she was away from her former life-style, the less she missed it.

She was growing up, she reflected, and she liked the idea. She supposed maturity meant recognizing what was really important. The camp was important, her friendship with Candy vital. The girls under their care for the summer, even the dastardly Roberta Snow, were what really mattered. She came to realize that even if everything she had once had was handed back to her, she would no longer be able to treat it in the same way.

She had changed. And even though she was certain there were still more changes to come, she liked the new Eden Carlbough. This Eden was independent, not financially, but internally. She'd never realized how dependent she had been on her father, her fiancé, the servants. The new Eden could cope with problems, large ones, small ones. Her hands were no longer elegantly manicured. The nails were neat, but short and rounded, unpainted. Practical, Eden thought as she held one up for inspection. Useful. She liked what she saw.

She continued her nightly ritual by walking to the stables. Inside it was cool and dark, smelling of leather, hay and horses. Just stepping inside helped to cement her confidence. This was her contribution. In most other areas, she still relied on pride and nerve, but here she had skill and knowledge.

She would check each of the six horses, then the tack, before she would consider her duties over for the day. Candy might be able to build a cathedral out of papier-mâché, but she knew nothing about strained tendons or split hooves.

Eden stopped at the first stall to stroke the roan gelding she called Courage. In her hand was a paper bag with six apple halves. It was a nightly ritual the horses had caught on to quickly. Courage leaned his head over the stall door and nuzzled her palm.

"Such a good boy," she murmured as she reached into the bag. "Some of the girls still don't know a bit from a stirrup, but we're going to change that." She held the apple in her palm and let him take it. While he chewed contentedly, Eden stepped into the stall to check him over. He'd been a bargain because of his age and his slight swayback. She hadn't been looking for thorough-breds, but for dependability and gentleness. Satisfied that his grooming had been thorough, she latched the stall door behind her and went to the next.

Next summer they'd have at least three more mounts. Eden smiled as she worked her way from stall to stall. She wasn't going to question whether there would be a Camp Liberty next summer. There would be, and she'd be part of it. A real part.

She realized that she'd brought little with her other than money and a flair for horses. It was Candy who had the training, Candy who had had the three younger sisters and a family that had possessed more tradition than money. Unlike Eden, Candy had always known she would have to earn her own way and had prepared for it. But Eden was a quick learner. By Camp Liberty's second season, she would be a partner in more than name.

Her ambition was already spiraling upward. In a few years, Camp Liberty would be renowned for its equestrian program. The name Carlbough would be respected again. There might even come a time when her Philadelphia contemporaries would send their children to her. The irony of it pleased her.

After the fifth apple had been devoured, Eden moved to the last stall. Here was Patience, a sweet-tempered, aging mare who would tolerate any kind of ineptitude in a rider as long as she received affection. Sympathetic to old bones and muscles, Eden often spent an extra hour rubbing the mare down with liniment.

"Here you are, sweetheart." As the horse gnawed the apple, Eden lifted each hoof for inspection. "A pretty sketchy job," she mumbled before drawing a hoof pick out of her back pocket. "Let's see, wasn't it little Marcie who rode you last? I suppose this means we have to have a discussion on responsibility." With a sigh, Eden switched to another hoof. "I hate discussions on responsibility. Especially when I'm giving them." Patience snorted sympathetically. "Well, I can't leave all the dirty work to Candy, can I? In any case, I don't think Marcie meant to be inconsiderate. She's still a bit nervous around horses. We'll have to show her what a nice lady you are. There. Want a rubdown?" After sticking the pick back in her pocket, Eden rested her cheek against the mare's neck. "Oh, me too, Patience. A nice long massage with some scented oil. You can just lie there with your eyes closed while all the kinks are worked out, then your skin feels so soft, your muscles so supple." With a quick laugh, Eden drew away. "Well, since you can't oblige me, I'll oblige you. Just let me get the liniment."

Giving the mare a final pat, she turned. Her breath caught on a gasp.

Chase Elliot leaned against the open stall door. Shadows fell across his face, deepening its hollows. In the dim light, his eyes were like sea foam. She would have taken a step backward in retreat, but the mare blocked her way. He smiled at her predicament.

That triggered her pride. She could be grateful for that. It had thrown her that, in the shadowed light, he was even more attractive, more…compelling than he had been in the sun. Not handsome, she amended quickly. Certainly not in the smooth, conventional sense, the sense she had always gauged men's looks by before. Everything about him was fundamental. Not simple, she thought. No, not simple, but basic. Basic, like his kiss that morning. Warmth prickled along her skin.

"I'd be happy to help you with the massage." He smiled again. "Yours, or the mare's."

"No, thank you." She became aware that she was even more disheveled than she had been at their first meeting, and that she smelled, all too obviously, of horse. "Is there something I can do for you, Mr. Elliot?"

He liked her style, Chase decided. She might be standing in a stall that could use a bit of cleaning, but she was still the lady of the drawing room. "You've got a good stock here. A bit on the mature side, but solid."

Eden had to ward off a surge of pleasure. His opinion hardly mattered. "Thank you. I'm sure you didn't come to look over the horses."

"No." But he stepped inside the stall. The mare shifted to accommodate him. "Apparently you know your way around them." He lifted a hand to run it down the mare's neck. There was a simple gold ring on his right hand. Eden recognized its age and value, as well as the strength of the man who wore it.

"Apparently." There was no way past him, so she linked her fingers together and waited. "Mr. Elliot, you haven't told me what you're doing here."

Chase's lips twitched as he continued to stroke the mare. Miss Philadelphia was nervous, he thought. She covered it well enough with frigid manners, but her nerves were jumping. It pleased him to know that she hadn't been able to brush off that quick, impulsive kiss any more than he had. "No, I haven't." Before she could avoid it, he reached down for her hand. An opal gleamed dully in the shadowed light, nestled in a circle of diamond chips that promised to catch heat and fire.

"Wrong hand for an engagement ring." He discovered that the fact pleased him, perhaps more than it should have. "I'd heard you and Eric Keeton were to be married last spring. Apparently it didn't come off."

She would like to have sworn, shouted, yelled. That's what *he* wanted, Eden told herself, letting her hand lie passive in his. "No, it didn't. Mr. Elliot, for a, let's say, country squire, you have boundless curiosity about Philadelphia gossip. Don't your apples keep you busy enough?"

He had to admire anyone who could shoot straight and smile. "I manage to eke out a bit of free time. Actually, I was interested because Keeton's a family connection."

"He is not."

There, he'd ruffled her. For the first time since her initial surprise, she was really looking at him. Take a good look, Chase thought. You won't see any resemblance. "Distant, certainly." Capturing her other hand, he turned the palms up. "My grandmother was a Winthrop, and a cousin of his grandmother. Your Philadelphia hands have a couple of blisters. You should take care."

"A Winthrop?" Eden was surprised enough at the name to forget her hands.

"We've thinned the blood a bit in the last few generations." She should be wearing gloves, he thought, as he touched a blister with his thumb. "Still, I'd expected an invitation and was curious why you dumped him."

"I didn't dump him." The words came out like poisoned honey. "But to satisfy your curiosity, and to use your own crude phrase, he dumped me. Now if you'd give me back my hands, I could finish for the day."

Chase obliged, but continued to block her way out of the stall. "I'd never considered Eric bright, but I'd never thought him stupid."

"What a delightful compliment. Please excuse me, Mr. Elliot."

"Not a compliment." Chase brushed at the bangs over her forehead. "Just an observation."

"Stop touching me."

"Touching's a habit of mine. I like your hair, Eden. It's soft, but it goes its own way."

"A veritable bouquet of compliments." She managed one small step backward. He had her pulse thudding again. She didn't want to be touched, not physically, not emotionally, not by anyone. Instinct warned her how easily he could do both. "Mr. Elliot—"

"Chase."

"Chase." She acknowledged this with a regal nod. "The morning bell goes off at six. I still have several things to do tonight, so if there's a purpose in your being here, could we get to it?"

"I came to bring you back your hat." Reaching into his back pocket, he pulled out the Phillies cap.

"I see." One more black mark against Roberta. "It's not mine, but I'd be happy to return it to its owner. Thank you for troubling."

"You were wearing it when you fell out of my tree." Chase ignored her outstretched hand and dropped the cap on her head. "Fits, too."

"As I've already explained—"

Eden's frigid retort was interrupted by the sound of running feet. "Miss Carlbough! Miss Carlbough!" Roberta, in an angelic pink nightgown and bare feet, skidded to a halt at the open stall. Beaming, she stared up at Chase. Her adolescent heart melted. "Hi."

"Hi."

"Roberta." Voice stern, teeth nearly clenched, Eden stepped forward. "It's almost an hour past lights-out."

"I know, Miss Carlbough. I'm sorry." When she smiled, Eden thought you could almost believe it. "I just couldn't get to sleep because I kept thinking about my cap. You promised I could have it back, but you never gave it to me. I helped Mrs. Petrie. Honest, you can ask. There were millions of pans, too. I even peeled potatoes, and—"

"Roberta!" The sharp tone was enough for the moment. "Mr. Elliot was kind enough to return your hat." Whipping it off her own head, Eden thrust it into the girl's hands. "I believe you should thank him, as well as apologize for trespassing."

"Gee, thanks." She treated him to a dazzling smile. "Are those your trees, really?"

"Yeah." With a fingertip, Chase adjusted the brim of her hat. He had a weakness for black sheep and recognized a kindred soul in Roberta.

"I think they're great. Your apples tasted a whole lot better than the ones we get at home."

"Roberta."

The quiet warning had the girl rolling her eyes, which only Chase could see. "I'm sorry I didn't show the proper respect for your property." Roberta turned her head to see whether Eden approved of the apology.

"Very nice, Roberta. Now straight back to bed."

"Yes, ma'am." She shot a last look at Chase. Her little heart fluttered. Crushing the cap down on her head, she raced to the door.

"Roberta." She whipped back around at the sound of Chase's voice. He grinned at her. "See you around."

"Yeah, see you." In love, Roberta floated off to her cabin. When the stable door slammed at her back, all Eden could manage was a sigh.

"It's no use," Chase commented.

"What isn't?"

"Pretending you don't get a kick out of her. A kid like that makes you feel good."

"You wouldn't be so sure of that if you'd seen what she can do with mashed potatoes." But Eden gave in enough to smile. "She's a monster, but an appealing one. Still, I have to admit, if we had twenty-seven Robertas in camp this summer, I'd end up in a padded room."

"Certain people just breed excitement."

Eden remembered the dinner hour. "Some call it chaos."

"Life flattens out quickly without a little chaos."

She looked at him, realizing she'd dropped her guard enough to have an actual conversation. And realizing as well that they'd stopped talking about Roberta. The stables suddenly seemed very quiet. "Well, now that we've gotten that settled, I think—"

He took a step forward. She took a step back. A smile played around his lips again as he reached for her hand. Eden bumped solidly into the mare before she managed to raise her free hand to his chest.

"What do you want?" Why was she whispering, and why was the whisper so tremulous?

He wasn't sure what he wanted. Once, quickly, he scanned her face before bringing his gaze back to hers with a jolt. Or perhaps he was. "To walk with you in the moonlight, I think. To listen to the owls hoot and wait for the nightingale."

The shadows had merged. The mare stood quietly, breathing softly. His hand was in Eden's hair now, as if it belonged there. "I have to go in." But she didn't move.

"Eden and the apple," he murmured. "I can't tell you how tempting I've found that combination. Come with me. We'll walk."

"No." Something was building inside her, too quickly. She knew he was touching more than her hand, more than her hair. He was reaching for something he should not have known existed.

"Sooner or later." He'd always been a patient man. He could wait for her the way he waited for a new tree to bear fruit. His fingers slid down to her throat, stroking once. He felt her quick shudder, heard the unsteady indrawn breath. "I'll be back, Eden."

"It won't make any difference."

Smiling, he brought her hand to his lips, turning it palm up. "I'll still be back."

She listened to his footsteps, to the creak of the door as he opened it, then shut it again.

Chapter 3

The camp was developing its own routine. Eden adjusted hers to it. Early hours, long, physical days and basic food were both a solace and a challenge. The confidence she'd once had to work at became real.

There were nights during the first month of summer that she fell into her bunk certain she would never be able to get up in the morning. Her muscles ached from rowing, riding and endless hiking. Her head spun from weekly encounters with ledgers and account books. But in the morning the sun would rise, and so would she.

Every day it became easier. She was young and healthy. The daily regimented exercise hardened muscles only touched on by occasional games of tennis. The weight she had lost over the months since her father's death gradually came back, so that her look of fragility faded.

To her surprise, she developed a genuine affection for the girls. They became individuals, not simply a group to be coped with or income on the books. It surprised her more to find that same affection returned.

Right from the start, Eden had been certain the girls would love Candy. Everyone did. She was warm, funny, talented. The most Eden had hoped for, for herself, was to be tolerated and respected. The day Marcie had brought her a clutch of wildflowers, Eden had been too stunned to do more than stammer a thank-you. Then there had been the afternoon she had given Linda Hopkins an extra half hour in the corral. After her first gallop, Linda had thrown herself into Eden's arms for a fierce and delightful hug.

So the camp had changed her life, in so many more ways than she'd expected.

The summer grew hot with July. Girls darted around the compound in shorts. Dips in the lake became a glorious luxury. Doors and windows stayed open at night to catch even the slightest breeze. Roberta found a garter snake and terrorized her cabin mates. Bees buzzed around the wildflowers and stings became common.

Days merged together, content, but never dull, so that it seemed possible that summer could last forever. As the time passed, Eden began to believe that Chase had forgotten his promise, or threat, to come back. She'd been careful to stay well within the borders of the camp herself. Though once or twice she'd been tempted to wander toward the orchards, she stayed away.

It didn't make sense for her to still be tense and uneasy. She could tell herself he'd only been a brief annoyance. Yet every time she went into the stables in the evening, she caught herself listening. And waiting.

* * *

Late in the evening, with the heat still shimmering, Eden stretched out on her bunk, fully dressed. Bribed by the promise of a bonfire the following night, the campers had quieted down early. Relaxed and pleasantly weary, Eden pictured it. Hot dogs flaming on sharpened sticks, marshmallows toasting, the blaze flickering heat over her face and sending smoke billowing skyward. Eden found herself looking forward to the evening every bit as much as the youngest camper. With her head pillowed on her folded arms, she stared up at the ceiling while Candy paced.

"I'm sure we could do it, Eden."

"Hmm?"

"The dance." Gesturing with the clipboard she was carrying, Candy stopped at the foot of the bunk. "The dance I've been talking about having for the girls. Remember?"

"Of course." Eden forced her mind back to business. "What about it?"

"I think we should go ahead with it. In fact, if it works out, I think it should be an annual event." Even after she plopped herself down on Eden's bed, her enthusiasm continued to bounce around the room. "The boys' camp is only twenty miles from here. I'm sure they'd go for it."

"Probably." A dance. That would mean refreshments for somewhere close to a hundred, not to mention music, decorations. She thought first of the red ink in the ledger, then about how much the girls would enjoy it. There had to be a way around the red ink. "I guess there'd be room in the mess area if we moved the tables."

"Exactly. And most of the girls have records with

them. We could have the boys bring some, too." She began to scrawl on her clipboard. "We can make the decorations ourselves."

"We'd have to keep the refreshments simple," Eden put in before Candy's enthusiasm could run away with her. "Cookies, punch, that sort of thing."

"We can plan it for the last week of camp. Kind of a celebrational send-off."

The last week of camp. How strange, when the first week had been so wearing, that the thought of it ending brought on both panic and regret. No, summer wouldn't last forever. In September there would be the challenge of finding a new job, a new goal. She wouldn't be going back to a teaching job as Candy was, but to want ads and résumés.

"Eden? Eden, what do you think?"

"About what?"

"About planning the dance for the last week of camp?"

"I think we'd better clear it with the boys' camp first."

"Honey, are you okay?" Leaning forward, Candy took Eden's hand. "Are you worried about going back home in a few weeks?"

"No. Concerned." She gave Candy's hand a squeeze. "Just concerned."

"I meant it when I told you not to worry about a job right away. My salary takes care of the rent on the apartment, and I still have a little piece of the nest egg my grandmother left me."

"I love you, Candy. You're the best friend I've ever had."

"The reverse holds true, Eden."

"For that reason, there's no way I'm going to sit around

while you work to pay the rent and put dinner on the table. It's enough that you've let me move in with you."

"Eden, you know I'm a lot happier sharing my apartment with you than I was living alone. If you look at it as a favor, you're going to feel pressured, and that's ridiculous. Besides, for the past few months, you were taking care of fixing all the meals."

"Only a small portion of which were edible."

"True." Candy grinned. "But I didn't have to cook. Listen, give yourself a little space. You'll need some time to find out what it is you want to do."

"What I want to do is work." With a laugh, Eden lay back on the bed again. "Surprise. I really want to work, to keep busy, to earn a living. The past few weeks have shown me how much I enjoy taking care of myself. I'm banking on getting a job at a riding stable. Maybe even the one I used to board my horse at. And if that doesn't pan out—" She shrugged her shoulders. "I'll find something else."

"You will." Candy set the clipboard aside. "And next year, we'll have more girls, a bigger staff and maybe even a profit."

"Next year, I'm going to know how to make a hurricane lamp out of a tuna can."

"And a pillow out of two washcloths."

"And pot holders."

Candy remembered Eden's one mangled attempt. "Well, maybe you should take it slow."

"There's going to be no stopping me. In the meantime, I'll contact the camp director over at—what's the name, Hawk's Nest?"

"Eagle Rock," Candy corrected her, laughing. "It'll be fun for us, too, Eden. They have counselors. *Male* counselors." Sighing, she stretched her arms to the ceiling. "Do you know how long it's been since I've spoken with a man?"

"You talked to the electrician just last week."

"He was a hundred and two. I'm talking about a man who still has all his hair and teeth." She touched her tongue to her upper lip. "Not all of us have passed the time holding hands with a man in the stables."

Eden plumped up her excuse for a pillow. "I wasn't holding hands. I explained to you."

"Roberta Snow, master spy, gave an entirely different story. With her, it appears to be love at first sight."

Eden examined the pad of callus on the ridge of her palm. "I'm sure she'll survive."

"Well, what about you?"

"I'll survive, too."

"No, I mean, aren't you interested?" After folding her legs under her, Candy leaned forward. "Remember, darling, I got a good look at the man when I was negotiating for the use of his lake. I don't think there's a woman alive who wouldn't sweat a bit after a look at those spooky green eyes."

"I never sweat."

Chuckling, Candy leaned back. "Eden, you're talking to the one who loves you best. The man was interested enough to track you down in the stables. Think of the possibilities."

"It's possible that he was returning Roberta's cap."

"And it's possible that pigs fly. Haven't you been tempted to wander over by the orchard, just once?"

"No." Only a hundred times. "Seen one apple tree, you've seen them all."

"The same doesn't hold true for an apple grower who's about six-two, with a hundred and ninety well-placed pounds and one of the most fascinating faces this side of the Mississippi." Concern edged into her voice. She had watched her friend suffer and had been helpless to do more than offer emotional support. "Have fun, Eden. You deserve it."

"I don't think Chase Elliot falls into the category of fun." Danger, she thought. Excitement, sexuality and, oh yes, temptation. Tossing her legs over the bunk, Eden walked to the window. Moths were flapping at the screen.

"You're gun-shy."

"Maybe."

"Honey, you can't use Eric as a yardstick."

"I'm not." With a sigh, she turned back. "I'm not pining or brooding over him, either."

The quick shrug was Candy's way of dismissing someone she considered a weasel. "That's because you were never really in love with him."

"I was going to marry him."

"Because it seemed the proper thing to do. I know you, Eden, like no one else. Everything was very simple and easy with Eric. It all fit—click, click, click."

Amused, Eden shook her head. "Is something wrong with that?"

"Everything's wrong with that. Love makes you giddy and foolish and achy. You never felt any of that with Eric." She spoke from the experience of a woman who'd fallen in love, and out again, a dozen times before she'd hit twenty. "You would have married him, and maybe you would even have been content. His tastes were compatible with yours. His family mixed well with yours."

Amusement fled. "You make it sound so cold."

"It was. But you're not." Candy raised her hands, hoping she hadn't gone too far. "Eden, you were raised a certain way, to be a certain way; then the roof collapsed. I can only guess at how traumatic that was. You've picked yourself up, but still you've closed pieces of yourself off. Isn't it time you put the past behind you, really behind you?"

"I've been trying."

"I know, and you've made a good start, with the camp, with your outlook. Maybe it's time you started looking for a little more, just for yourself."

"A man?"

"Some companionship, some sharing, some affection. You're too smart to think that you need a man to make things work, but to cut them off because one acted like a weasel isn't the answer, either." She rubbed at a streak of red paint on her fingernail. "I guess I still believe that everyone needs someone."

"Maybe you're right. Right now I'm too busy pasting myself back together and enjoying the results. I'm not ready for complications. Especially when they're six foot two."

"You were always the romantic one, Eden. Remember the poetry you used to write?"

"We were children." Restless, Eden moved her shoulders. "I had to grow up."

"Growing up doesn't mean you have to stop dreaming." Candy rose. "We've started one dream here, together. I want to see you have other dreams."

"When the time's right." Touched, Eden kissed Candy's cheek. "We'll have your dance and charm your counselors."

"We could invite some neighbors, just to round things out."

"Don't press your luck." Laughing, Eden turned toward the door. "I'm going for a walk before I check on the horses. Leave the light on low, will you?"

The air was still, but not quiet. The first nights Eden had spent in the hills, the country quiet had disturbed her. Now, she could hear and appreciate the night music. The chorus of crickets in soprano, the tenor crying of an owl, the occasional bass lowing of the cows on a farm half a mile away all merged into a symphony accompanied by the rustling of small animals in the brush. The three-quarter moon and a galaxy of stars added soft light and dramatic shadows. The erratic yellow beams of an army of fireflies was a nightly light show.

As she strolled toward the lake, she heard the rushing song of peepers over the softer sound of lapping water. The air smelled as steamy as it felt, so she rounded the edge of the lake toward the cooler cover of trees.

With her mind on her conversation with Candy, Eden bent to pluck a black-eyed Susan. Twisting the stem between her fingers, she watched the petals revolve around the dark center.

Had she been a romantic? There had been poetry, dreamy, optimistic poetry, often revolving around love. Troubadour love, she thought now. The sort that meant long, wistful glances, sterling sacrifices and purity. Romantic, but unrealistic, Eden admitted. She hadn't written any poetry in a long time.

Not since she had met Eric, Eden realized. She had gone from dreamy young girl to proper young woman, exchanging verses for silver patterns. Now both the dreamy girl and the proper woman were gone.

That was for the best, Eden decided, and she tossed her flower onto the surface of the lake. She watched it float lazily.

Candy had been right. It had not been a matter of love with Eric, but of fulfilling expectations. When he had turned his back on her, he had broken not her heart, but her pride. She was still repairing it.

Eric had given her a suitable diamond, sent her roses at the proper times and had never been at a loss for a clever compliment. That wasn't romance, Eden mused, and it certainly wasn't love. Perhaps she'd never really understood either.

Was romance white knights and pure maidens? Was it Chopin and soft lights? Was it the top of the Ferris wheel? Maybe she'd prefer the last after all. With a quiet laugh, Eden wrapped her arms around herself and held her face up to the stars.

"You should do that more often."

She whirled, one hand pressing against her throat. Chase stood a few feet away at the edge of the trees, the edge of the shadows. It flashed through her mind that this was the third time she had seen him and the third time he had taken her by surprise. It was a habit she wanted to break.

"Do you practice startling people, or is it a natural gift?"

"I can't remember it happening much before you." The fact was, he hadn't come up on her, but she on him. He'd been walking since dusk, and had stopped on the banks of the lake to watch the water and to think of her. "You've been getting some sun." Her hair seemed lighter, more fragile against the honeyed tone of her skin. He wanted to touch it, to see if it was still as soft and fragrant.

"Most of the work is outdoors." It amazed her that she had to fight the urge to turn and run. There was something mystical, even fanciful, about meeting him here in the moonlight, by the water. Almost as if it had been fated.

"You should wear a hat." He said it absently, distracted by the pounding of his own heart. She might have been an illusion, long slender arms and legs gleaming in the moonlight, her hair loose and drenched with it. She wore white. Even the simple shorts and shirt seemed to glimmer. "I'd wondered if you walked here."

He stepped out of the shadows. The monotonous song of the crickets seemed to reach a crescendo. "I thought it might be cooler."

"Some." He moved closer. "I've always been fond of hot nights."

"The cabins tend to get stuffy." Uneasy, she glanced back and discovered she had walked farther than she'd intended. The camp, with its comforting lights and company, was very far away. "I didn't realize I'd crossed over onto your property."

"I'm only a tyrant about my trees." She was less of an illusion up close, more of a woman. "You were laughing before. What were you thinking of?"

Her mouth was dry. Even as she backed away, he seemed to be closer. "Ferris wheels."

"Ferris wheels? Do you like the drop?" Satisfying his own need, he reached for her hair. "Or the climb?"

At his touch, her stomach shot down to her knees. "I have to get back."

"Let's walk."

To walk with you in the moonlight. Eden thought of his words, and of fate. "No, I can't. It's late."

"Must be all of nine-thirty." Amused, he took her hand, then immediately turned it over. There was a hardening ridge of calluses on the pad beneath her fingers. "You've been working."

"Some people make a living that way."

"Don't get testy." He turned her hand back to run a thumb over her knuckles. Was it a talent of his, Eden wondered, to touch a woman in the most casual of ways and send her blood pounding? "You could wear gloves," Chase went on, "and keep your Philadelphia hands."

"I'm not in Philadelphia." She drew her hand away. Chase simply took her other one. "And since I'm pitching hay rather than serving tea, it hardly seems to matter."

"You'll be serving tea again." He could see her, seated in some fussy parlor, wearing pink silk and holding a china pot. But, for the moment, her hand was warm in his. "The moon's on the water. Look."

Compelled, she turned her head. There were such things as moonbeams. They gilded the dark water of the lake and silvered the trees. She remembered some old legend about three women, the moonspinners, who spun the moon on spindles. More romance. But even the new, practical Eden couldn't resist.

"It's lovely. The moon seems so close."

"Some things aren't as close as they seem; others aren't so far away."

He began to walk. Because he still had her hand, and

because he intrigued her, Eden walked with him. "I suppose you've always lived here." Just small talk, she told herself. She didn't really care.

"For the most part. This has always been headquarters for the business." He turned to look down at her. "The house is over a hundred years old. You might find it interesting."

She thought of her home and of the generations of Carlboughs who had lived there. And of the strangers who lived there now. "I like old houses."

"Are things going well at camp?"

She wouldn't think of the books. "The girls keep us busy." Her laugh came again, low and easy. "That's an understatement. We'll just say their energy level is amazing."

"How's Roberta?"

"Incorrigible."

"I'm glad to hear it."

"Last night she painted one of the girls while the girl was asleep."

"Painted?"

Eden's laugh came again, low and easy. "The little darling must have copped a couple of pots of paint from the art area. When Marcie woke up, she looked like an Indian preparing to attack a wagon train."

"Our Roberta's inventive."

"To say the least. She told me she thought it might be interesting to be the first woman chief justice."

He smiled at that. Imagination and ambition were the qualities he most admired. "She'll probably do it."

"I know. It's terrifying."

"Let's sit. You can see the stars better."

Stars? She'd nearly forgotten who she was with and why she had wanted to avoid being with him. "I don't think I—" Before she'd gotten the sentence out, he'd tugged her down on a soft, grassy rise. "One wonders why you bother to ask."

"Manners," he said easily as he slipped an arm around her shoulders. Even as she stiffened, he relaxed. "Look at the sky. How often do you notice it in the city?"

Unable to resist, she tilted her face up. The sky was an inky black backdrop for countless pinpoints of lights. They spread, winking, shivering, overhead with a glory that made Eden's throat ache just in the looking. "It isn't the same sky that's over the city."

"Same sky, Eden. It's people who change." He stretched out on his back, crossing his legs. "There's Cassiopeia."

"Where?" Curious, Eden searched, but saw only stars without pattern.

"You can see her better from here." He pulled her closer to him, and before she could protest, he was pointing. "There she is. Looks like a W this time of year."

"Yes!" Delighted, she reached for his wrist and outlined the constellation herself. "I've never been able to find anything in the sky."

"You have to look first. There's Pegasus." Chase shifted his arm. "He has a hundred and sixty-six stars you can view with the naked eye. See? He's flying straight up."

Eyes narrowed, she concentrated on finding the pattern. Moonlight splashed on her face. "Oh yes, I see." She shifted a bit closer to guide his hand again. "I named my first pony Pegasus. Sometimes I'd imagine he sprouted wings and flew. Show me another."

He was looking at her, at the way the stars reflected in her eyes, at the way her mouth softened so generously with a smile. "Orion," he murmured.

"Where?"

"He stands with his sword behind him and his shield lifted in front. And a red star, thousands of times brighter than the sun, is the shoulder of his sword arm."

"Where is he? I—" Eden turned her head and looked directly into Chase's eyes. She forgot the stars and the moonlight and the soft, sweet grass beneath her. The hand on his wrist tightened until the rhythm of his pulse was the rhythm of hers.

Her muscles contracted and held as she braced for the kiss. But his lips merely brushed against her temple. Warmth spread through her as softly as the scent of honeysuckle spread through the air. She heard an owl call out to the night, to the stars, or to a lover.

"What are we doing here?" she managed.

"Enjoying each other." Without rushing, his lips moved over her face.

Enjoying? That was much too mild a word for what was burning through her. No one had ever made her feel like this, so weak and hot, so strong and desperate. His lips were soft, the hand that rested on the side of her face was hard. Beneath his, her heart began to gallop uncontrolled. Eden's fingers slipped off the reins.

She turned her head with a moan and found his mouth with hers. Her arms went around him, holding him close as her lips parted in demand. In all her life she had never known true hunger, not until now. This was breathless, painful, glorious.

He'd never expected such unchecked passion. He'd

been prepared to go slowly, gently, as the innocence he'd felt in her required. Now she was moving under him, her fingers pressing and kneading the muscles of his back, her mouth hot and willing on his. The patience that was so much a part of him drowned in need.

Such new, such exciting sensations. Her body gave as his pressed hard against it. Gods and goddesses of the sky guarded them. He smelled of the grass and the earth, and he tasted of fire. Night sounds roared in her head, and her own sigh was only a dim echo when his lips slid down to her throat.

Murmuring his name, Eden combed her fingers through his hair. He wanted to touch her, all of her. He wanted to take her now. When her hand came to rest on his face, he covered it with his own and felt the smooth stone of her ring.

There was so much more he needed to know. So little he was sure of. Desire, for the moment, couldn't be enough. Who was she? He lifted his head to look down at her. Who the hell was she, and why was she driving him mad?

Pulling himself back, he tried to find solid ground. "You're full of surprises, Eden Carlbough of the Philadelphia Carlboughs."

For a moment, she could only stare. She'd had her ride on the Ferris wheel, a wild, dizzying ride. Somewhere along the line, she'd been tossed off to spiral madly in the air. Now she'd hit the ground, hard. "Let me up."

"I can't figure you, Eden."

"You aren't required to." She wanted to weep, to curl up into a ball and weep, but she couldn't focus on the reason. Anger was clearer. "I asked you to let me up."

He rose, holding out a hand to help her. Ignoring it, Eden got to her feet. "I've always felt it was more constructive to shout when you're angry."

She shot him one glittering look. Humiliation. It was something she'd sworn she would never feel again. "I'm sure you do. If you'll excuse me."

"Damn it." He caught her arm and swung her back to face him. "Something was happening here tonight. I'm not fool enough to deny that, but I want to know what I'm getting into."

"We were enjoying each other. Wasn't that your term?" Nothing more, Eden repeated over and over in her head. Nothing more than a moment's enjoyment. "We've finished now, so good night."

"We're far from finished. That's what worries me."

"I'd say that's your problem, Chase." But a ripple of fear—of anticipation—raced through her, because she knew he was right.

"Yeah, it's my problem." My God, how had he passed so quickly from curiosity to attraction to blazing need? "And because it is, I've got a question. I want to know why Eden Carlbough is playing at camp for the summer rather than cruising the Greek Isles. I want to know why she's cleaning out stables instead of matching silver patterns and planning dinner parties as Mrs. Eric Keeton."

"My business." Her voice rose. The new Eden wasn't as good as the old one at controlling emotion. "But if you're so curious, why don't you call one of your family connections? I'm sure any of them would be delighted to give you all the details."

"I'm asking you."

"I don't owe you any explanations." She jerked her

arm away and stood trembling with rage. "I don't owe you a damn thing."

"Maybe not." His temper had cooled his passion and cleared his head. "But I want to know who I'm making love with."

"That won't be an issue, I promise you."

"We're going to finish what we started here, Eden." Without stepping closer, he had her arm again. The touch was far from gentle, far from patient. "That I promise you."

"Consider it finished."

To her surprise and fury, he only smiled. His hand eased on her arm to one lingering caress. Helpless against her response, she shivered. "We both know better than that." He touched a finger to her lips, as if reminding her what tastes he'd left there. "Think of me."

He slipped back into the shadows.

Chapter 4

It was a perfect night for a bonfire. Only a few wispy clouds dragged across the moon, shadowing it, then freeing it. The heat of the day eased with sunset, and the air was balmy, freshened by a calm, steady breeze.

The pile of twigs and sticks that had been gathered throughout the day had been stacked, tepeelike, in a field to the east of the main compound. In the clearing, it rose from a wide base to the height of a man. Every one of the girls had contributed to the making of it, just as every one of them circled around the bonfire now, waiting for the fire to catch and blaze. An army of hot dogs and marshmallows was laid out on a picnic table. Stacked like swords were dozens of cleaned and sharpened sticks. Nearby was the garden hose with a tub full of water, for safety's sake.

Candy held up a long kitchen match, drawing out the

drama as the girls began to cheer. "The first annual bonfire at Camp Liberty is about to begin. Secure your hot dogs to your sticks, ladies, and prepare to roast."

Amid the giggles and gasps, Candy struck the match, then held it to the dry kindling at the base. Wood crackled. Flames licked, searched for more fuel, and spread around and around, following the circle of starter fluid. As they watched, fire began its journey up and up. Eden applauded with the rest.

"Fabulous!" Even as she watched, smoke began to billow. Its scent was the scent of autumn, and that was still a summer away. "I was terrified we wouldn't get it started."

"You're looking at an expert." Catching her tongue between her teeth, Candy speared a hot dog with a sharpened stick. Behind her, the bonfire glowed red at the center. "The only thing I was worried about was rain. But just look at those stars. It's perfect."

Eden tilted her head back. Without effort, without thought, she found Pegasus. He was riding the night sky just as he'd been riding it twenty-four hours before. One day, one night. How could so much have happened? Standing with her face lifted to the breeze and her hands growing warm from the fire, she wondered if she had really experienced that wild, turbulent moment with Chase.

She had. The memories were too ripe, too real for dreams. The moment had happened, and all the feelings and sensations that had grown from it. Deliberately she turned her gaze to a riot of patternless stars.

It didn't change what she remembered, or what she still felt. The moment had happened, she thought again, and it had passed. Yet, somehow, she wasn't certain it was over.

"Why does everything seem different here, Candy?"

"Everything *is* different here." Candy took a deep breath, drawing in the scents of smoke, drying grass and roasting meat. "Isn't it marvelous? No stuffy parlors, no boring dinner parties, no endless piano recitals. Want a hot dog?"

Because her mouth was watering, Eden accepted the partially blackened wiener. "You simplify things, Candy." Eden ran a thin line of ketchup along the meat and stuck it in a bun. "I wish I could."

"You will once you stop thinking you're letting down the Carlbough name by enjoying a hot dog by a bonfire." When Eden's mouth dropped open, Candy gave her a friendly pat. "You ought to try the marshmallows," she advised before she wandered off to find another stick.

Is that what she was doing? Eden wondered, chewing automatically. Maybe, in a way that wasn't quite as basic as Candy had said, it was. After all, she had been the one who had sold the house that had been in the family for four generations. In the end, it had been she who had inventoried the silver and china, the paintings and the jewelry for auction. So, in the end, it had been she who had liquidated the Carlbough tradition to pay off debts and to start a new life.

Necessary. No matter how the practical Eden accepted the necessity, the grieving Eden still felt the loss, and the guilt.

With a sigh, Eden stepped back. The scene that played out in front of her was like a memory from her own childhood. She could see the column of gray smoke rising toward the sky, twirling and curling. At the core of the tower of wood, the fire was fiercely gold and greedy. The smell of outdoor cooking was strong and summery, as it had been during her own weeks at Camp Forden for Girls. For a moment, there was regret that she couldn't step back into those memories of a time when life was simple and problems were things for parents to fix.

"Miss Carlbough."

Brought out of a half-formed dream, Eden glanced down at Roberta. "Hello, Roberta. Are you having fun?"

"It's super!" Roberta's enthusiasm was evident from the smear of ketchup on her chin. "Don't you like bonfires?"

"Yes, I do." Smiling, she looked back at the crackling wood, one hand dropping automatically to Roberta's shoulder. "I like them a lot."

"I thought you looked sort of sad, so I made you a marshmallow."

The offering dripped, black and shriveled, from the end of a stick. Eden felt her throat close up the same way it had when another girl had offered her a clutch of wildflowers. "Thanks, Roberta. I wasn't sad really, I was just remembering." Gingerly, Eden pulled the melted, mangled marshmallow from the stick. Half of it plopped to the ground on the way to her mouth.

"They're tricky," Roberta observed. "I'll make you another one."

Left with the charred outer hull, Eden swallowed valiantly. "You don't have to bother, Roberta."

"Oh, I don't mind." She looked up at Eden with a glowing, generous grin. Somehow, all her past crimes didn't seem so important. "I like to do it. I thought camp was going to be boring, but it's not. Especially the horses. Miss Carlbough…" Roberta looked down at the ground and seemed to draw her courage out of her toes. "I guess I'm not as good as Linda with the horses, but I wondered if maybe you could—well, if I could spend some more time at the stables."

"Of course you can, Roberta." Eden rubbed her thumb and forefinger together, trying fruitlessly to rid herself of the goo. "And you don't even have to bribe me with marshmallows."

"Really?"

"Yes, really." Attracted despite herself, Eden ruffled Roberta's hair. "Miss Bartholomew and I will work it into your schedule."

"Gee, thanks, Miss Carlbough."

"But you'll have to work on your posting."

Roberta's nose wrinkled only a little. "Okay. But I wish we could do stuff like barrel racing. I've seen it on TV."

"Well, I don't know about that, but you might progress to small jumps before the end of camp."

Eden had the pleasure of seeing Roberta's eyes saucer with pleasure. "No fooling?"

"No fooling. As long as you work on your posting."

"I will. And I'll be better than Linda, too. Wow, jumps." She spun in an awkward pirouette. "Thanks a lot, Miss Carlbough. Thanks a lot."

She was off in a streak, undoubtedly to spread the word. If Eden knew Roberta, and she was beginning to, she was certain the girl would soon have talked herself into a gold medal for equestrian prowess at the next Olympic Games.

But, as she watched Roberta spin from group to group, Eden realized she wasn't thinking of the past any longer; nor was she regretting. She was smiling. As one of the counselors began to strum a guitar, Eden licked marshmallow goop from her fingers.

"Need some help with that?"

With her fingers still in her mouth, Eden turned. She should have known he'd come. Perhaps, in her secret thoughts, she had hoped he would. Now she found herself thrusting her still-sticky fingers behind her back.

He wondered if she knew how lovely she looked, with the fire at her back and her hair loose on her shoulders. There was a frown on her face now, but he hadn't missed that one quick flash of pleasure. If he kissed her now, would he taste that sweet, sugary flavor she had been licking from her fingers? Through it would he find that simmering, waiting heat he'd tasted once before? The muscles in his stomach tightened, even as he dipped his thumbs into his pockets and looked away from her toward the fire.

"Nice night for a bonfire."

"Candy claims she arranged it that way." Confident there was enough distance between them, and that there were enough people around them, Eden allowed herself to relax. "We weren't expecting any company."

"I spotted your smoke."

That made her glance up and realize how far the smoke might travel. "I hope it didn't worry you. We notified the fire department." Three girls streaked by behind them. Chase glanced their way and had them lapsing into giggles. Eden caught her tongue in her cheek. "How long did it take you to perfect it?"

With a half smile, Chase turned back to her. "What?"

"The deadly charm that has females crumpling at your feet?"

"Oh, that." He grinned at her. "I was born with it."

The laugh came out before she could stop it. To cover her lapse, Eden crossed her arms and took a step backward. "It's getting warm."

"We used to have a bonfire on the farm every Halloween. My father would carve the biggest pumpkin in the patch and stuff some overalls and a flannel shirt with straw. One year he dressed himself up as the Headless Horseman and gave every kid in the neighborhood a thrill." Watching the fire, he remembered and wondered why until tonight he hadn't thought of continuing the tradition. "My mother would give each of the kids a caramel apple, then we'd sit around the fire and tell ghost stories until we'd scared ourselves silly. Looking back, I think my father got a bigger kick out of it than any of us kids."

She could see it, just as he described, and had to smile again. For her, Halloween had been tidy costume parties where she'd dressed as a princess or ballerina. Though the memories were still lovely, she couldn't help wishing she'd seen one of the bonfires and the Headless Horseman.

"When we were planning tonight, I was as excited as any of the girls. I guess that sounds foolish."

"No, it sounds promising." He put a hand to her cheek, turning her slightly toward him. Though she stiffened, her skin was warm and soft. "Did you think of me?"

There it was again—that feeling of drowning, of floating, of going under for the third time. "I've been busy." She told herself to move away, but her legs didn't respond. The sound of singing and strumming seemed to be coming from off in the distance, with melody and lyrics she couldn't quite remember. The only thing that was close and real was his hand on her cheek.

"I-it was nice of you to drop by," she began, struggling to find solid ground again.

"Am I being dismissed?" He moved his hand casually from her cheek to her hair.

"I'm sure you have better things to do." His fingertip skimmed the back of her neck and set every nerve end trembling. "Stop."

The smoke billowed up over her head. Light and shadow created by the fire danced over her face and in her eyes. He'd thought of her, Chase reminded himself. Too much. Now he could only think what it would be like to make love with her near the heat of the fire, with the scent of smoke, and night closing in.

"You haven't walked by the lake."

"I told you, I've been busy." Why couldn't she make her voice firm and cool? "I have a responsibility to the girls, and the camp, and—"

"Yourself?" How badly he wanted to walk with her again, to study the stars and talk. How badly he wanted to taste that passion and that innocence again. "I'm a very patient man, Eden. You can only avoid me for so long."

"Longer than you think," she murmured, letting out a sigh of relief as she spotted Roberta making a beeline for them.

"Hi!" Delighted with the quick fluttering of her heart, Roberta beamed up at Chase.

"Hi, Roberta," he said. She was thrilled that he'd remembered her name. He gave her a smile, and his attention, without releasing Eden's hair. "You're taking better care of your cap, I see."

She laughed and pushed up the brim. "Miss Carlbough said if I wandered into your orchard again,
she'd hold my cap for ransom. But if you invited us
to come on a tour, that would be educational,
wouldn't it?"

"Roberta." Why was it the child was always one step
ahead of everyone else? Eden lifted her brow in a
quelling look.

"Well, Miss Bartholomew said we should think of
interesting things." Roberta put her most innocent look
to good use. "And I think the apple trees are interesting."

"Thanks." Chase thought he heard Eden's teeth
clench. "We'll give it some thought."

"Okay." Satisfied, Roberta stuck out a wrinkled black
tube. "I made you a hot dog. You have to have a hot dog
at a bonfire."

"Looks terrific." Accepting it, he pleased Roberta by
taking a generous bite. "Thanks." Only Chase and his
stomach knew that the meat was still cold on the inside.

"I got some marshmallows and sticks, too." She
handed them over. "It's more fun to do it yourself, I
guess." Because she was on the border between childhood and womanhood, Roberta picked up easily on the
vibrations around her. "If you two want to be alone, you
know, to kiss and stuff, no one's in the stables."

"Roberta!" Eden pulled out her best camp director's
voice. "That will do."

"Well, my parents like to be alone sometimes."
Undaunted, she grinned at Chase. "Maybe I'll see
you around."

"You can count on it, kid." As Roberta danced off
toward a group of girls, Chase turned back. The moment

he took a step toward her, Eden extended her skewered marshmallow toward the fire. "Want to go kiss and stuff?"

It was the heat of the fire that stung her cheeks with color, Eden assured herself. "I suppose you think it would be terribly amusing for Roberta to go home and report that one of the camp directors spent her time in the stables with a man. That would do a lot for Camp Liberty's reputation."

"You're right. You should come to my place."

"Go away, Chase."

"I haven't finished my hot dog. Have dinner with me."

"I've had a hot dog already, thank you."

"I'll make sure hot dogs aren't on the menu. We can talk about it tomorrow."

"We will not talk about it tomorrow." It was anger that made her breathless, just as it was anger that made her unwise enough to turn toward him. "We will not talk about anything tomorrow."

"Okay. We won't talk." To show how reasonable he was, he bent down and closed the conversation, his mouth covering hers. He wasn't holding her, but it took her brain several long, lazy seconds before it accepted the order to back away.

"Don't you have any sense of propriety?" she managed in a strangled voice.

"Not much." He made up his mind, looking down at her eyes, dazed and as blue as his lake, that he wasn't going to take no for an answer—to any question. "We'll make it about nine tomorrow morning at the entrance to the orchard."

"Make what?"

"The tour." He grinned and handed her his stick. "It'll be educational."

Though she was in an open field, Eden felt her back press into a corner. "We have no intention of disrupting your routine."

"No problem. I'll pass it on to your co-director before I go back. That way, you'll be sure to be coordinated."

Eden took a long breath. "You think you're very clever, don't you?"

"Thorough, just thorough, Eden. By the way, your marshmallow's on fire."

With his hands in his pockets, he strolled off while she blew furiously on the flaming ball.

She'd hoped for rain but was disappointed. The morning dawned warm and sunny. She'd hoped for support but was faced with Candy's enthusiasm for a field trip through one of the most prestigious apple orchards in the country. The girls were naturally delighted with any shift in schedule, so as they walked as a group the short distance to the Elliot farm, Eden found herself separated from the excitement.

"You could try not to look as though you're walking to the guillotine." Candy plucked a scrawny blue flower from the side of the road and stuck it in her hair. "This is a wonderful opportunity—for the girls," she added quickly.

"You managed to convince me of that, or else I wouldn't be here."

"Grumpy."

"I'm not grumpy," Eden countered. "I'm annoyed at being manipulated."

"Just a small piece of advice." Picking another flower, Candy twirled it. "If I'd been manipulated by a man, I'd make certain he believed it was my idea in the first place. Don't you think it would throw him off if you walked up to the gates with a cheery smile and boundless enthusiasm?"

"Maybe." Eden mulled the idea over until her lips began to curve. "Yes, maybe."

"There now. With a little practice, you'll find out that deviousness is much better in some cases than dignity."

"I wouldn't have needed either if you'd let me stay behind."

"Darling, unless I miss my guess, a certain apple baron would have plucked you up from whatever corner you'd chosen to hide in, tossed you over his wonderfully broad shoulder and dragged you along on our little tour, like it or not." Pausing, Candy let a sigh escape. "Now that I think about it, that would have been more exciting."

Because she was well able to picture it herself, Eden's mood hardened again. "At least I thought I could count on support from my best friend."

"And you can. Absolutely." With easy affection, Candy draped an arm over Eden's shoulder. "Though why you think you need my support when you have a gorgeous man giving you smoldering kisses, I can't imagine."

"That's just it!" Because several young heads turned when she raised her voice, Eden fought for calm again. "He had no business pulling something like that in front of everyone."

"I suppose it is more fun in private."

"Keep this up, and you may find that garter snake in your underwear yet."

"Just ask him if he's got a brother, or a cousin. Even an uncle. Ah, here we are," she continued before Eden could reply. "Now smile and be charming, just like you were taught."

"You're going to pay for this," Eden promised her in an undertone. "I don't know how, I don't know when, but you'll pay."

They brought the group to a halt when the road forked. On the left were stone pillars topped with an arching wrought-iron sign that read ELLIOT. Sloping away from the pillars was a wall a foot thick and high as a man. It was old and sturdy, proving to Eden that the penchant for privacy hadn't begun with Chase.

The entrance road, smooth and well-maintained, ribboned back over the crest of a hill before it disappeared. Along the road were trees, not apple but oak, older and sturdier than the wall.

It was the continuity that drew her, the same symmetry she had seen and admired in the groves. The stone, the trees, even the road, had been there for generations. Looking, Eden understood his pride in them. She, too, had once had a legacy.

Then he strode from behind the wall and she fought back even that small sense of a common ground.

In a T-shirt and jeans, he looked lean and capable. There was a faint sheen of sweat on his arms that made her realize he'd already been working that morning. Drawn against her will, she dropped her gaze to his hands, hands that were hard and competent and unbearably gentle on a woman's skin.

"Morning, ladies." He swung the gates open for them.

"Oh Lord, he's something," Eden heard one of the counselors mumble. Remembering Candy's advice, she straightened her shoulders and fixed on her most cheerful smile.

"This is Mr. Elliot, girls. He owns the orchards we'll tour today. Thank you for inviting us, Mr. Elliot."

"My pleasure—Miss Carlbough."

The girlish murmurs of agreement became babbles of excitement as a dog sauntered to Chase's side. His fur was the color of apricots and glistened as though it had been polished in the sunlight. The big, sad eyes studied the group of girls before the dog pressed against Chase's leg. Eden had time to think that a smaller man might have been toppled. The dog was no less than three feet high at the shoulder. More of a young lion than a house pet, she thought. When he settled to sit at Chase's feet, Chase didn't have to bend to lay a hand on the dog's head.

"This is Squat. Believe it or not, he was the runt of his litter. He's a little shy."

Candy gave a sigh of relief when she saw the enormous tail thump the ground. "But friendly, right?"

"Squat's a pushover for females." His gaze circled the group. "Especially so many pretty ones. He was hoping he could join the tour."

"He's neat." Roberta made up her mind instantly. Walking forward, she gave the dog's head a casual pat. "I'll walk with you, Squat."

Agreeable, the dog rose to lead the way.

There was more to the business of apples than Eden had imagined. It wasn't all trees and plump fruit to be plucked and piled into baskets for market. Harvesting wasn't limited to autumn with the variety of types that were planted. The season, Chase explained, had been extended into months, from early summer to late fall.

They weren't just used for eating and baking. Even cores and peelings were put to use for cider, or dried and shipped to Europe for certain champagnes. As they walked, the scent of ripening fruit filled the air, making more than one mouth water.

The Tree of Life, Eden thought as the scent tempted her. Forbidden fruit. She kept herself surrounded by girls and tried to remember that the tour was educational.

He explained that the quick-maturing trees were planted in the forty-foot spaces between the slow growers, then cut out when the space was needed. A practical business, she remembered, organized, with a high level of utility and little waste. Still, it had the romance of apple blossoms in spring.

Masses of laborers harvested the summer fruit. While they watched the men and machines at work, Chase answered questions.

"They don't look ripe," Roberta commented.

"They're full-size." Chase rested a hand on her shoulder as he chose an apple. "The changes that take place after the fruit's reached maturity are mainly chemical. It goes on without the tree. The fruit's hard, but the seeds are brown. Look." Using a pocketknife with casual skill, he cut the fruit in half. "The apples we harvest now are superior to the ones that hang longer." Reading Roberta's expression correctly, Chase tossed her half the fruit. The other half Squat took in one yawning bite.

"Maybe you'd like to pick some yourself." The reaction was positive, and Chase reached up to demonstrate. "Twist the fruit off the stem. You don't want to break the twig and lose bearing wood."

Before Eden could react, the girls had scattered to

nearby trees. She was facing Chase. Perhaps it was the way his lips curved. Perhaps it was the way his eyes seemed so content to rest on hers, but her mind went instantly and completely blank.

"You have a fascinating business." She could have kicked herself for the inanity of it.

"I like it."

"I, ah…" There must be a question, an intelligent question, she could ask. "I suppose you ship the fruit quickly to avoid spoilage."

He doubted that either of them gave two hoots about apples at the moment, but he was willing to play the game. "It's stored right after picking at thirty-two degrees Fahrenheit. I like your hair pulled back like that. It makes me want to tug on the string and watch it fall all over your shoulders."

Her pulse began to sing, but she pretended she hadn't heard. "I'm sure you have various tests to determine quality."

"We look for richness." Slowly, he turned the fruit over in his hand, but his gaze roamed to her mouth. "Flavor." He watched her lips part as if to taste. "Firmness," he murmured, as he circled her throat with his free hand. "Tenderness."

Her breath seemed to concentrate, to sweeten into the sound of a sigh. It was almost too late when she bit it off. "It would be best if we stuck to the subject at hand."

"Which subject?" His thumb traced along her jawline.

"Apples."

"I'd like to make love with you in the orchards, Eden, with the sun warm on your face and the grass soft at your back."

It terrified her that she could almost taste what it would be like, to be with him, alone. "If you'll excuse me."

"Eden." He took her hand, knowing he was pushing too hard, too fast, but unable to stop himself. "I want you. Maybe too much."

Though his voice was low, hardly more than a whisper, she felt her nerves jangling. "You should know you can't say those things to me here, now. If the children—"

"Have dinner with me."

"No." On this, she told herself she would stand firm. She would not be manipulated. She would not be maneuvered. "I have a job, Chase, one that runs virtually twenty-four hours a day for the next few weeks. Even if I wanted to have dinner with you, which I don't, it would be impossible."

He considered all this reasonable. But then, a great many smoke screens were. "Are you afraid to be alone with me? Really alone."

The truth was plain and simple. She ignored it. "You flatter yourself."

"I doubt a couple hours out of an evening would disrupt the camp's routine, or yours."

"You don't know anything about the camp's routine."

"I know that between your partner and the counselors, the girls are more than adequately supervised. And I know that your last riding lesson is at four o'clock."

"How did you—"

"I asked Roberta," he said easily. "She told me you have supper at six, then a planned activity or free time from seven to nine. Lights-out is at ten. You usually spend your time after supper with the horses. And sometimes you ride out at night when you think everyone's asleep."

She opened her mouth, then shut it again, having no idea what to say. She had thought those rides exclusively hers, exclusively private.

"Why do you ride out alone at night, Eden?"

"Because I enjoy it."

"Then tonight you can enjoy having dinner with me."

She tried to remember there were girls beneath the trees around them. She tried to remember that a display of temper was most embarrassing for the person who lost control. "Perhaps you have some difficulty understanding a polite refusal. Why don't we try this? The last place I want to be tonight, or at any other time, is with you."

He moved his shoulders before he took a step closer. "I guess we can just settle all this now. Here."

"You wouldn't…" She didn't bother to finish the thought. By now she knew very well what he would dare. One quick look around showed her that Roberta and Marcie were leaning against the trunk of a tree, happily munching apples and enjoying the show. "All right, stop it." So much for not being manipulated. "I have no idea why you insist on having dinner with someone who finds you so annoying."

"Me, either. We'll discuss it tonight. Seven-thirty." Tossing Eden the apple, he strolled over toward Roberta.

Eden hefted the fruit. She even went so far as to draw a mental bull's-eye on the back of his head. With a sound of disgust, she took a hefty bite instead.

Chapter 5

Vengefully, Eden dragged a brush through her hair. Despite the harsh treatment, it sprang back softly to wisp around her face and wave to her shoulders. She wouldn't go to any trouble as she had for other dates and dinners, but leave it loose and unstyled. Though he was undoubtedly too hardheaded to notice that sort of female subtlety.

She didn't bother with jewelry, except for the simple pearl studs she often wore around camp. In an effort to look cool, even prim, she wore a high-necked white blouse, regretting only the lace at the cuffs. Matching it with a white skirt, she tried for an icy look. The result was an innocent fragility she couldn't detect in the one small mirror on the wall.

Intending on making it plain that she had gone to no trouble for Chase's benefit, she almost ignored makeup. Grumbling to herself, Eden picked up her blusher. Basic feminine vanity, she admitted; then she added a touch of clear gloss to her lips. There was, after all, a giant step between not fussing and looking like a hag. She was reaching for her bottle of perfume before she stopped herself. No, that was definitely fussing. He would get soap, and soap only. She turned away from the mirror just as Candy swung through the cabin door.

"Wow." Stopping in the doorway, Candy took a long, critical look. "You look terrific."

"I do?" Brow creased, Eden turned back to the mirror. "Terrific wasn't exactly what I was shooting for. I wanted something along the lines of prim."

"You couldn't look prim if you wore sackcloth and ashes, any more than I could look delicate even with lace at my wrists."

With a sound of disgust, Eden tugged at the offending lace. "I knew it. I just knew it was a mistake. Maybe I can rip it off."

"Don't you dare." Laughing, Candy bounded into the room to stop Eden from destroying her blouse. "Besides, it isn't the clothes that are important. It's the attitude, right?"

Eden gave the lace a last tug. "Right. Candy, are you sure everything's going to be under control here? I could still make excuses."

"Everything's already under control." Candy flopped down on her bunk, then began to peel the banana she held. "In fact, things are great. I've just taken a five-minute break to see you off and stuff my face." She took a big bite to prove her point. "Then," she continued over a mouthful of banana, "we're getting together in the mess area to take an inventory of our record collection for the dance. The girls want some practice time before the big night."

"You could probably use extra supervision."

Candy waved her half-eaten banana. "Everyone's going to be in the same four walls for the next couple of hours. You go enjoy your dinner and stop worrying. Where are you going?"

"I don't know." She stuffed some tissue in her bag. "And I really don't care."

"Come on, after nearly six weeks of wholesome but god-awful boring food, aren't you just a little excited about the prospect of oysters Rockefeller or escargots?"

"No." She began to clasp and unclasp her bag. "I'm only going because it was simpler than creating a scene."

Candy broke off a last bite of banana. "Certainly knows how to get his own way, doesn't he?"

"That's about to end." Eden closed her purse with a snap. "Tonight."

At the sound of an approaching car, Candy propped herself up on an elbow. She noticed Eden nervously biting her lower lip, but she only gestured toward the door with her banana peel. "Well, good luck."

Eden caught the grin and paused, her hand on the screen door. "Whose side are you on, anyway?"

"Yours, Eden." Candy stretched, and prepared to go rock and roll. "Always."

"I'll be back early."

Candy grinned, wisely saying nothing as the screen door slammed shut.

However hard Eden might have tried to look remote, icy, disinterested, the breath clogged up in Chase's lungs the moment she stepped outside. They were still an hour from twilight, and the sun's last rays shot through her hair. Her skirt swirled around bare legs honey-toned after long days outdoors. Her chin was lifted, perhaps in anger, perhaps in defiance. He could only see the elegant line of her throat.

The same slowly drumming need rose up inside him the moment she stepped onto the grass.

She'd expected him to look less…dangerous in more formal attire. Eden discovered she had underestimated him again. The muscles in his arms and shoulders weren't so much restricted as enhanced by the sports jacket. The shirt, either by design or good fortune, matched his eyes and was left open at the throat. Slowly and easily he smiled at her, and her lips curved in automatic response.

"I imagined you looking like this." In truth, he hadn't been sure she would come, or what he might have done if she had locked herself away in one of the cabins and refused to see him. "I'm glad you didn't disappoint me."

Feeling her resolve weaken, Eden made an effort to draw back. "I made a bargain," she began, only to fall silent when he handed her a bunch of anemones freshly picked from the side of the road. He wasn't supposed to be sweet, she reminded herself. She wasn't supposed to be vulnerable to sweetness. Still, unable to resist, she buried her face in the flowers.

That was a picture he would carry with him forever, Chase realized. Eden, with wildflowers clutched in both hands; her eyes, touched with both pleasure and confusion, watching him over the petals.

"Thank you."

"You're welcome." Taking one of her hands, he

brought it to his lips. She should have pulled away. She knew she should. Yet there was something so simple, so right in the moment—as if she recognized it from some long-ago dream. Bemused, Eden took a step closer, but the sound of giggling brought her out of the spell.

Immediately she tried to pull her hand away. "The girls." She glanced around quickly enough to catch the fielder's cap as it disappeared around the corner of the building.

"Well, then, we wouldn't want to disappoint them?" Turning her hand over, Chase pressed a kiss to her palm. Eden felt the heat spread.

"You're being deliberately difficult." But she closed her hand as if to capture the sensation and hold it.

"Yes." He smiled, but resisted the impulse to draw her into his arms and enjoy the promise he'd seen so briefly in her eyes.

"If you'd let me go, I'd like to put the flowers in water."

"I'll do it." Candy left her post by the door and came outside. Even Eden's glare didn't wipe the smile from her face. "They're lovely, aren't they? Have a good time."

"We'll do that." Chase linked his fingers with Eden's and drew her toward his car. She told herself the sun had been in her eyes. Why else would she have missed the low-slung white Lamborghini parked beside the cabin. She settled herself in the passenger's seat with a warning to herself not to relax.

The moment the engine sprang to life, there was a chorus of goodbyes. Every girl and counselor had lined up to wave them off. Eden disguised a chuckle with a cough.

"It seems this is one of the camp's highlights this summer."

Chase lifted a hand out of the open window to wave back. "Let's see if we can make it one of ours."

Something in his tone made her glance over just long enough to catch that devil of a smile. Eden made up her mind then and there. No, she wouldn't relax, but she'd be damned if she'd be intimidated either. "All right." She leaned back in her seat, prepared to make the best of a bad deal. "I haven't had a meal that wasn't served on a tray in weeks."

"I'll cancel the trays."

"I'd appreciate it." She laughed, then assured herself that laughing wasn't really relaxing. "Stop me if I start stacking the silverware." The breeze blowing in the open window was warm and as fresh as the flowers Chase had brought her. Eden allowed herself the pleasure of lifting her face to it. "This is nice, especially when I was expecting a pickup truck."

"Even country bumpkins can appreciate a well-made machine."

"That's not what I meant." Ready with an apology, she turned, but saw he was smiling. "I suppose you wouldn't care if it was."

"I know what I am, what I want and what I can do." As he took a curve he slowed. His eyes met hers briefly. "But the opinions of certain people always matter. In any case, I prefer the mountains to traffic jams. What do you prefer, Eden?"

"I haven't decided." That was true, she realized with a jolt. In a matter of weeks her priorities, and her hopes, had changed direction. Musing on that, she almost missed the arching ELLIOT sign when Chase turned between the columns. "Where are we going?"

"To dinner."

"In the orchard?"

"In my house." With that he changed gears and had the car cruising up the gravel drive.

Eden tried to ignore the little twist of apprehension she felt. True, this wasn't the crowded, and safe, restaurant she had imagined. She'd shared private dinners before, hadn't she? She'd been raised from the cradle to know how to handle any social situation. But the apprehension remained. Dinner alone with Chase wouldn't be, couldn't possibly be, like any other experience.

Even as she was working out a polite protest, the car crested the hill. The house rose into view.

It was stone. She couldn't know it was local stone, quarried from the mountains. She saw only that it was old, beautifully weathered. At first glance, it gave the appearance of being gray, but on a closer look colors glimmered through. Amber, russet, tints of green and umber. The sun was still high enough to make the chips of mica and quartz glisten. There were three stories, with the second overhanging the first by a skirting balcony. Eden could see flashes of red and buttercup yellow from the pots of geraniums and marigolds. She caught the scent of lavender even before she saw the rock garden.

A wide, sweeping stone stairway, worn slightly in the center, led to double glass doors of diamond panes. A redwood barrel was filled with pansies that nodded in the early evening breeze.

It was nothing like what she had expected, and

yet…the house, and everything about it, was instantly recognizable.

His own nervousness caught Chase off guard. Eden said nothing when he stopped the car, still nothing when he got out to round the hood and open her door. It mattered, more than he had ever imagined it could, what she thought, what she said, what she felt about his home.

She held her hand out for his in a gesture he knew was automatic. Then she stood beside him, looking at what was his, what had been his even before his birth. Tension lodged in the back of his neck.

"Oh, Chase, it's beautiful." She lifted her free hand to shield her eyes from the sun behind the house. "No wonder you love it."

"My great-grandfather built it." The tension had dissolved without his being aware of it. "He even helped quarry the stone. He wanted something that would last and that would carry a piece of him as long as it did."

She thought of the home that had been her family's for generations, feeling the too-familiar burning behind her eyes. She'd lost that. Sold it. The need to tell him was almost stronger than pride, because in that moment she thought he might understand.

He felt her change in mood even before he glanced down and saw the glint of tears in her eyes. "What is it, Eden?"

"Nothing." No, she couldn't tell him. Some wounds were best left hidden. Private. "I was just thinking how important some traditions are."

"You still miss your father."

"Yes." Her eyes were dry now, the moment past. "I'd love to see inside."

He hesitated a moment, knowing there had been more and that she'd been close to sharing it with him. He could wait, Chase told himself, though his patience was beginning to fray. He would have to wait until she took that step toward him rather than away from him.

With her hand still in his, he climbed the steps to the door. On the other side lay a mountain of apricot fur known as Squat. Even after Chase opened the door, the mound continued to snore.

"Are you sure you should have such a vicious watchdog unchained?"

"My theory is most burglars wouldn't have the nerve to step over him." Catching Eden around the waist, Chase lifted her up and over.

The stone insulated well against the heat, so the hall was cool and comfortable. High, beamed ceilings gave the illusion of unlimited space. A Monet landscape caught her eye, but before she could comment on it, Chase was leading her through a set of mahogany doors.

The room was cozily square, with window seats recessed into the east and west walls. Instantly Eden could imagine the charm of watching the sun rise or set. Comfort was the theme of the room, with its range of blues from the palest aqua to the deepest indigo. Hand-hooked rugs set off the American antiques. There were fresh flowers here, too, spilling out of a Revere Ware bowl. It was a touch she hadn't expected from a bachelor, particularly one who worked with his hands.

Thoughtful, she crossed the room to the west window. The slanting sun cast long shadows over the buildings he had taken them through that morning. She remembered the conveyor belts, the busy sorters and packers, the noise. Behind her was a small, elegant room with pewter bowls and wild roses.

Peace and challenge, she realized, and she sighed without knowing why. "I imagine it's lovely when the sun starts to drop."

"It's my favorite view." His voice came from directly behind her, but for once she didn't stiffen when he rested his hands on her shoulders. He tried to tell himself it was just coincidence that she had chosen to look out that window, but he could almost believe that his own need for her to see and understand had guided her there. It wouldn't be wise to forget who she was and how she chose to live. "There's no Symphony Hall or Rodin Museum."

His fingers gently massaged the curve of her shoulders. But his voice wasn't as patient. Curious, she turned. His hands shifted to let her slide through, then settled on her shoulders again. "I don't imagine they're missed. If they were, you could visit, then come back to this." Without thinking, she lifted her hand to brush the hair from his forehead. Even as she caught herself, his hand closed around her wrist. "Chase, I—"

"Too late," he murmured; then he kissed each of her fingers, one by one. "Too late for you. Too late for me."

She couldn't allow herself to believe that. She couldn't accept the softening and opening of her emotions. How badly she wanted to let him in, to trust again, to need again. How terrifying it was to be vulnerable. "Please don't do this. It's a mistake for both of us."

"You're probably right." He was almost sure of it himself. But he brushed his lips over the pulse that hammered in her wrist. He didn't give a damn. "Everyone's entitled to one enormous mistake."

"Don't kiss me now." She lifted a hand but only curled her fingers into his shirt. "I can't think."

"One has nothing to do with the other."

When his mouth touched hers, it was soft, seeking. *Too late.* The words echoed in her head even as she lifted her hands to his face and let herself go. This is what she had wanted, no matter how many arguments she had posed, no matter how many defenses she had built. She wanted to be held against him, to sink into a dream that had no end.

He felt her fingers stream through his hair and had to force himself not to rush her. Desire, tensed and hungry, had to be held back until it was tempered with acceptance and trust. In his heart he had already acknowledged that she was more than the challenge he had first considered her. She was more than the summer fling he might have preferred. But as her slim, soft body pressed against his, as her warm, willing mouth opened for him, he could only think of how he wanted her, now, when the sun was beginning to sink toward the distant peaks to the west.

"Chase." It was the wild, drumming beat of her heart that frightened her most. She was trembling. Eden could feel it start somewhere deep inside and spread out until it became a stunning combination of panic and excitement. How could she fight the first and give in to the second? "Chase, please."

He had to draw himself back, inch by painful inch. He hadn't meant to take either of them so far, so fast. Yet perhaps he had, he thought as he ran a hand down her hair. Perhaps he had wanted to push them both toward an answer that still seemed just out of reach.

"The sun's going down." His hands weren't quite

steady when he turned her toward the window again. "Before long, the light will change."

She could only be grateful that he was giving her time to regain her composure. Later she would realize how much it probably had cost him.

They stood a moment in silence, watching the first tints of rose spread above the mountains. A loud, rasping cough had her already-tense nerves jolting.

"S'cuze me."

The man in the doorway had a grizzled beard that trailed down to the first button of his red checked shirt. Though he was hardly taller than Eden, his bulk gave the impression of power. The folds and lines in his face all but obscured his dark eyes. Then he grinned, and she caught the glint of a gold tooth.

So this was the little lady who had the boss running around in circles. Deciding she was prettier than a barrelful of prime apples, he nodded to her by way of greeting. "Supper's ready. Unless you want to eat it cold, you best be moving along."

"Eden Carlbough, Delaney." Chase only lifted a brow, knowing Delaney had already sized up the situation. "He cooks and I don't, which is why I haven't fired him yet."

This brought on a cackle. "He hasn't fired me because I wiped his nose and tied his shoes."

"We could add that that was close to thirty years ago."

She recognized both affection and exasperation. It pleased her to know someone could exasperate Chase Elliot. "It's nice to meet you, Mr. Delaney."

"Delaney, ma'am. Just Delaney." Still grinning, he pulled on his beard. "Mighty pretty," he said to Chase.

"It's smarter to think of settling down with someone who isn't an eyesore at breakfast. Supper's going to get cold," he added. Then he was gone.

Though Eden had remained politely silent during Delaney's statement, it took only one look at Chase's face to engender a stream of laughter. The sound made Chase think more seriously about gagging Delaney with his own beard.

"I'm glad you're amused."

"Delighted. It's the first time I've ever seen you speechless. And I can't help being pleased not to be considered an eyesore." Then she disarmed him by offering him her hand. "Supper's going to get cold."

Instead of the dining room, Chase led her out to a jalousied porch. Two paddle fans circled overhead, making the most of the breeze that crept in the slanted windows. A wind chime jingled cheerfully between baskets of fuchsia.

"Your home is one surprise after another," Eden commented as she studied the plump love seats and the glass-and-wicker table. "Every room seems fashioned for relaxation and stunning views."

The table was set with colorful stoneware. Though the sun had yet to drop behind the peaks, two tapers were already burning. There was a single wild rose beside her plate.

Romance, she thought. This was the romance she had once dreamed of. This was the romance she must now be very wary of. But, wary or not, she picked up the flower and smiled at him. "Thank you."

"Did you want one, too?" As she laughed, Chase drew back her chair.

"Sit down. Sit down. Eat while it's hot." Despite his bulk, Delaney bustled into the room. In his large hands was an enormous tray. Because she realized how easily she could be mowed down, Eden obeyed. "Hope you got an appetite. You could use a little plumping up, missy. Then, I've always preferred a bit of healthy meat on female bones."

As he spoke, he began to serve an exquisite seafood salad. "Made my special, Chicken Delaney. It'll keep under the covers if you two don't dawdle over the salad. Apple pie's on the hot plate, biscuits in the warmer." He stuck a bottle of wine unceremoniously in an ice bucket. "That's the fancy wine you wanted." Standing back, he took a narrowed-eyed glance around before snorting with satisfaction. "I'm going home. Don't let my chicken get cold." Wiping his hands on his jeans, he marched to the door and let it swing shut behind him.

"Delaney has amazing style, doesn't he?" Chase took the wine from the bucket to pour two glasses.

"Amazing," Eden agreed, finding it amazing enough that those gnarled hands had created anything as lovely as the salad in front of her.

"He makes the best biscuits in Pennsylvania." Chase lifted his glass and toasted her. "And I'd put his Beef Wellington up against anyone's."

"Beef Wellington?" With a shake of her head, Eden sipped her wine. It was cool, just a shade tart. "I hope you'll take it the right way when I say he looks more like the type who could charcoal a steak over a backyard grill." She dipped her fork in the salad and sampled it. "But…"

"Appearances can be deceiving," Chase finished for her, pleased with the way her eyes half shut as she tasted. "Delaney's been cooking here as long as I can remember. He lives in a little cottage my grandfather helped him build about forty years ago. Nose-wiping and shoe-tying aside, he's part of the family."

She only nodded, looking down at her plate for a moment as she remembered how difficult it had been to tell her longtime servants she was selling out. Perhaps they had never been as familiar or as informal as Chase's Delaney, but they, too, had been part of the family.

It was there again, that dim candle glow of grief he'd seen in her eyes before. Wanting only to help, he reached over to touch her hand. "Eden?"

Quickly, almost too quickly, she moved her hand and began to eat again. "This is wonderful. I have an aunt back home who would shanghai your Delaney after the first forkful."

Home, he thought, backing off automatically. Philadelphia was still home.

The Chicken Delaney lived up to its name. As the sun set, the meal passed easily, even though they disagreed on almost every subject.

She read Keats and he read Christie. She preferred Bach and he Haggard, but it didn't seem to matter as the glass walls filtered the rosy light of approaching twilight. The candles burned lower. The wine shimmered in crystal, inviting one more sip. Close and clear and quick came the two-tone call of a quail.

"That's a lovely sound." Her sigh was easy and content. "If things are quiet at camp, we can hear the birds in the evening. There's a whippoorwill who's taken to singing right outside the cabin window. You can almost set your watch by her."

"Most of us are creatures of habit," he murmured. He wondered about her, what habits she had, what habits she had changed. Taking her hand, he turned it up. The ridge of callus had hardened. "You didn't take my advice."

"About what?"

"Wearing gloves."

"It didn't seem worth it. Besides…" Letting the words trail off, she lifted her wine.

"Besides?"

"Having calluses means I did something to earn them." She blurted it out, then sat swearing at herself and waiting for him to laugh.

He didn't. Instead he sat silently, passing his thumb over the toughened skin and watching her. "Will you go back?"

"Go back?"

"To Philadelphia."

It was foolish to tell him how hard she'd tried not to think about that. Instead, she answered as the practical Eden was supposed to. "The camp closes down the last week in August. Where else would I go?"

"Where else?" he agreed, but when he released her hand she felt a sense of loss rather than relief. "Maybe there comes a time in everyone's life when they have to take a hard look at the options." He rose, and her hands balled into fists. He took a step toward her, and her heart rose up to her throat. "I'll be back."

Alone, she let out a long, shaky breath. What had she been expecting? she asked herself. What had she been hoping for? Her legs weren't quite steady when she rose, but it could have been the wine. But wine would have made her warm, and she felt a chill. To ward it off, she rubbed her arms with her hands. The sky was a quiet, deepening blue but for a halo of scarlet along the horizon. She concentrated on that, trying not to imagine how it would look when the stars came out.

Maybe they would look at the stars together again. They could look, picking out the patterns, and she would again feel that click that meant her needs and dreams were meshing. With his.

Pressing a hand to her lips, she struggled to block off that train of thought. It was only that the evening had been lovelier than she had imagined. It was only that they had more in common than she had believed possible. It was only that he had a gentleness inside him that softened parts of her when she least expected it. And when he kissed her, she felt as though she had the world pulsing in the palm of her hand.

No. Uneasy, she wrapped her hands around her forearms and squeezed. She was romanticizing again, spinning daydreams when she had no business dreaming at all. She was just beginning to sort out her life, to make her own place. It wasn't possible that she was looking to him to be any part of it.

She heard the music then, something low and unfamiliar that nonetheless had tiny shivers working their way up her spine. She had to leave, she thought quickly. And right away. She had let the atmosphere get to her. The house, the sunset, the wine. Him. Hearing his footsteps, she turned. She would tell him she had to get back. She would thank him for the evening, and…escape.

When he came back into the room, she was standing beside the table so that the candlelight flickered over her skin. Dusk swirled behind her with its smoky magic. The scent of wild roses from the bush outside the window seemed to sigh into the room. He wondered, if he touched her now, if she would simply dissolve in his hands.

"Chase, I think I'd better—"

"Shh." She wouldn't dissolve, he told himself as he went to her. She was real, and so was he. One hand captured hers, the other slipping around her waist. After one moment of resistance, she began to move with him. "One of the pleasures of country music is dancing to it."

"I, ah, I don't know the song." But it felt so good, so very good, to sway with him while darkness fell.

"It's about a man, a woman and passion. The best songs are."

She shut her eyes. She could feel the brush of his jacket against her cheek, the firm press of his hand at her waist. He smelled of soap, but nothing a woman would use. This had a tang that was essentially masculine. Wanting to taste, she moved her head so that her lips rested against his neck.

His pulse beat there, quick, surprising her. Forgetting caution, she nestled closer and felt its sudden rise in speed. As her own raced to match it, she gave a murmur of pleasure and traced it with the tip of her tongue.

He started to draw her away. He meant to. When he'd left her, he'd promised himself that he would slow the pace to one they could both handle. But now she was cuddled against him, her body swaying, her fingers straying to his neck, and her mouth... With an oath, Chase dragged her closer and gave in to hunger.

The kiss was instantly torrid, instantly urgent. And

somehow, though she had never experienced anything like it, instantly familiar. Her head tilted back in surrender. Her lips parted. Here and now, she wanted the fire and passion that had only been hinted at.

Perhaps he lowered her to the love seat, perhaps she drew him to it, but they were wrapped together, pressed against the cushions. An owl hooted once, then twice, then gave them silence.

He'd wanted to believe she could be this generous. He'd wanted to believe his lips would touch hers and find unrestricted sweetness. Now his mind spun with it. Whatever he had wanted, whatever he had dreamed of, was less, so much less than what he now held in his arms.

He stroked a hand down her body and met trembling response. With a moan, she arched against him. Through the sheer fabric of her blouse, he could feel the heat rising to her skin, enticing him to touch again and yet again.

He released the first button of her blouse, then the second, following the course with his lips. She shivered with anticipation. Her lace cuffs brushed against his cheeks as she lifted her hands to his hair. It seemed her body was filling, flooding with sensations she'd once only imagined. Now they were so real and so clear that she could feel each one as it layered over the next.

The pillows at her back were soft. His body was hard and hot. The breeze that jingled the wind chime overhead was freshened with flowers. Behind her closed eyes came the flicker and glow of candlelight. In teams of thousands, the cicadas began to sing. But more thrilling, more intense, was the sound of her name whispering from him as he pressed his lips against her skin.

Suddenly, searing, his mouth took hers again. In the

kiss she could taste everything, his need, his desire, the passion that teetered on the edge of sanity. As her own madness hovered, she felt her senses swimming with him. And she moaned with the ecstasy of falling in love.

For one brief moment, she rose on it, thrilled with the knowledge that she had found him. The dream and the reality were both here. She had only to close them both in her arms and watch them become one.

Then the terror of it fell on her. She couldn't let it be real. How could she risk it? Once she had given her trust and her promise, if not her heart. And she had been betrayed. If it happened again, she would never recover. If it happened with Chase, she wouldn't want to.

"Chase, no more." She turned her face away and tried to clear her head. "Please, this has to stop."

Her taste was still exploding in his mouth. Beneath his, her body was trembling with a need he knew matched his own. "Eden, for God's sake." With an effort that all but drained him, he lifted his head to look down at her. She was afraid. He recognized her fear immediately and struggled to hold back his own needs. "I won't hurt you."

That almost undid her. He meant it, she was sure, but that didn't mean it wouldn't happen. "Chase, this isn't right for me. For either of us."

"Isn't it?" Tension knotted in his stomach as he drew her toward him. "Can you tell me you didn't feel how right it was a minute ago?"

"No." It was both confusion and fear that had her dragging her hands through her hair. "But this isn't what I want. I need you to understand that this can't be what I want. Not now."

"You're asking a hell of a lot."

"Maybe. But there isn't any choice."

That infuriated him. She was the one who had taken his choice away, simply by existing. He hadn't asked her to fall into his life. He hadn't asked her to become the focus of it before he had a chance for a second breath. She'd given in to him to the point where he was half-mad for her. Now she was drawing away. And asking him to understand.

"We'll play it your way." His tone chilled as he drew away from her.

She shuddered, recognizing instantly that his anger could be lethal. "It's not a game."

"No? Well, in any case, you play it well."

She pressed her lips together, understanding that she deserved at least a part of the lash. "Please, don't spoil what happened."

He walked to the table and, lifting his glass, studied the wine. "What did happen?"

I fell in love with you. Rather than answer him, she began to button her blouse with nerveless fingers.

"I'll tell you." He tossed back the remaining wine, but it didn't soothe him. "Not for the first time in our fascinating relationship, you blew hot and cold without any apparent reason. It makes me wonder if Eric backed out of the marriage out of self-defense."

He saw her fingers freeze on the top button of her blouse. Even in the dim light, he could watch the color wash out of her face. Very carefully, he set his glass down again. "I'm sorry, Eden. That was uncalled-for."

The fight for control and composure was a hard war, but she won. She made her fingers move until the button was in place, then, slowly, she rose. "Since you're so interested, I'll tell you that Eric jilted me for more practical reasons. I appreciate the meal, Chase. It was lovely. Please thank Delaney for me."

"Damn it, Eden."

When he started forward, her body tightened like a bow. "If you could do one thing for me, it would be to take me back now and say nothing. Absolutely nothing."

Turning, she walked away from the candlelight.

Chapter 6

During the first weeks of August, the camp was plagued with one calamity after another. The first was an epidemic of poison ivy. Within twenty-four hours, ten of the girls and three of the counselors were coated with calamine lotion. The sticky heat did nothing to make the itching more bearable.

Just as the rashes started to fade came three solid days of rain. As the camp was transformed into a muddy mire, outdoor activities were canceled. Tempers soared. Eden broke up two hair-pulling battles in one day. Then, as luck would have it, lightning hit one of the trees and distracted the girls from their boredom.

By the time the sun came out, they had enough pot holders, key chains, wallets and pillows to open their own craft shop.

Men with Jeeps and chain saws came to clear away

the debris from the tree. Eden wrote out a check and prayed the last crisis was over.

It was doubtful the check had even been cashed when the secondhand restaurant stove she and Candy had bought stopped working. In the three days the parts were on order, cooking was done in true camp style— around an open fire.

The gelding, Courage, developed an infection that settled in his lungs. Everyone in camp worried about him and fussed over him and pampered him. The vet dosed him with penicillin. Eden spent three sleepless nights in the stables, nursing him and waiting for the crisis to pass.

Eventually the horse's appetite improved, the mud in the compound dried and the stove was back in working order. Eden told herself that the worst had to be over as the camp's routine picked up again.

Yet oddly, the lull brought out a restlessness she'd been able to ignore while the worst was happening. At dusk, she wandered to the stables with her sackful of apples. It wasn't hard to give a little extra attention to Courage. He'd gotten used to being pampered during his illness. Eden slipped him a carrot to go with the apple.

Still, as she worked her way down the stalls, she found the old routine didn't keep her mind occupied. The emergencies over the past couple of weeks had kept her too busy to take a second breath, much less think. Now, with calm settling again, thinking was unavoidable.

She could remember her evening with Chase as if it had been the night before. Every word spoken, every touch, every gesture, was locked in her mind as it had been when it had been happening. The rushing, tumbling sensation of falling in love was just as vital now, and just as frightening.

She hadn't been prepared for it. Her life had always been a series of preparations and resulting actions. Even her engagement had been a quiet step along a well-paved road. Since then, she'd learned to handle the detours and the roadblocks. But Chase was a sudden one-way street that hadn't been on any map.

It didn't matter, she told herself as she finished Patience's rubdown. She would navigate this and swing herself back in the proper direction. Having her choices taken away at this point in her life wasn't something she would tolerate. Not even when the lack of choice seemed so alluring and so right.

"I thought I'd find you here." Candy leaned against the stall door to give the mare a pat. "How was Courage tonight?"

"Good." Eden walked to the little sink in the corner to wash liniment from her hands. "I don't think we have to worry about him anymore."

"I'm glad to know that you'll be using your bunk instead of a pile of hay."

Eden pressed both hands to the small of her back and stretched. No demanding set of tennis had ever brought on this kind of ache. Strangely enough, she liked it. "I never thought I'd actually look forward to sleeping in that bunk."

"Well, now that you're not worried about the gelding, I can tell you I'm worried about you."

"Me?" Eden looked for a towel and, not finding one, dried her hands on her jeans. "Why?"

"You're pushing yourself too hard."

"Don't be silly. I'm barely pulling my weight."

"That stopped being even close to the truth the second week of camp." Now that she'd decided to speak up, Candy took a deep breath. "Damn it, Eden, you're exhausted."

"Tired," Eden corrected her. "Which is nothing a few hours on that miserable bunk won't cure."

"Look, it's okay if you want to avoid the issue with everyone else, even with yourself. But don't do it with me."

It wasn't often Candy's voice took on that firm, no-nonsense tone. Eden lifted a brow and nodded. "All right, what is the issue?"

"Chase Elliot," Candy stated, and she saw Eden freeze up. "I didn't hound you with questions the night you came back from dinner."

"And I appreciate that."

"Well, don't, because I'm asking now."

"We had dinner, talked a bit about books and music, then he brought me back."

Candy closed the stall door with a creak. "I thought I was your friend."

"Oh, Candy, you know you are." With a sigh, Eden closed her eyes a moment. "All right, we did exactly what I said we did, but somewhere between the talk and the ride home, things got a little out of hand."

"What sort of things?"

Eden found she didn't even have the energy to laugh. "I've never known you to pry."

"I've never known you to settle comfortably into depression."

"Am I?" Eden blew her bangs out of her eyes. "God, maybe I am."

"Let's just say that you've jumped from one problem to the next in order to avoid fixing one of your own." Taking a step closer, Candy drew Eden down on a small bench. "So let's talk."

"I'm not sure I can." Linking her hands, Eden looked down at them. The opal ring that had once been her mother's winked back at her. "I promised myself after Papa died and everything was in such a mess that I would handle things and find the best way to solve the problems. I've needed to solve them myself."

"That doesn't mean you can't lean on a friend."

"I've leaned on you so much I'm surprised you can walk upright."

"I'll let you know when I start limping. Eden, unless my memory's faulty, we've taken turns leaning on each other since before either of us could walk. Tell me about Chase."

"He scares me." With a long breath, Eden leaned back against the wall. "Everything's happening so fast, and everything I feel seems so intense." Dropping the last of her guard, she turned her face to Candy's. "If things had worked out differently, I'd be married to another man right now. How can I even think I might be in love with someone else so soon?"

"You're not going to tell me you think you're fickle." The last thing Eden had expected was Candy's bright, bubbling laughter, but that was what echoed off the stable walls. "Eden, I'm the fickle one, remember? You've always been loyal to a fault. Wait, I can see you're getting annoyed, so let's take this logically." Candy crossed her ankles and began to count off on her fingers.

"First, you were engaged to Eric—the slime—because

of all the reasons we've discussed before. It seemed the proper thing to do. Were you in love with him?"

"No, but I thought—"

"Irrelevant. No is the answer. Second, he showed his true colors, the engagement's been off for months, and you've met a fascinating, attractive man. Now, let's even take it a step further." Warming up to the subject, Candy shifted on the bench. "Suppose—God forbid—that you had actually been madly in love with Eric. After he had shown himself to be a snake, your heart would have been broken. With time and effort, you would have pulled yourself back together. Right?"

"I certainly like to think so."

"So we agree."

"Marginally."

That was enough for Candy. "Then, heart restored, if you'd met a fascinating and attractive man, you would have been equally free to fall for him. Either way, you're in the clear." Satisfied, Candy rose and dusted her palms on her jeans. "So what's the problem?"

Not certain she could explain, or even make sense of it herself, Eden looked down at her hands. "Because I've learned something. Love is a commitment, it's total involvement, promises, compromises. I'm not sure I can give those things to anyone yet. And if I were, I don't know if Chase feels at all the same way."

"Eden, your instincts must tell you he does."

With a shake of her head, she rose. She did feel better having said it all out loud, but that didn't change the bottom line. "I've learned not to trust my instincts, but to be realistic. Which is why I'm going to go hit the account books."

"Oh, Eden, give it a break."

"Unfortunately, I had to give it a break during the poison ivy, the lightning, the stove breakdown and the vet visits." Hooking her arm through Candy's, she started to walk toward the door. "You were right, and talking it out helped, but practicality is still the order of the day."

"Meaning checks and balances."

"Right. I'd really like to get to it. The advantage is I can frazzle my brain until the bunk really does feel like a feather bed."

Candy pushed open the door, then squared her shoulders. "I'll help."

"Thanks, but I'd like to finish them before Christmas."

"Oh, low blow, Eden."

"But true." She latched the door behind them. "Don't worry about me, Candy. Talking about it cleared my head a bit."

"Doing something about it would be better, but it's a start. Don't work too late."

"A couple of hours," Eden promised.

The office, as Eden arrogantly called it, was a small side room off the kitchen. After switching on the gooseneck lamp on the metal army-surplus desk, she adjusted the screen, flap up. As an afterthought, she switched the transistor radio on the corner of the desk to a classical station. The quiet, familiar melodies would go a long way toward calming her.

Still, as always, she drew in a deep breath as she took her seat behind the desk. Here, she knew too well, things were black-and-white. There were no multiple choices, no softening the rules as there could be in other areas of the camp. Figures were figures and facts were facts. It was up to her to tally them.

Opening the drawers, she pulled out invoices, the business checkbook and the ledger. She began systematically sorting and entering as the tape spilled out of the adding machine at her elbow.

Within twenty minutes, she knew the worst. The additional expenses of the past two weeks had stretched their capital to the limit. No matter how many ways Eden worked the numbers, the answer was the same. They weren't dead broke, but painfully close to it. Wearily, she rubbed the bridge of her nose between her thumb and forefinger.

They could still make it, she told herself. She pressed her hand down on the pile of papers, letting her palm cover the checks and balances. By the skin of their teeth, she thought, but they could still make it. If there were no more unexpected expenses. And if, she continued, the pile seeming to grow under her hand, she and Candy lived frugally over the winter. She imagined the pile growing another six inches under her restraining hand. If they got the necessary enrollments for the next season, everything would turn around.

Curling her fingers around the papers, she let out a long breath. If one of those *if*s fell through, she still had some jewelry that could be sold.

The lamplight fell across her opal-and-diamond ring, but she looked away, feeling guilty at even considering selling it. But she would. If her other choices were taken away, she would. What she wouldn't do was give up.

The tears began so unexpectedly that they fell onto the blotter before she knew she had shed them. Even as she wiped them away, new ones formed. There was no one to see, no one to hear. Giving in, Eden laid her head on the piles of bills and let the tears come.

They wouldn't change anything. With tears would come no fresh ideas or brilliant answers, but she let them come anyway. Quite simply, her strength had run out.

He found her like that, weeping almost soundlessly over the neat stacks of paper. At first Chase only stood there, with the door not quite shut at his back. She looked so helpless, so utterly spent. He wanted to go to her, but held himself back. He understood that the tears would be private. She wouldn't want to share them, particularly not with him. And yet, even as he told himself to step back, he moved toward her.

"Eden."

Her head shot up at the sound of her name. Her eyes were drenched, but he saw both shock and humiliation in them before she began to dry her cheeks with the backs of her hands.

"What are you doing here?"

"I wanted to see you." It sounded simple enough, but didn't come close to what was moving inside him. He wanted to go to her, to gather her close and fix whatever was wrong. He stuck his hands in his pockets and remained standing just inside the door. "I just heard about the gelding this morning. Is he worse?"

She shook her head, then struggled to keep her voice calm. "No, he's better. It wasn't as serious as we thought it might be."

"That's good." Frustrated by his inability to think of something less inane, he began to pace. How could he offer comfort when she wouldn't share the problem?

Her eyes were dry now, but he knew it was pride, and pride alone, that held her together. The hell with her pride, he thought. He needed to help.

When he turned back, he saw she had risen from the desk. "Why don't you tell me about it?"

The need to confide in him was so painfully strong that she automatically threw up the customary shield. "There's nothing to tell. It's been a rough couple of weeks. I suppose I'm overtired."

It was more than that, he thought, though she did look exhausted. "The girls getting to you?"

"No, really, the girls are fine."

Frustrated, he looked for another answer. The radio was playing something slow and romantic. Glancing toward it, Chase noticed the open ledger. The tail of adding-machine tape was spilling onto the floor. "Is it money? I could help."

Eden closed the book with a snap. Humiliation was a bitter taste at the back of her throat. At least it dried the last of her tears. "We're fine," she told him in a voice that was even and cool. "If you'd excuse me, I still have some work to do."

Rejection was something Chase had never fully understood until he'd met her. He didn't care for it. Nodding slowly, he searched for patience. "It was meant as an offer, not an insult." He would have turned and left her then, but the marks of weeping and sleeplessness gave her a pale, wounded look. "I'm sorry about the trouble you've been having the past year, Eden. I knew you'd lost your father, but I didn't know about the estate."

She wanted, oh so badly, to reach out, to let him gather her close and give her all the comfort she needed.

She wanted to ask him what she should do, and have him give her the answers. But wouldn't that mean that all the months of struggling for self-sufficiency had been for nothing? She straightened her shoulders. "It isn't necessary to be sorry."

"If you had told me yourself, it would have been simpler."

"It didn't concern you."

He didn't so much ignore the stab of hurt as turn it into annoyance. "Didn't it? I felt differently—feel differently. Are you going to stand there and tell me there's nothing between us, Eden?"

She couldn't deny it, but she was far too confused, far too afraid, to try to define the truth. "I don't know how I feel about you, except that I don't want to feel anything. Most of all, I don't want your pity."

The hands in his pockets curled into fists. He didn't know how to handle his own feelings, his own needs. Now she was treating them as though they didn't matter. He could leave, or he could beg. At the moment, Chase saw no choice between the two. "Understanding and pity are different things, Eden. If you don't know that, there's nothing else to say."

Turning, he left her. The screen door swished quietly behind him.

For the next two days, Eden functioned. She gave riding instructions, supervised meals and hiked the hills with groups of girls. She talked and laughed and listened, but the hollowness that had spread inside her when the door had closed at Chase's back remained.

Guilt and regret. Those were the feelings she couldn't

shake, no matter how enthusiastically she threw herself into her routine. She'd been wrong. She'd known it even as it was happening, but pride had boxed her in. He had offered to help. He had offered to care, and she'd refused him. If there was a worse kind of selfishness, she couldn't name it.

She'd started to phone him, but hadn't been able to dial the number. It hadn't been pride that had held her back this time. Every apology that formed in her mind was neat and tidy and meaningless. She couldn't bear to give him a stilted apology, nor could she bear the possibility that he wouldn't care.

Whatever had started to grow between them, she had squashed. Whatever might have been, she had cut off before it had begun to flower. How could she explain to Chase that she'd been afraid of being hurt again? How could she tell him that when he'd offered help and understanding she'd been afraid to accept it because it was so easy to be dependent?

She began to ride out alone at night again. Solitude didn't soothe her as it once had; it only reminded her that she had taken steps to insure that she would remain alone. The nights were warm, with the lingering scent of honeysuckle bringing back memories of a night where there had been pictures in the sky. She couldn't look at the stars without thinking of him.

Perhaps that was why she rode to the lake, where the grass was soft and thick. Here she could smell the water and wild blossoms. The horse's hooves were muffled, and she could just hear the rustle of wings in flight— some unseen bird in search of prey or a mate.

Then she saw him.

The moon was on the wane, so he was only a shadow, but she knew he was watching her. Just as she had known, somehow, that she would find him there tonight. Reining in, she let the magic take her. For the moment, even if it were only a moment, she would forget everything but that she loved him. Tomorrow would take care of itself.

She slid from the horse and went to him.

He said nothing. Until she touched him, he wasn't sure she wasn't a dream. In silence, she framed his face in her hands and pressed her lips to his. No dream had ever tasted so warm. No illusion had ever felt so soft.

"Eden—"

With a shake of her head, she cut off his words. There were weeks of emptiness to fill, and no questions that needed answering. Rising on her toes, she kissed him again. The only sound was her sigh as his arms finally came around her. She discovered a bottomless well of giving inside her. Something beyond passion, something beyond desire. Here was comfort, strength and the understanding she had been afraid to accept.

His fingers trailed up to her hair, as if each touch reassured him she was indeed real. When he opened his eyes again, his arms wouldn't be empty, but filled with her. Her cheek rubbed his, smooth skin against a day's growth of beard. With her head nestled in a curve of his shoulder, she watched the wink and blink of fireflies and thought of stars.

They stood in silence while an owl hooted and the horse whinnied in response.

"Why did you come?" He needed an answer, one he could take back with him when she had left him again.

"To see you." She drew away, wanting to see his face. "To be with you."

"Why?"

The magic shimmered and began to dim. With a sigh, she drew back. Dreams were for sleeping, Eden reminded herself. And questions had to be answered. "I wanted to apologize for the way I behaved before. You were being kind." Searching for words, she turned to pluck a leaf from the tree that shadowed them. "I know how I must have seemed, how I sounded, and I am sorry. It's difficult, still difficult for me to…" Restless, she moved her shoulders. "We were able to muffle most of the publicity after my father died, but there was a great deal of gossip, of speculation and not-so-quiet murmurs."

When he said nothing, she shifted again, uncomfortable. "I suppose I resented all of that more than anything else. It became very important to me to prove myself, that I could manage, even succeed. I realize that I've become sensitive about handling things myself and that when you offered to help, I reacted badly. I apologize for that."

Silence hung another moment before he took a step toward her. Eden thought he moved the way the shadows did. Silently. "That's a nice apology, Eden. Before I accept it, I'd like to ask if the kiss was part of it."

So he wasn't going to make it easy for her. Her chin lifted. She didn't need an easy road any longer. "No."

Then he smiled and circled her throat with his hand. "What was it for then?"

The smile disturbed her more than the touch, though it was the touch she backed away from. Strange how you could take one step and find yourself sunk to the hips. "Does there have to be a reason?" When she walked toward the edge of the lake, she saw an owl swoop low over the water. That was the way she felt, she realized.

As if she were skimming along the surface of something that could take her in over her head. "I wanted to kiss you, so I did."

The tension he'd lived with for weeks had vanished, leaving him almost light-headed. He had to resist the urge to scoop her up and carry her home, where he'd begun to understand she belonged. "Do you always do what you want?"

She turned back with a toss of her head. She'd apologized, but the pride remained. "Always."

He grinned, nudging a smile from her. "So do I."

"Then we should understand each other."

He trailed a finger down her cheek. "Remember that."

"I will." Steady again, she moved past him to the gelding. "We're having a dance a week from Saturday. Would you like to come?"

His hand closed over hers on the reins. "Are you asking me for a date?"

Amused, she swung her hair back before settling a foot in the stirrup. "Certainly not. We're short of chaperons."

She bent her leg to give herself a boost into the saddle, but found herself caught at the waist. She dangled in midair for a moment before Chase set her on the ground again, turning her to face him. "Will you dance with me?"

She remembered the last time they had danced and saw from the look in his eyes that he did as well. Her heart fluttered in the back of her dry throat, but she lifted a brow and smiled. "Maybe."

His lips curved, then descended slowly to brush against hers. She felt the world tilt, then steady at an angle only lovers understand. "A week from Saturday," he murmured, then lifted her easily into the saddle. His hand remained over hers another moment. "Miss me."

He stayed by the water until she was gone and the night was silent again.

Chapter 7

The last weeks of summer were hot and long. At night, there was invariably heat lightning and rumbling thunder, but little rain. Eden pushed herself through the days, blocking out the uncertainty of life after September.

She wasn't escaping, she told herself. She was coping with one day at a time. If she had learned one important lesson over the summer, it was that she could indeed make changes, in herself and in her life.

The frightened and defeated woman who had come to Camp Liberty almost as if it were a sanctuary would leave a confident, successful woman who could face the world on her own terms.

Standing in the center of the compound, she ran her hands down her narrow hips before dipping them into the pockets of her shorts. Next summer would be even better, now that they'd faced the pitfalls and learned how to maneuver around them. She knew she was skipping over months of her life, but found she didn't want to dwell on the winter. She didn't want to think of Philadelphia and snowy sidewalks, but of the mountains and what she had made of her life there.

If it had been possible, she would have found a way to stay behind during the off-season. Eden had begun to understand that only necessity and the need for employment were taking her back east. It wasn't her home any longer.

With a shake of her head, Eden pushed away thoughts of December. The sun was hot and bright. She could watch it shimmer on the surface of Chase's lake and think of him.

She wondered what would have happened if she had met him two years earlier when her life had been so ordered and set and mapped-out. Would she have fallen in love with him then? Perhaps it was all a matter of timing; perhaps she would have given him a polite how-do-you-do and forgotten him.

No. Closing her eyes, she could recall vividly every sensation, every emotion he'd brought into her life. Timing had nothing to do with something so overwhelming. No matter when, no matter where, she would have fallen in love with him. Hadn't she fought it all along, only to find her feelings deepening?

But she'd thought herself in love with Eric, too.

She shivered in the bright sun and watched a jay race overhead. Was she so shallow, so cold, that her feelings could shift and change in the blink of an eye? That was what held her back and warned her to be cautious. If Eric hadn't turned his back on her, she would have married him. His ring would be on her finger even now. Eden glanced down at her bare left hand.

But that hadn't been love, she reassured herself. Now she knew what love felt like, what it did to heart and mind and body. And yet… How did he feel? He cared, and he wanted, but she knew enough of love now to understand that wasn't enough. She, too, had once cared and wanted. If Chase was in love with her, there wouldn't be any *before*. Time would begin now.

Don't be a fool, she told herself with a flash of annoyance. That kind of thinking would only make her drift back to dependence. There was a before for both of them, and a future. There was no way of being sure that the future would merge with what she felt today.

But she wanted to be a fool, she realized with a quick, delicious shudder. Even if only for a few weeks, she wanted to absorb and concentrate all those mad feelings. She'd be sensible again. Sensible was for January, when the wind was sharp and the rent had to be paid. In a few days she would dance with him, smile up at him. She would have that one night of the summer to be a fool.

Kicking off her shoes, Eden plucked them up in one hand and ran the rest of the way to the dock. Girls, already separated into groups, were waiting for the signal to row out into the lake.

"Miss Carlbough!" In her camp uniform and her familiar cap, Roberta hopped up and down on the grass near the rowboats. "Watch this." With a quick flurry of motion, she bent over, kicked up her feet and stood on her head. "What do you think?" she demanded through teeth clenched with effort. Her triangular face reddened.

"Incredible."

"I've been practicing." With a grunt, Roberta tumbled onto the grass. "Now, when my mom asks what I did at camp, I can stand on my head and show her."

Eden lifted a brow, hoping Mrs. Snow got a few more details. "I'm sure she'll be impressed."

Still sprawled on the grass, arms splayed out to the sides, Roberta stared up at Eden. She was just old enough to wish that her hair was blond and wavy. "You look real pretty today, Miss Carlbough."

Touched, and more than a little surprised, Eden held out a hand to help Roberta up. "Why, thank you, Roberta. So do you."

"Oh, I'm not pretty, but I'm going to be once I can wear makeup and cover my freckles."

Eden rubbed a thumb over Roberta's cheek. "Lots of boys fall for freckles."

"Maybe." Roberta tucked that away to consider later. "I guess you're soft on Mr. Elliot."

Eden dropped her hand back in her pocket. "Soft on?"

"You know." To demonstrate, Roberta sighed and fluttered her eyes. Eden wasn't sure whether to laugh or give the little monster a shove into the lake.

"That's ridiculous."

"Are you getting married?"

"I haven't the vaguest idea where you come up with such nonsense. Now into the boat. Everyone's ready to go."

"My mom told me people sometimes get married when they're soft on each other."

"I'm sure your mother's quite right." Hoping to close the subject, Eden helped Roberta into their assigned rowboat, where Marcie and Linda were already waiting. "However, in this case, Mr. Elliot and I barely know each other. Everyone hook their life jackets, please."

"Mom said she and Daddy fell in love at first sight." Roberta hooked on the preserver, though she thought it was a pain when she swam so well. "They kiss all the time."

"I'm sure that's nice. Now—"

"I used to think it was kind of gross, but I guess it's okay." Roberta settled into her seat and smiled. "Well, if you decide not to marry Mr. Elliot, maybe I will."

Eden was busy locking in the oars, but she glanced up. "Oh?"

"Yeah. He's got a neat dog and all those apple trees." Roberta adjusted the brim of her cap over her eyes. "And he's kind of pretty." The two girls beside her giggled in agreement.

"That's certainly something to think about." Eden began to row. "Maybe you can discuss the idea with your mother when you get home."

"'Kay. Can I row first?"

Eden could only be grateful that the girl's interest span was as fast-moving as the rest of her. "Fine. You and I will row out. Marcie and Linda can row back."

After a bit of drag and a few grunts, Roberta matched her rhythm to Eden's. As the boat began to glide, it occurred to Eden that she was rowing with the same three girls who had started the adventure in the apple orchard. With a silent chuckle, she settled into sync with Roberta and let her mind drift.

What if she had never gone up in that tree? Absently, she touched her lower lip with her tongue, recalling the taste and feel of Chase. If she had it to do over, would she run in the opposite direction?

Smiling, Eden closed her eyes a moment, so that the sun glowed red under her lids. No, she wouldn't run. Being able to admit it, being able to be sure of it, strengthened her confidence. She wouldn't run from Chase, or from anything else in life.

Perhaps she was soft on him, as Roberta had termed it. Perhaps she could hug that secret to herself for a little while. It would be wonderful if things could be as simple and uncomplicated as Roberta made them. Love equaled marriage, marriage equaled happiness. Sighing, Eden opened her eyes and watched the surface of the lake. For a little while she could believe in poetry and dreams.

Daydreams… They were softer and even more mystical than dreams by night. It had been a long time since Eden had indulged in them. Now the girls were chattering and calling to their friends in the other boats. Someone was singing, deliberately off-key. Eden's arms moved in a steady rhythm as the oars cut smoothly into the water and up into the air again.

So she was floating…dreaming with her eyes open… silk and ivory and lace. The glitter of the sun on water was like candlelight. The call of crows was music to dance by.

She was riding on Pegasus. High in a night sky, his white wings effortlessly cut through the air. She could taste the cool, thin wind that took them through clouds. Her hair was free, flying behind her, twined with flowers. More clouds, castle-like, rose up in the distance, filmy and gray and secret. Their secrets were nothing to her. She had freedom for the first time, full, unlimited freedom.

And he was with her, riding the sky through snatches of light and dark. Higher, still higher they rose, until the earth was only mist beneath them. And the stars were flowers, the white petals of anemones that she could reach out and pick as the whim struck her.

When she turned in his arms, she was his without boundaries. All restrictions, all doubts, had been left behind in the climb.

"Hey, look. It's Squat!"

Eden blinked. The daydream disintegrated. She was in a rowboat, with muscles that were just beginning to ache from exertion. There were no flowers, no stars, only water and sky.

They'd rowed nearly the width of the lake. A portion of Chase's orchard spread back from the shore, and visible was one of the greenhouses he had taken the camp through on the day of the tour. Delighted with the company, Squat dashed back and forth in the shallow water near the lake's edge. His massive paws scattered a flurry of water that coated him until he was a sopping, shaggy mess.

Smiling as the girls called out greetings to the dog, Eden wondered if Chase was home. What did he do with his Sundays? she thought. Did he laze around the house with the paper and cups of coffee? Did he switch on the ball game, or go out for long, solitary drives? Just then, as if to answer her questions, he and Delaney joined the dog on the shore. Across the water, Eden felt the jolt as their eyes met.

Would it always be like that? Always stunning, always fresh? Always immediate? Inhaling slowly, she coaxed her pulse back to a normal rate.

"Hey, Mr. Elliot!" Without a thought for the consequences, Roberta dropped her oar and jumped up. Excitement had her bouncing up and down as the boat teetered.

"Roberta." Acting by instinct, Eden locked her oars. "Sit down, you'll turn us over." Eden started to grab for her hand as the other girls took Roberta's lead and jumped to their feet.

"Hi, Mr. Elliot!"

The greeting rang out in unison, just before the boat tipped over.

Eden hit the water headfirst. After the heat of the sun it seemed shockingly cold, and she surfaced sputtering with fury. With one hand, she dragged the hair out of her eyes and focused on the three bobbing heads. The girls, buoyed by their life jackets, waved unrepentantly at the trio on shore.

Eden grabbed the edge of the upended boat. "Roberta!"

"Look, Miss Carlbough." Apparently the tone, said through gritted teeth, passed over the girl's head. "Squat's coming out."

"Terrific." Treading water, Eden plucked Roberta by the arm and tried to drag her back to the capsized boat. "Remember the rules of boating safety. Stay here." Eden went for the next girl, but twisted her head to see the dog paddling toward them. Uneasy with his progress, she looked back toward shore.

Her request that Chase call back his dog caught in her throat as she spotted his grin. Though she couldn't hear the words, she saw Delaney turn to him with some remark. It was enough to see Chase throw back his head and laugh. That sound carried.

"Want some help?" he called out.

Eden pulled at the next giggling girl. "Don't put yourself out," she began, then shrieked when Squat laid a wet, friendly nose on her shoulder. Her reaction seemed to amuse everyone, dog included. Squat began to bark enthusiastically in her ear.

Fresh pandemonium broke out as the girls began to splash water at each other and the dog. Eden found herself caught in the crossfire. In the other boats, campers and counselors looked on, grinning or calling out encouraging words. Squat paddled circles around her as she struggled to restore some kind of order.

"All right, ladies. Enough." That earned her a mouthful of lake. "It's time to right the boat."

"Can Squat take a ride with us?" Roberta giggled as he licked water from her face.

"No."

"That hardly seems fair."

Eden nearly submerged before Chase gripped her arm. She'd been too busy trying to restore order and her own dignity to notice that he'd swum the few yards from shore. "He came out to help."

His hair was barely damp, while hers was plastered to her head. Chase hooked an arm around her waist to ease her effort to tread water.

"You'd better right the boat," he said to the girls, who immediately fell to doing so with a vengeance. "Apparently you do better with horses." His voice was soft and amused in Eden's ear.

She started to draw away, but her legs tangled with his. "If you and that monster hadn't been on shore—"

"Delaney?"

"No, not Delaney." Frustrated, Eden pushed at her hair.

"You're beautiful when you're wet. Makes me wonder why I haven't thought of swimming with you before."

"We're not supposed to be swimming, we're supposed to be boating."

"Either way, you're beautiful."

She wouldn't be moved. Even though the girls had already righted the boat, Eden knew she was in over her head. "It's that dog," she began. Even as she said it, the girls were climbing back into the boat and urging Squat to join them.

"Roberta, I said—" Chase gently dunked her. Surfacing, she heard him striking the bargain.

"We'll swim back. You bring Squat. He likes boats."

"I said—" Again, she found herself under water. This time when she came up for air, she gave Chase her full attention. The swing she took at him was slow and sluggish because of the need to tread water.

He caught her fist and kissed it. "Beat you back."

Narrowing her eyes, Eden gave him a shove before striking out after the boat. The water around her ears muffled the sound of Squat's deep barking and the girls' excited cheering. With strong, even strokes, she kept a foot behind the boat and made certain the girls behaved.

Less than twenty feet from shore, Chase caught her by the ankle. Laughing and kicking, Eden found herself tangled in his arms.

"You cheat." As he rose, he swept her off her feet so that her accusation ended in another laugh. His bare chest was cool and wet under her palms. His hair was dripping so that the sunlight was caught in each separate drop of water. "I won."

"Wrong." She should have seen it coming. Without

effort, he pitched her back in the lake. Eden landed bottom first. "I won."

Eden stood to shake herself off. Managing to suppress a smile, she nodded toward the whooping girls. "And that, ladies, is a classic example of poor sports-manship." She reached up to squeeze the water out of her hair, unaware that her shirt clung to every curve. Chase felt his heart stop. She waded toward shore, with the clear lake water clinging to her tanned legs. "Good afternoon, Delaney."

"Ma'am." He gave her a gold, flashing grin. "Nice day for a swim."

"Apparently."

"I was about to pick me some blackberries for jam." He cast his gaze over the three dripping girls. "If I had some help, could be I'd have a jar or so extra for some neighbors."

Before Eden could consent or refuse, all the girls and Squat were jumping circles around her. She had to admit that a ten- or fifteen-minute break would make the row back to camp a little more appealing. "Ten minutes," she told them before turning back to signal to the other boats.

Delaney toddled off, sandwiched between girls who were already barraging him with questions. As they dis-appeared into a cluster of trees, a startled flock of birds whizzed out. She laughed, turning back to see Chase staring at her.

"You're a strong swimmer."

She had to clear her throat. "I think I've just become more competitive. Maybe I should keep an eye on the girls so—"

"Delaney can handle them." He reached out to brush a bead of water from her jawline. Beneath his gentle touch, she shivered. "Cold?"

More than the sun had taken the lake's chill from her skin. Eden managed to shake her head. "No." But when his hands came to her shoulders, she stepped back.

He wore only cutoffs, faded soft from wear. The shirt he had peeled off before diving into the lake had been tossed carelessly to the ground. "You don't feel cold," he murmured as he stroked his hands down her arms.

"I'm not." She heard the laughter beyond the trees. "I really can't let them stay long. They'll have to change."

Patient, Chase took her hand. "Eden, you're going to end up in the lake again if you keep backing up." He was frightening her. Frustrated, he struggled not to push. It seemed that every time he thought he'd gained her trust, he saw that quick flash of anxiety in her eyes again. He smiled, hoping the need that was roiling inside him didn't show. "Where are your shoes?"

Off-balance, she looked down and stared at her own bare feet. Slowly, her muscles began to relax again. "At the bottom of your lake." Laughing, she shook her wet hair back, nearly destroying him. "Roberta always manages to keep things exciting. Why don't we give them a hand with the berry-picking."

His arm came across her body to take her shoulder before she could move past him. "You're still backing away, Eden." Lifting a hand, he combed his fingers through her sleek, wet hair until they rested at the base of her neck. "It's hard to resist you this way, with your face glowing and your eyes aware and just a bit frightened."

"Chase, don't." She put her hand to his.

"I want to touch you." He shifted so that the full length of her body was against his. "I need to touch you." Through the wet cotton, she could feel the texture of his skin on hers. "Look at me, Eden." The slightest pressure of his fingers brought her face up to his. "How close are you going to let me get?"

She could only shake her head. There weren't any words to describe what she was feeling, what she wanted, what she was still too afraid to need. "Chase, don't do this. Not here, not now." Then she could only moan, as his mouth traveled with a light, lazy touch over her face.

"When?" He had to fight the desire to demand rather than to ask, to take rather than to wait. "Where?" This time the kiss wasn't lazy, but hard, bruising. Eden felt rational thought spiral away even as she groped for an answer. "Don't you think I know what happens to you when we're like this?" His voice thickened as his patience stretched thinner and thinner. "Good God, Eden, I need you. Come with me tonight. Stay with me."

Yes, yes. Oh, yes. How easy it would be to say it, to give in, to give everything without a thought for tomorrow. She clung to him a moment, wanting to believe dreams were possible. He was so solid, so real. But so were her responsibilities.

"Chase, you know I can't." Fighting for rationality, she drew away. "I have to stay at camp."

Before she could move away again, he caught her face in his hands. She thought his eyes had darkened, a stormier green now, with splashes of gold from the sun. "And when summer's over, Eden? What then?"

What then? How could she have the answer, when

the answer was so cold, so final? It wasn't what she wanted, but what had to be. If she was to keep her promise to herself, to make her life work, there was only one answer. "Then I'll go back, back to Philadelphia, until next summer."

Only summers? Was that all she was willing to give? It was the panic that surprised him and kept the fury at bay. When she left, his life would be empty. He took her shoulders again, fighting back the panic.

"You'll come to me before you go." It wasn't a question. It wasn't a demand. It was a simple statement. The demand she could have rebelled against; the question she could have refused.

"Chase, what good would it do either of us?"

"You'll come to me before you go," he repeated. Because if she didn't, he'd follow her. There would be no choice.

Chapter 8

Red and white crepe paper streamed from corner to corner, twined together in elongated snakes of color. Balloons, bulging with air from energetic young lungs, were crowded into every available space. Stacked in three uneven towers were all the records deemed fit to play.

Dance night was only a matter of hours away.

Under Candy's eagle eye, tables were carried outside, while others were grouped strategically around the mess area. This simple chore took twice as long as it should have, as girls had to stop every few feet to discuss the most important aspect of the evening: boys.

Although her skills with paint and glue were slim at best, Eden had volunteered for the decorating committee—on the understanding that her duties were limited to hanging and tacking what was already made. In addition to the crepe paper and balloons, there were banners and paper flowers that the more talented members of campers and staff had put together by hand. The best of these was a ten-foot banner dyed Camp Liberty red and splashed with bold letters that spelled out WELCOME TO CAMP LIBERTY'S ANNUAL SUMMER DANCE.

Candy had already taken it for granted that it would be the first of many. In her better moods, Eden hoped she was right. In her crankier ones, she wondered if they could swing a deal with the boys' camp to split the cost of refreshments. For the moment, she pushed both ideas aside, determined to make this dance the best-decorated one in Pennsylvania.

Eden let an argument over which records had priority run its course below her as she climbed a stepladder to secure more streamers. Already, the record player at the far end of the room was blaring music.

It was silly. She told herself that yet again as she realized she was as excited about the evening as any of the girls. She was an adult, here only to plan, supervise and chaperon. Even as she reminded herself of this, her thoughts ran forward to the evening, when the mess area would be filled with people and noise and laughter. Like the girls below her, her thoughts kept circling back to vital matters—like what she should wear.

It was fascinating to realize that this simple end-of-the-summer dance in the mountains was more exciting for her than her own debutante ball. That she had taken lightly, as the next step along the path that had been cleared for her before she was born. This was new, untried and full of possibilities.

It all centered on Chase. Eden was nearly ready to

accept that as a new song blared into life. Since it was one she'd heard dozens of times before, she began to hum along with it. Her ponytail swayed with the movement as she attached another streamer.

"We'll ask Miss Carlbough." Eden heard the voices below, but paid little attention, as she had a tack in her mouth and five feet of crepe paper held together by her thumb. "She always knows, and if she doesn't, she finds out."

She had started to secure the tack, but as the statement drifted up to her, she stopped pushing. Was that really the way the girls saw her? Dependable? With a half laugh, she sent the tack home. To her, the statement was the highest of compliments, a sign of faith.

She'd done what she had set out to do. In three short months, she had accomplished something she had never done in all her years of living. She had made something of herself, by herself. And, perhaps more importantly, for herself.

It wasn't going to stop here. Eden dropped the rest of the tacks into her pocket. The summer might be nearly over, but the challenge wasn't. Whether she was in South Mountain or Philadelphia, she wasn't going to forget what it meant to grow. Twisting on the ladder, she started down to find out what it was the girls had wanted to ask her. On the second rung, she stopped, staring.

The tall, striking woman strode into the mess. The tail of her Hermès scarf crossed the neck of a cerise suit and trailed on behind. Her bone-white hair was perfect, as was the double strand of pearls that lay on her bosom. Tucked in the crook of one arm was a small piece of white fluff known as BooBoo.

"Aunt Dottie!" Delighted, Eden scrambled down from the ladder. In seconds she was enveloped by Dottie's personal scent, an elusive combination of Paris and success. "Oh, it's wonderful to see you." Drawing back from the hug, Eden studied the lovely, strong-boned face. Even now, she could see shadows of her father in the eyes and around the mouth. "You're the last person I expected to see here."

"Darling, have you grown thorns in the country?"

"Thorns? I—oh." Laughing, Eden reached in her pocket. "Thumbtacks. Sorry."

"The hug was worth a few holes." Taking Eden's hand, she stepped back to make her own study. Though her face remained passive, she let out a quiet sigh of relief. No one knew how many restless nights she'd spent worrying over her brother's only child. "You look beautiful. A little thin, but with marvelous color." With Eden's hand still in hers, she glanced around the room. "But darling, what an odd place you've chosen to spend the summer."

"Aunt Dottie." Eden just shook her head. Throughout the weeks and months after her father's death, Dottie had stubbornly refused to accept Eden's decision not to use Dottie's money as a buffer, her home as a refuge. "If I have marvelous color, credit the country air."

"Hmm." Far from convinced, Dottie continued to look around as a new record plopped down to continue the unbroken cycle of music. "I've always considered the south of France country enough."

"Aunt Dottie, tell me what you're doing here. I'm amazed you could even find the place."

"It wasn't difficult. The chauffeur reads a map very

well." Dottie gave the fluff in her arms a light pat. "BooBoo and I felt an urge for a drive to the country."

"I see." And she did. Like everyone else she had left behind, Eden knew that her aunt considered her camp venture an impulse. It would take more than one summer to convince Dottie, or anyone else, that she was serious. After all, it had taken her most of the summer to convince herself.

"Yes, and since I was in the neighborhood…" Dottie let that trail off. "What a chic outfit," she commented, taking in Eden's paint-spattered smock and tattered sneakers. "Then, perhaps bohemian's coming back. What do you have there?"

"Crepe paper. It goes with the thumbtacks." Eden extended her hand. BooBoo regally allowed her head to be patted.

"Well, give them both to one of these charming young ladies and come see what I've brought you."

"Brought me?" Obeying automatically, Eden handed over the streamers. "Start these around the tables, will you, Lisa?"

"Do you know," Dottie began as she linked her arm through Eden's, "the nearest town is at least twenty miles from here? That is if one could stretch credibility and call what we passed through a town. There, there, BooBoo, I won't set you down on the nasty ground." She cuddled the dog as they stepped outside. "BooBoo's a bit skittish out of the city, you understand."

"Perfectly."

"Where was I? Oh yes, the town. It had one traffic light and a place called Earl's Lunch. I was almost curious enough to stop and see what one did at Earl's Lunch."

Eden laughed, and leaned over to kiss Dottie's cheek. "One eats a small variety of sandwiches and stale potato chips and coffee while exchanging town gossip."

"Marvelous. Do you go often?"

"Unfortunately, my social life's been a bit limited."

"Well, your surprise might just change all that." Turning, Dottie gestured toward the canary-yellow Rolls parked in the main compound. Eden felt every muscle, every emotion freeze as the man straightened from his easy slouch against the hood.

"Eric."

He smiled, and in a familiar gesture, ran one hand lightly over his hair. Around him, a group of girls had gathered to admire the classic lines of the Rolls and the classic looks of Eric Keeton.

His smile was perfectly angled as he walked toward her. His walk was confident, just a shade too conservative for a swagger. As she watched him, Eden saw him in the clear light of disinterest. His hair, several shades darker than her own, was perfectly styled for the boardroom or the country club. Casual attire, which included pleated slacks and a polo shirt, fit neatly over his rather narrow frame. Hazel eyes, which had a tendency to look bored easily, smiled and warmed now. Though she hadn't offered them, he took both her hands.

"Eden, how marvelous you look."

His hands were soft. Strange, she had forgotten that. Though she didn't bother to remove hers, her voice was cool. "Hello, Eric."

"Lovelier than ever, isn't she, Dottie?" Her stiff greeting didn't seem to disturb him. He gave her hands an intimate little squeeze. "Your aunt was worried about you. She expected you to be thin and wan."

"Fortunately, I'm neither." Now, carefully, deliberately, Eden removed her hands. She would have been greatly pleased, though she had no way of knowing it, that her eyes were as cold as her voice. It was so easy to turn away from him. "Whatever possessed you to drive all this way, Aunt Dottie? You weren't really worried?"

"A tad." Concerned with the ice in her niece's voice, Dottie touched Eden's cheek. "And I did want to see the—the place where you spent the summer."

"I'll give you a tour."

A thin left brow arched in a manner identical to Eden's. "How charming."

"Aunt Dottie!" Red curls bouncing, Candy raced around the side of the building. "I knew it had to be you." Out of breath and grinning broadly, Candy accepted Dottie's embrace. "The girls were talking about a yellow Rolls in the compound. Who else could it have been?"

"As enthusiastic as ever." Dottie's smile was all affection. She might not have always understood Candice Bartholomew, but she had always been fond of her. "I hope you don't mind a surprise visit."

"I love it." Candy bent down to the puff of fur. "Hi, BooBoo." Straightening, she let her gaze drift over Eric. "Hello, Eric." Her voice dropped an easy twenty-five degrees. "Long way from home."

"Candy." Unlike Dottie, he had no fondness for Eden's closest friend. "You seem to have paint all over your hands."

"It's dry," she said, carelessly, and somewhat regretfully. If the paint had been wet, she would have greeted him more personally.

"Eden's offered to take us on a tour." Dottie was well aware of the hostility. She'd driven hundreds of miles from Philadelphia for one purpose. To help her niece find happiness. If it meant she had to manipulate...so much the better. "I know Eric's dying to look around, but if I could impose on you—" She laid her hand on Candy's. "I'd really love to sit down with a nice cup of tea. BooBoo, too. The drive was a bit tiring."

"Of course." Manners were their own kind of trap. Candy sent Eden a look meant to fortify her. "We'll use the kitchen, if you don't mind the confusion."

"My dear, I thrive on it." With that she turned to smile at Eden and was surprised by the hard, knowing look in Eden's eyes.

"Go right ahead, Aunt Dottie. I'll show Eric what the camp has to offer."

"Eden, I—"

"Go have your tea, darling." She kissed Dottie's cheek. "We'll talk later." She turned, leaving Eric to follow or not. When he fell into step beside her, she began. "We've six sleeping cabins this season, with plans to add two more for next summer. Each cabin has an Indian name to keep it distinct."

As they passed the cabins, she saw that the anemones were still stubbornly blooming. They gave her strength. "Each week, we have a contest for the neatest cabin. The reward is extra riding time, or swimming time, or whatever the girls prefer. Candy and I have a small shower in our cabin. The girls share facilities at the west end of the compound."

"Eden." Eric cupped her elbow in his palm in the same manner he had used when strolling down Broad Street. She gritted her teeth, but didn't protest.

"Yes?" The cool, impersonal look threw him off. It took him only a moment to decide it meant she was hiding a broken heart.

"What have you been doing with yourself?" He waved his hand in a gesture that took in the compound and the surrounding hills. "Here?"

Holding on to her temper, Eden decided to take the question literally. "We've tried to keep the camp regimented, while still allowing for creativity and fun. Over the past few weeks, we've found that we can adhere fairly tightly to the schedule as long as we make room for fresh ideas and individual needs." Pleased with herself, she dipped her hands into the pockets of her smock. "We're up at six-thirty. Breakfast is at seven sharp. Daily inspection begins at seven-thirty and activities at eight. For the most part, I deal with the horses and stables, but when necessary, I can pitch in and help in other areas."

"Eden." Eric stopped her by gently tightening his fingers on her elbow. Turning to him, she watched the faint breeze ruffle his smooth, fair hair. She thought of the dark confusion of Chase's hair. "It's difficult to believe you've spent your summer camping out in a cabin and overseeing a parade of girls on horseback."

"Is it?" She merely smiled. Of course it was difficult for him. He owned a stable, but he'd never lifted a pitchfork. Rather than resentment, Eden felt a stirring of pity. "Well, there's that, among a few other things such as hiking, smoothing over cases of homesickness and poison ivy, rowing, giving advice on teenage romance and fashion, identifying fifteen different varieties of local wildflowers and seeing that a group of girls has fun. Would you like to see the stables?" She headed off without waiting for his answer.

"Eden." He caught her elbow again. It took all her willpower not to jab it back into his soft stomach. "You're angry. Of course you are, but I—"

"You've always had a fondness for good horseflesh." She swung the stable door open so that he had to back off or get a faceful of wood. "We've two mares and four geldings. One of the mares is past her prime, but I'm thinking of breeding the other. The foals would interest the girls and eventually become part of the riding stock. This is Courage."

"Eden, please. We have to talk."

She stiffened when his hands touched her shoulders. But she was calm, very calm, when she turned and removed them. "I thought we were talking."

He'd heard the ice in her voice before, and he understood it. She was a proud, logical woman. He'd approach her on that level. "We have to talk about us, darling."

"In what context?"

He reached for her hand, giving a small shrug when she drew it away. If she had accepted him without a murmur, he would have been a great deal more surprised. For days now, he'd been planning exactly the proper way to smooth things over. He'd decided on regretful, with a hint of humble thrown in.

"You've every right to be furious with me, every right to want me to suffer."

His tone, soft, quiet, understanding, had her swallowing a ball of heat. Indifference, she reminded herself, disinterest, was the greatest insult she could hand him. "It doesn't really concern me if you suffer or not." That wasn't quite true, she admitted. She wouldn't be averse to seeing him writhe a bit. That was because he had come, she realized. Because he had had the gall to come and assume she'd be waiting.

"Eden, you have to know that I have suffered, suffered a great deal. I would have come before, but I wasn't sure you'd see me."

This was the man she had planned to spend her life with. This was the man she had hoped to have children with. She stared at him now, unsure whether she was in the midst of a comedy or a tragedy. "I'm sorry to hear that, Eric. I don't see any reason why you should have suffered. You were only being practical, after all."

Soothed by her placid attitude, he stepped toward her. "I admit that, rightly or wrongly, I was practical." His hands slid up her arms in an old gesture that made her jaw clench. "These past few months have shown me that there are times when practical matters have to take second place."

"Is that so?" She smiled at him, surprised that he couldn't feel the heat. "What would go first?"

"Personal…" He stroked a finger over her cheek. "Much more personal matters."

"Such as?"

His lips were curved as his mouth lowered. She felt the heat of anger freeze into icy disdain. Did he think her a fool? Could he believe himself so irresistible? Then she nearly did laugh, as she realized the answer to both questions was yes.

She let him kiss her. The touch of his lips left her totally unmoved. It fascinated her that, only a few short months before, his kisses had warmed her. It had been nothing like the volcanic heat she experienced with Chase, but there had been a comfort and an easy pleasure. That was all she had thought there was meant to be.

Now there was nothing. The absence of feeling in itself dulled the edge of her fury. She was in control. Here, as in other areas of her life, she was in control. Though his lips coaxed, she simply stood, waiting for him to finish.

When he lifted his head, Eden put her hands on his arms to draw herself away. It was then she saw Chase just inside the open stable door.

The sun was at his back, silhouetting him, blinding her to the expression on his face. Even so, her mouth was dry as she stared, trying to see through shadow and sun. When he stepped forward, his eyes were on hers.

Explanations sprang to her tongue, but she could only shake her head as his gaze slid over her and onto Eric.

"Keeton." Chase nodded, but didn't extend his hand. He knew if he had the other man's fingers in his he would take pleasure in breaking them, one by one.

"Elliot." Eric returned the nod. "I'd forgotten. You have land around here, don't you?"

"A bit." Chase wanted to murder him, right there in the stables, while Eden watched. Then he would find it just as satisfying to murder her.

"You must know Eden, then." Eric placed a hand on her shoulder in a casually possessive movement. Chase followed the gesture before looking at her again. Her instinctive move to shrug away Eric's hand was stopped by the look. Was it anger she saw there, or was it disgust?

"Yes. Eden and I have run into each other a few times." He dipped his hands into his pockets as they balled into fists.

"Chase was generous enough to allow us to use his lake." Her right hand groped for her left until they were clasped together. "We had a tour of his orchards." Though pride suffered, her eyes pleaded with him.

"Your land must be very near here." Eric hadn't missed the exchange of looks. His hand leaned more heavily on Eden's shoulder.

"Near enough."

Then they were looking at each other, not at her. Somehow that, more than anything, made her feel as though she'd been shifted to the middle. If there was tension and she was the cause of it, she wanted to be able to speak on her own behalf. But the expression in Chase's eyes only brought confusion. The weight of Eric's hand only brought annoyance. Moving away from Eric, she stepped toward Chase.

"Did you want to see me?"

"Yes." But he'd wanted more than that, a great deal more. Seeing her in Eric's arms had left him feeling both murderous and empty. He wasn't ready to deal with either yet. "It wasn't important."

"Chase—"

"Oh, hello." The warmth in Candy's voice came almost as a shock. She stepped through the doorway with Dottie at her side. "Aunt Dottie, I want you to meet our neighbor, Chase Elliot."

Even as Dottie extended her hand, her eyes were

narrowed speculatively. "Elliot? I'm sure I know that name. Yes, yes, didn't we meet several years ago? You're Jessie Winthrop's grandson."

Eden watched his lips curve, his eyes warm, but he wasn't looking at her. "Yes, I am, and I remember you very well, Mrs. Norfolk. You haven't changed."

Dottie's laugh was low and quick. "It's been fifteen years if it's been a day. I'd say there's been a change or two. You were about a foot shorter at the time." She sized him up approvingly in a matter of ten seconds. "It's apples, isn't it? Yes, of course, it is. Elliot's."

And, oh my God, she realized almost as quickly, I've brought Eric along and jammed up the works. A person would have to have a three-inch layer of steel coating not to feel the shock waves bouncing around the stables.

What could be done, she told herself, could be undone. Smiling, she looked at her niece. "Candy's been telling me about the social event of the season. Are we all invited?"

"Invited?" Eden struggled to gather her scattered wits. "You mean the dance?" She had to laugh. Her aunt was standing in the stables in Italian shoes and a suit that had cost more than any one of the horses. "Aunt Dottie, you don't intend to stay here?"

"Stay here?" The white brows shot up. "I should say not." She twisted the pearls at her neck as she began to calculate. She didn't intend to bunk down in a cabin, but neither was she about to miss the impending fireworks. "Eric and I are staying at a hotel some miles away, but I'd be heartbroken if you didn't ask us to the party tonight." She put a friendly hand on Chase's arm. "You're coming, aren't you?"

He knew a manipulator when he saw one. "Wouldn't miss it."

"Wonderful." Dottie slid Candy's hand back into the crook of her arm, then patted it. "We're all invited then."

Fumbling, Candy looked from Eric to Eden. "Well, yes, of course, but—"

"Isn't this sweet?" Dottie patted her hand again. "We'll have a delightful time. Don't you think so, Eden?"

"Delightful," Eden agreed, wondering if she could hitch a ride out of town.

Chapter 9

Eden had problems—big problems. But not the least of them were the sixty adolescents in the mess hall. However she handled Eric, however she managed to explain herself to Chase, sixty young bodies couldn't be put on hold.

The boys arrived in vans at eight o'clock. Unless Eden missed her guess, they were every bit as nervous as the girls. Eden remembered her own cotillion days, the uncertainty and the damp palms. The blaring music helped cover some of the awkwardness as the boys' counselors trooped them in.

The refreshment table was loaded. There was enough punch stored in the kitchen to bathe in. Candy gave a brief welcoming speech to set the tone, the banners and the paper flowers waving at her back. A fresh record was set spinning on the turntable. Girls stood on one side of the room, boys on the other.

The biggest problem, naturally, was that no one wanted to go first. Eden had worked that out by making up two bowls of corresponding numbers. Boys picked from one, girls from another. You matched, you danced. It wasn't imaginative, but it was expedient.

When the first dance was half over, she slipped into the kitchen to check on backup refreshments, leaving Candy to supervise and to mingle with the male counselors.

When she returned, the dance floor wasn't as crowded, but this time the partners had chosen for themselves.

"Miss Carlbough?"

Eden turned her head as she bent to place a bowl of chips in an empty space on the long crowded table. Roberta's face was spotless. Her thatch of wild hair had been tamed into a bushy ponytail and tied with a ribbon. She had little turquoise stars in her ears to match a ruffled and not-too-badly-wrinkled blouse. The dusting of freckles over her face had been partially hidden by a layer of powder. Eden imagined she had conned it out of one of the older girls, but let it pass.

"Hi, Roberta." Plucking two pretzels from a bowl, she handed one over. "Aren't you going to dance?"

"Sure." She glanced over her shoulder, confident and patient. "I wanted to talk to you first."

"Oh?" It didn't appear that she needed a pep talk. Eden had already seen the skinny, dark-haired boy Roberta had set her sights on. If Eden was any judge, he didn't stand a chance. "What about?"

"I saw that guy in the Rolls."

Eden's automatic warning not to speak with her mouth full was postponed. "You mean Mr. Keeton?"

"Some of the girls think he's cute."

"Hmm." Eden nibbled on her own pretzel.

"A couple of them said you were soft on him. They think you had a lovers' quarrel, you know, like Romeo and Juliet or something. Now he's come to beg you to forgive him, and you're going to realize that you can't live without him and go off and get married."

The pretzel hung between two fingers as Eden listened. After a moment, she managed to clear her throat. "Well, that's quite a scenario."

"I said it was baloney."

Trying not to laugh, she bit into the pretzel. "Did you?"

"You're smart, all the girls say so." Reaching behind Eden, she took a handful of chips. "I said you were too smart to be soft on the guy in the Rolls, because he's not nearly as neat as Mr. Elliot." Roberta glanced over her shoulder as if in confirmation. "He's shorter, too."

"Yes." Eden had to bite her lip. "Yes, he is."

"He doesn't look like he'd jump in the lake to fool around."

The last statement had Eden trying to imagine Eric diving into the cool waters of the lake half-dressed. Or bringing her a clutch of wildflowers. Or finding pictures in the sky. Her lips curved dreamily. "No, Eric would never do that."

"That's why I knew it was all baloney." Roberta devoured the chips. "When Mr. Elliot comes, I'm going to dance with him, but now I'm going to dance with Bobby." Shooting Eden a smile, she walked across the room and grabbed the hand of the lanky, dark-haired boy. As Eden had thought, he didn't have a chance.

She watched the dancing, but thought of Chase. It came to her all at once that he was the only man she knew whom she hadn't measured against her father. Comparisons had never occurred to her. She hadn't measured Chase against anyone but had fallen in love with him for himself. Now all she needed was the courage to tell him.

"So this is how young people entertain themselves these days."

Eden turned to find Dottie beside her. For Camp Liberty's summer dance, she had chosen mauve lace. The pearls had been exchanged for a single, sensational ruby. BooBoo had a clip of rhinestones—Eden sincerely hoped they were only rhinestones—secured on top of her head. Feeling a wave of affection, Eden kissed her aunt. "Are you settled into your hotel?"

"So to speak." Accepting a potato chip, Dottie took her own survey. The powder-blue voile was the essence of simplicity with its cap sleeves and high neck, but Dottie approved the way it depended on the wearer for its style. "Thank God you haven't lost your taste."

Laughing, Eden kissed her again. "I've missed you. I'm so glad you came."

"Are you?" Always discreet, Dottie led her toward the screen door. "I was afraid you weren't exactly thrilled to see me here." She let the screen whoosh shut as they stepped onto the porch. "Particularly with the surprise I brought you."

"I was glad to see you, Aunt Dottie."

"But not Eric."

Eden leaned back on the rail. "Did you think I would be?"

"Yes." She sighed, and brushed at the bodice of her lace. "I suppose I did. It only took five minutes to realize what a mistake I'd made. Darling, I hope you understand I was trying to help."

"Of course I do, and I love you for it."

"I thought that whatever had gone wrong between you would have had time to heal over." Forgetting herself, Dottie offered BooBoo the rest of the chip. "To be honest, the way he's been talking to me, I was sure by bringing him to you I'd be doing the next-best thing to saving your life."

"I can imagine," Eden murmured.

"So much for grand gestures." Dottie moved her shoulders so that the ruby winked. "Eden, you never told me why you two called off the wedding. It was so sudden."

Eden opened her mouth, then closed it again. There was no reason to hurt and infuriate her aunt after all these months. If she told her now, it would be for spite or, worse, for sympathy. Eric was worth neither. "We just realized we weren't suited."

"I always thought differently." There was a loud blast of music and a chorus of laughter. Dottie cast a glance over her shoulder. "Eric seems to think differently, too. He's been to see me several times in recent weeks."

Pushing the heavy fall of hair from her shoulders, Eden walked to the edge of the porch. Perhaps Eric had discovered that the Carlbough name wasn't so badly tarnished after all. It gave her no pleasure to be cynical, but it was the only answer that seemed right. It wouldn't have taken him long to realize that eventually she would come into money again, through inheritances. She swallowed her bitterness as she turned back to her aunt.

"He's mistaken, Aunt Dottie. Believe me when I say

he doesn't have any genuine feelings for me. Perhaps he thinks he does," she added, when she saw the frown centered between Dottie's brows. "I'd say it's a matter of habit. I didn't love Eric." Her hands outstretched, she went to take her aunt's. "I never did. It's taken me some time to understand that I was going to marry him for all the wrong reasons—because it was expected, because it was easy. And…" She drew in her breath. "Because I mistakenly thought he was like Papa."

"Oh, darling."

"It was my mistake, so most of it was my fault." Now that it was said, and said aloud, she could accept it. "I always compared the men I dated with Papa. He was the kindest, most caring man I've ever known, but even though I loved and admired him, it was wrong of me to judge other men by him."

"We all loved him, Eden." Dottie drew Eden into her arms. "He was a good man, a loving man. A gambler, but—"

"I don't mind that he was a gambler." Now, when she drew back, Eden could smile. "I know if he hadn't died so suddenly, he'd have come out on top again. But it doesn't matter, Aunt Dottie, because I'm a gambler, too." She turned so that her gesture took in the camp. "I've learned how to make my own stake."

"How like him you are." Dottie was forced to draw a tissue out of her bag. "When you insisted on doing this, even when I first came here today, I could only think my poor little Eden's gone mad. Then I looked, really looked, at your camp, at the girls, at you, and I could see you'd made it work." After one inelegant sniff, she stuffed the tissue back in her bag. "I'm proud of you, Eden. Your father would have been proud of you."

Now it was Eden's eyes that dampened. "Aunt Dottie, I can't tell you how much that means to me. After he died and I had to sell everything, I felt I'd betrayed him, you, everyone."

"No." Dottie cupped Eden's chin in her hand. "What you did took tremendous courage, more than I had. You know how badly I wanted to spare you all of that."

"I know, and I appreciate it, but it had to be this way."

"I think I understand that now. I want you to know that I hurt for you, Eden, but I was never ashamed. Even now, knowing you don't need it, I'll tell you that my house is yours whenever you like."

"Knowing that is enough."

"And I expect this to be the finest camp in the east within five years."

Eden laughed again, and all the weight she'd carried with her since her father's death slipped off her shoulders. "It will be."

With a nod, Dottie took a step along the rail and looked out at the compound. "I do believe you should have a pool. Girls should have regulated, regimented swimming lessons. Splashing in the lake doesn't meet those standards. I'm going to donate one."

Eden's back went up immediately. "Aunt Dottie—"

"In your father's name." Dottie paused and cocked a brow. "Yes, I can see you won't argue with that. If I can donate a wing to a hospital, I can certainly donate a swimming pool in my brother's name to my favorite niece's camp. In fact, my accountant's going to be thrilled. Now, would you like Eric and me to go?"

Barely recovered from being so neatly maneuvered, Eden only sighed. "Having Eric here means nothing now. I want you to stay as long as you like."

"Good. BooBoo and I are enjoying ourselves." Dottie bent down to nuzzle in the dog's fur. "The delightful thing about BooBoo is that she's so much more tractable than any of my children were. Eden, one more thing before I go inside and absorb culture. I would swear that I felt, well, how to put it? One might almost say earth tremors when I walked into the stables this afternoon. Are you in love with someone else?"

"Aunt Dottie—"

"Answer enough. I'll just add my complete approval, not that it matters. BooBoo was quite charmed."

"Are you trying to be eccentric?"

With a smile, Dottie shifted the bundle in her arms. "When you can't rely on beauty any longer, you have to fall back on something. Ah, look here." She stepped aside as the Lamborghini cruised up. Lips pursed, Dottie watched Chase climb out. "Hello again," she called. "I admire your taste." She gave Eden a quick pat. "Yes, I do. I think I'll just pop inside and try some punch. It isn't too dreadful, is it?"

"I made it myself."

"Oh." Dottie rolled her eyes. "Well, I've some gambler in me as well."

Bracing herself, Eden turned toward Chase. "Hello. I'm glad you could—"

His mouth covered hers so quickly, so completely, that there wasn't even time for surprise. She might think of the hard possessiveness of the kiss later, but for now she just slid her hands up his back so that she could grip his shoulders. Instantly intense, instantly real, instantly right.

She hadn't felt this with Eric. That was what Chase told himself as she melted against him. She'd never felt this with anyone else. And he was going to be damn sure she didn't. Torn between anger and need, he drew her away.

"What—" She had to stop and try again. "What was that for?"

He gathered her hair in his hand to bring her close again. His lips tarried a breath from hers. "As someone once said to me, I wanted to kiss you. Any objections?"

He was daring her. Her chin angled in acceptance. "I can't think of any."

"Mull it over. Get back to me." With that, he propelled her toward the lights and music.

She didn't like to admit that cowardice might be part of the reason she carefully divided her time between the girls and the visiting counselors. Eden told herself it was a matter of courtesy and responsibility. But she knew she needed to have her thoughts well in hand before she spoke privately with Chase again.

She watched him dance with Roberta and wanted to throw herself into his arms and tell him how much she loved him. How big a fool would that make her? He hadn't asked about Eric, so how could she explain? It hummed through her mind that if he hadn't asked, it didn't matter to him. If it didn't matter, he wasn't nearly as involved as she was. Still, she told herself that before the evening was over she would find the time to talk it through with him, whether he wanted to hear it or not.

She just wanted to wait until she was sure she could do a good job of it.

There was no such confusion about the evening in general. The summer dance was a hit. Plans between the camp coordinators were already under way to make it an annual event. Already Candy was bubbling with ideas for more joint ventures.

As always, Eden would let Candy plan and organize; then she would tidy up the details.

By keeping constantly on the move, Eden avoided any direct confrontation with Eric or Chase. Of course they spoke, even danced, but all in the sanctuary of the crowded mess hall. Eric's conversation had been as mild as hers, but there had been something dangerous in Chase's eyes. It was that, and the memory of that rocketing kiss, that had her postponing the inevitable.

"I guess you like her a lot," Roberta ventured as she saw Chase's gaze wander toward Eden yet again.

"What?" Distracted, Chase looked back at his dance partner.

"Miss Carlbough. You're soft on her. She's so pretty," Roberta added with only the slightest touch of envy. "We voted her the prettiest counselor, even though Miss Allison has more—" She caught herself, realizing suddenly that you didn't discuss certain parts of a woman's anatomy with a man, even with Mr. Elliot. "More, ah…"

"I get the picture." Charmed, as always, Chase swung her in a quick circle.

"Some of the other girls think Mr. Keeton's a honey."

"Oh?" Chase's smile turned into a sneer as he glanced at the man in question.

"I think his nose is skinny."

"It was almost broken," Chase muttered.

"And his eyes are too close together," Roberta added for good measure. "I like you a lot better."

Touched, and remembering his first crush, Chase tugged on her ponytail to tilt her face to his. "I'm pretty soft on you, too."

From her corner, Eden watched the exchange. She saw Chase bend down and saw Roberta's face explode into smiles. A sigh nearly escaped her before she realized she was allowing herself to be envious of a twelve-year-old. With a shake of her head, she told herself that it was the strain of keeping herself unavailable that was beginning to wear on her. The music never played below loud. Uncountable trips to the kitchen kept the refreshment table full. Boys and girls shouted over the music to make themselves heard.

Five minutes, she told herself. She would steal just five quiet, wonderful minutes by herself.

This time, when she slipped back into the kitchen, she kept going. The moist summer air soothed her the moment she stepped outside. It smelled of grass and honeysuckle. Grateful for the fresh air after the cloying scent of fruit punch, Eden breathed deeply.

Tonight, the moon was only a sliver in the sky. She realized she had seen it change, had watched its waning and waxing more in the past three months than she had in all of her life. This was true of more than the moon. She would never look at anything else exactly the same way again.

She stood for a moment, finding the pictures in the sky that Chase had shown her. With the air warm on her face, she wondered if there would ever be a time when he would show her more.

As she crossed the grass, the light was silvery. From behind her came the steady murmur of music and voices. She found an old hickory tree and leaned against it, enjoying the solitude and the distance.

This was what warm summer nights were for, she thought. For dreams and wishes. No matter how cold it got during the winter, no matter how far away summer seemed, she would be able to take this night out of her memory and live it again.

The creak and swish of the back door cut through her concentration.

"Eric." She straightened, not bothering to disguise the irritation in her voice.

He came to her until he, too, stood under the hickory. Starlight filtered through the leaves to mix with the shadows. "I've never known you to leave a party."

"I've changed."

"Yes." Her eyes were calm and direct. He shifted uncomfortably. "I've noticed." When he reached out to touch her, she didn't step back. She didn't even feel his touch. "We never finished talking."

"Yes, we did. A long time ago."

"Eden." Moving cautiously, he lifted a finger to trace her jawline. "I've come a long way to see you, to make things right between us."

Eden merely tilted her head to the side. "I'm sorry you were inconvenienced, but there's nothing to make right." Oddly, the anger, even the bitterness, had become diluted. It had started weakening, she knew, when he had kissed her that afternoon. Looking at him now, she felt detached, as if he were someone she'd known only vaguely. "Eric, it's foolish for either of us to drag this out. Let's just leave things alone."

"I admit I was a fool." He blocked her exit, as if by simply continuing in the same vein he could put things back in the order he wanted. "Eden, I hurt you, and I'm sorry, but I was thinking of you as well as myself."

She wanted to laugh, but found she didn't even have the energy to give him that much. "Of me, Eric? All right, have it your way. Thank you and goodbye."

"Don't be difficult," he said, displaying a first trace of impatience. "You know how difficult it would have been for you to go through with the wedding while the scandal was still fresh in everyone's mind."

That stopped her, more than his hand had. She leaned back against the tree and waited. Yes, there was still a trace of anger, she discovered. It was mild, and buried quite deep, but it was still there. Perhaps it would be best to purge everything from her system. "Scandal. By that I assume you mean my father's poor investments."

"Eden." He moved closer again to put a comforting hand on her arm. "Your position changed so dramatically, so abruptly, when your father died and left you…"

"To earn my own way," she finished for him. "Yes, we can agree on that. My position changed. Over the past few months I've become grateful for that." There was annoyance now, but only as if he were a pesky fly she had to swat away. "I've learned to expect things from myself and to realize money had very little to do with the way I was living."

She saw by his frown that he didn't understand, would never understand the person who had grown up from the ashes of that old life. "You might find this amazing, Eric, but I don't care what anyone thinks about my altered circumstances. For the first time in my life, I have what I want, and I earned it myself."

"You can't expect me to believe that this little camp is what you want. I know you, Eden." He twined a lock of hair around his finger. "The woman I know would never choose something like this over the life we could have together in Philadelphia."

"You might be right again." Slowly, she reached up to untangle his hand from her hair. "But I'm no longer the woman you knew."

"Don't be ridiculous." For the first time he felt a twinge of panic. The one thing he had never considered was driving hundreds of miles to be humiliated. "Come back to the hotel with me tonight. Tomorrow we can go back to Philadelphia and be married, just as we always planned."

She studied him for a moment, trying to see if there was some lingering affection for her there, some true emotion. No, she decided almost at once. She wished it had been true, for then she could have had some kind of respect for him.

"Why are you doing this? You don't love me. You never did, or you couldn't have turned your back on me when I needed you."

"Eden—"

"No, let me finish. Let's finish this once and for all." She pushed him back a foot with an impatient movement of her hands. "I'm not interested in your apologies or your excuses, Eric. The simple truth is you don't matter to me."

It was said so calmly, so bluntly, that he very nearly

believed it. "You know you don't mean that, Eden. We were going to be married."

"Because it was convenient for both of us. For that much, Eric, I'll share the blame with you."

"Let's forget blame, Eden. Let me show you what we can have."

She held him off with a look. "I'm not angry anymore, and I'm not hurt. The simple fact is, Eric, I don't love you, and I don't want you."

For a moment, he was completely silent. When he did speak, Eden was surprised to hear genuine emotion in his voice. "Find someone to replace me so soon, Eden?"

She could almost laugh. He had jilted her almost two steps from the altar, but now he could act out the role of betrayed lover. "This grows more and more absurd, but no, Eric, it wasn't a matter of replacing you, it was a matter of seeing you for what you are. Don't make me explain to you what that is."

"Just how much does Chase Elliot have to do with all of this?"

"How dare you question me?" She started past him, but this time he grabbed her arm, and his grip wasn't gentle. Surprised by his refusal to release her, she stepped back and looked at him again. He was a child, she thought, who had thrown away a toy and was ready to stamp his feet now that he wanted it back and couldn't have it. Because her temper was rising, she fell back on her attitude of icy detachment. "Whatever is or isn't between Chase and me is none of your concern."

This cool, haughty woman was one he recognized. His tone softened. "Everything about you concerns me."

Weary, she could only sigh. "Eric, you're embarrassing yourself."

Before she could rid herself of him again, the screen door opened for a second time.

"Apparently I'm interrupting again." Hands in pockets, Chase stepped down from the porch.

"You seem to be making a habit of it." Eric released Eden, only to step between her and Chase. "You should be able to see that Eden and I are having a private conversation. They do teach manners, even here in the hills, don't they?"

Chase wondered if Eric would appreciate his style of manners. No, he doubted the tidy Philadelphian would appreciate a bloody nose. But then, he didn't give a damn what Eric appreciated. He'd taken two steps forward before Eden realized his intent.

"The conversation's over," she said quickly, stepping between them. She might as well have been invisible. As she had felt herself being shifted to the middle that afternoon, now she felt herself being nudged aside.

"Seems you've had considerable time to say what's on your mind." Chase rocked back on his heels, keeping his eyes on Eric.

"I don't see what business it is of yours how long I speak with my fiancée."

"Fiancée!" Eden's outraged exclamation was also ignored.

"You've let some months slip past you, Keeton." Chase's voice remained mild. His hands remained in his pockets. "Some changes have been made."

"Changes?" This time Eden turned to Chase, with no better results. "What are you talking about?"

Calmly, without giving her a glance, he took her hand. "You promised me a dance."

Instantly, Eric had her other arm. "We haven't finished."

Chase turned back, and for the first time the danger in his eyes was as clear as glass. "Yes, you have. The lady's with me."

Infuriated, Eden yanked herself free of both of them. "Stop it!" She'd had enough of being pulled in two directions without being asked if she wanted to move in either. For the first time in her life, she forgot manners, courtesy and control and did what Chase had once advised. When you're mad, he'd said, yell.

"You are both so *stupid*!" A toss of her head had the hair flying into her eyes to be dragged back impatiently. "How dare you stand here like two half-witted dogs snarling over the same bone? Don't either of you think I'm capable of speaking my own mind, making my own decisions? Well, I've got news for both of you. I can speak my own mind just fine. You." She turned to face Eric. "I meant every word I said to you. Understand? *Every single word.* I tried to phrase things as politely as possible, but if you push, let me warn you, you won't receive the same courtesy again."

"Eden, darling—"

"No, no, no!" She slapped away the hand he held out to her. "You dumped me the moment things got rough. If you think I'll take you back now, after you've shown yourself to be a weak, callous, insensitive—" oh, what was Candy's word? "—weasel," she remembered with relish, "you're crazy. And if you dare, if you *dare* touch me again, I'll knock your caps loose."

God, what a woman, Chase thought. He wondered

how soon he could take her into his arms and show her
how much he loved her. He'd always thought her beautiful, almost ethereal; now she was a Viking. More than
he'd wanted anything in his life, he wanted to hold that
passion in his arms and devour it. He was smiling at her
when she whirled on him.

"And you." Taking a step closer to Chase, she began
to stab him in the chest with her finger. "You go find
someone else to start a common brawl over. I'm not flattered by your Neanderthal attempts at playing at the
white knight."

It wasn't quite what he'd had in mind. "For God's
sake, Eden, I was—"

"Shut up." She gave him another quick jab. "I can
take care of myself, Mr. Macho. And if you think I appreciate your interference in my affairs, you're
mistaken. If I wanted some—some muscle-flexing he-
man to clean up after me, I'd rent one."

Sucking in a deep breath, she turned to face both of
them. "The two of you have behaved with less common
sense than those children in there. Just for future refer-
ence, I don't find it amusing that two grown men should
feel it necessary for their egos to use me as a Ping-Pong
ball. I make my own choices, and I've got one for you,
so listen carefully. I don't want either one of you."

Turning on her heel, she left them standing under the
hickory, staring after her.

Chapter 10

The last day of the session was pandemonium. There was packing and tears and missing shoes. Each cabin gave birth to its own personal crisis. Gear had to be stored until the following summer, and an inventory had to be made of kitchen supplies.

Beds were stripped. Linen was laundered and folded. Eden caught herself sniffling over a pillowcase. Somehow, during the first inventory, they came up short by two blankets and counted five towels more than they'd started with.

Eden decided to leave her personal packing until after the confusion had died down. It even crossed her mind to spend one last night in camp and leave fresh the following morning. She told herself it was more practical, even more responsible, for one of them to stay behind so that a last check could be made of the empty cabins. In truth, she just couldn't let go.

She wasn't ready to admit that. Leaving the laundry area for the stables, she began counting bridles. The only reason she was considering staying behind, she lectured herself, was to make certain all the loose ends were tied up. As she marked numbers on her clipboard, she struggled to block out thoughts of Chase. He certainly had nothing to do with her decision to remain behind. She counted snaffle bits twice, got two different totals, then counted again.

Impossible man. She slashed the pencil over the paper, marking and totaling until she was satisfied. Without pausing, she started a critical study of reins, checking for wear. A good rubbing with saddle soap was in order, she decided. That was one more reason to stay over one more night. But, as it often had during the past week, her confrontation with Chase and Eric ran through her mind.

She had meant everything she'd said. Just reaffirming that satisfied her. Every single word, even though she had shouted it, had come straight from the heart. Even after seven days her indignation, and her resolve, were as fresh as ever.

She had simply been a prize to be fought over, she remembered, as indignation began to simmer toward rage. Is that all a woman was to a man, something to yank against his side and stretch his ego on? Well, that wasn't something she would accept. She had only truly forged her own identity in recent months. That wasn't something she was going to give up, or even dilute, for anyone, for any man.

Fury bubbling, Eden crossed over to inspect the saddles. Eric had never loved her. Now, more than ever, that was crystal clear. Even without love, without caring, he'd wanted to lay some sort of claim. My woman. My property. My *fiancée*! She made a sound, somewhere between disgust and derision, that had one of the horses blowing in response.

If her aunt hadn't taken him away, Eden wasn't sure what she might have done. And, at this point, she was equally unsure she wouldn't have enjoyed it immensely.

But worse, a hundred times worse, was Chase. As she stared into space, her pencil drummed a rapid rat-a-tat-tat on the clipboard. He'd never once spoken of love or affection. There had been no promises asked or given, and yet he'd behaved just as abominably as Eric.

That was where the comparison ended, she admitted, as she pressed the heel of her hand to her brows. She was in love with Chase. Desperately in love. If he'd said a word, if he'd given her a chance to speak, how different things might have been. But now she was discovering that leaving him was infinitely more difficult than it had been to leave Philadelphia.

He hadn't spoken; he hadn't asked. The compromises she might have made for him, and only him, would never be needed now. Whatever might have been was over, she told herself, straightening her shoulders. It was time for new adjustments, new plans and, again, a new life. She had done it once, and she could do it again.

"Plans," she muttered to herself as she studied the clipboard again. There were so many plans to make for the following season. It would be summer again before she knew it.

Her fingers clutched the pencil convulsively. Was that how she would live her life, from summer to summer? Would there only be emptiness in between, emptiness and waiting? How many times would she come back and walk along the lake hoping to see him?

No. This was the mourning period. Eden closed her eyes for a moment and waited for the strength to return. You couldn't adjust and go on unless you'd grieved first. That was something else she had learned. So she would grieve for Chase. Then she would build her life.

"Eden. Eden, are you in there?"

"Right here." Eden turned as Candy rushed into the tack room.

"Oh, thank God."

"What now?"

Candy pressed a hand to her heart as if to push her breath back. "Roberta."

"Roberta?" Her stomach muscles balled like a fist. "Is she hurt?"

"She's gone."

"What do you mean, gone? Did her parents come early?"

"I mean gone." Pacing, Candy began to tug on her hair. "Her bags are all packed and stacked in her cabin. She's nowhere in camp."

"Not again." More annoyed than worried now, Eden tossed the clipboard aside. "Hasn't that child learned anything this summer? Every time I turn around she's off on a little field trip of her own."

"Marcie and Linda claim that she said she had something important to take care of before she left." Candy lifted her hands, then let them fall. "She didn't tell them what she was up to, that I'm sure of. You and I both know that she might only have gone to pick some flowers for her mother, but—"

"We can't take any chances," Eden finished.

"I've got three of the counselors out looking, but I thought you might have some idea where she could have gone before we call out the marines." She paused to catch her breath. "What a way to round out the summer."

Eden closed her eyes a minute to concentrate. Conversations with Roberta scattered through her memory until she focused on one in particular. "Oh, no." Her eyes shot open. "I think I know where she's gone." She was already rushing out of the tack room as Candy loped to keep up.

"Where?"

"I'll need to take the car. It'll be quicker." Thinking fast, Eden dashed to the rear of their cabin, where the secondhand compact was parked under a gnarled pear tree. "I'd swear she's gone to say goodbye to Chase, but make sure the orchard gets checked."

"Already done, but—"

"I'll be back in twenty minutes."

"Eden—"

The gunning of the motor drowned out Candy's words. "Don't worry, I'll bring the little darling back." She set her teeth. "If I have to drag her by her hair."

"Okay, but—" Candy stepped back as the compact shot forward. "Gas," she said with a sigh as Eden drove away. "I don't think there's much gas in the tank."

Eden noticed that the sky was darkening and decided to blame Roberta for that as well. She would have sworn an oath that Roberta had gone to see Chase one last time.

A three-mile hike would never have deterred a girl of Roberta's determination.

Eden drove under the arching sign, thinking grimly of what she would say to Roberta once she had her. The pleasure she got from that slid away as the car bucked and sputtered. Eden looked down helplessly as it jolted again, then stopped dead. The needle of the gas gauge registered a flat *E*.

"Damn!" She slapped a hand on the steering wheel, then let out a yelp. Padded steering wheels weren't part of the amenities on cars as old as this one. Nursing her aching wrist, she stepped out of the car just as the first blast of thunder shook the air. As if on cue, a torrent of rain poured down.

For a moment, Eden merely stood beside the stalled car, her throbbing hand at her mouth, while water streamed over her. Her clothes were soaked through in seconds. "Perfect," she mumbled; then, on the heels of that: "Roberta." Casting one furious look skyward, she set off at a jogging run.

Lightning cracked across the sky like a whip. Thunder bellowed in response. Each time, Eden's heart leaped toward her throat. As each step brought her closer to Chase's home, her fear mounted.

What if she'd been wrong? What if Roberta wasn't there, but was caught somewhere in the storm, wet and frightened? What if she was lost or hurt? Her breath began to hitch as anxiety ballooned inside her.

She reached Chase's door, soaked to the skin and terrified.

Her pounding at the door sounded weak against the cannoning thunder. Looking back over her shoulder,

Eden could see nothing but a solid wall of rain. If Roberta was out there, somewhere… Whirling back, she pounded with both fists, shouting for good measure.

When Chase opened the door, she nearly tumbled over his feet. He took one look at her soaked, bedraggled figure and knew he'd never seen anything more beautiful in his life. "Well, this is a surprise. Get you a towel?"

Eden grabbed his shirt with both hands. "Roberta," she managed, trying to convey everything with one word.

"She's in the front room." Gently, he pushed the hair out of her eyes. "Relax, Eden, she's fine."

"Oh, thank God." Near tears, Eden pressed her fingers to her eyes. But when she lowered them, her eyes were dry and furious. "I'll murder her. Right here, right now. Quickly."

Before she could carry through with her threat, Chase stepped in front of her. Now that he'd had a good taste of her temper, he no longer underestimated it. "I think I have an idea how you feel, but don't be too rough on her. She came by to propose."

"Just move aside, or I'll take you down with her." She shoved him aside and strode past him. The moment she stood in the doorway, Eden drew a breath. "Roberta." Each syllable was bitten off. The girl on the floor stopped playing with the dog and looked up.

"Oh, hi, Miss Carlbough." She grinned, apparently pleased with the company. After a moment her teeth dropped down to her lower lip. Though perhaps an optimist, Roberta was no fool. "You're all wet, Miss Carlbough."

The low sound deep in Eden's throat had Squat's ears pricking. "Roberta," she said again as she started forward.

Squat moved simultaneously. Drawing up short, Eden gave the dog a wary glance. He sat now, his tail thumping, directly between Eden and Roberta. "Call off your dog," she ordered without bothering to look at Chase.

"Oh, Squat wouldn't hurt you." Roberta scurried across the floor to leap lovingly on his neck. Squat's tail thumped even harder. Eden thought for a moment that he was smiling. She was certain she'd gotten a good view of his large white teeth. "He's real friendly," Roberta assured her. "Just hold your hand out and he'll sniff it."

And take it off at the wrist—which was giving her enough trouble as it was. "Roberta," Eden began again, staying where she was. "After all these weeks, aren't you aware of the rules about leaving camp?"

"Yes, ma'am." Roberta hooked an arm around Squat's neck. "But it was important."

"That isn't the point." Eden folded her hands. She was aware of how she looked, how she sounded, and she knew that if she turned her head she would see Chase grinning at her. "Rules have a purpose, Roberta. They aren't made up just to spoil your fun, but to see to order and safety. You've broken one of the most important ones today, and not for the first time. Miss Bartholomew and I are responsible for you. Your parents expect, and rightfully so, that we'll…"

Eden trailed off as Roberta listened, solemn-eyed. She opened her mouth again, prepared to complete the lecture, but only a shuddering breath came out. "Roberta, you scared me to death."

"Gee, I'm sorry, Miss Carlbough." To Eden's surprise, Roberta jumped up and dashed across the room to throw her arms around Eden's waist. "I didn't mean to, really. I guess I didn't think anyone would miss me before I got back."

"Not miss you?" A laugh, a little shaky, whispered out as Eden pressed a kiss to the top of Roberta's head. "You monster, don't you know I've developed radar where you're concerned?"

"Yeah?" Roberta squeezed hard.

"Yeah."

"I am sorry, Miss Carlbough, really I am." She drew back so that her freckled, triangular face was tilted to Eden's. "I just had to see Chase for a minute." She sent Eden an intimate, feminine glance that had Eden looking quickly over at Chase.

"Chase?" Eden repeated, knowing her emphasis on Roberta's use of the first name would get her nowhere.

"We had a personal matter to discuss." Chase dropped down onto the arm of a chair. He wondered if Eden had any idea how protectively she was holding Roberta.

Though it was difficult, Eden managed to display some dignity in her dripping clothes. "I realize it's too much to expect a twelve-year-old to show a consistent sense of responsibility, but I would have expected more from you."

"I called the camp," he said, taking the wind out of her sails. "Apparently I just missed catching you. They know Roberta's safe." Rising, he walked over and grabbed the tail of her T-shirt. A flick of the wrist had water dripping out. "Did you walk over?"

"No." Annoyed that he had done exactly what he should have done, Eden smacked his hand away. "The car…" She hesitated, then decided to lie. "Broke down." She turned to frown at Roberta again. "Right before the storm."

"I'm sorry you got wet," Roberta said again.

"And so you should be."

"Didn't you put gas in the car? It was out, you know."

Before Eden could decide to murder her after all, they were interrupted by the blast of a horn.

"That'll be Delaney." Chase walked to the window to confirm it. "He's going to run Roberta back to camp."

"That's very kind of him." Eden held her hand out for Roberta's. "I appreciate all the trouble."

"Just Roberta." Chase caught Eden's hand before she could get away from him again. Ready and willing, or kicking and screaming, he was holding on to what he needed. "You'd better get out of those wet clothes before you come down with something."

"As soon as I get back to camp."

"My mother says you catch a chill if your feet stay wet." Roberta gave Squat a parting hug. "See you next year," she said to Chase, and for the first time Eden saw a hint of shyness. "You really will write?"

"Yeah." Chase bent down, tilted her head and kissed both cheeks. "I really will write."

Her freckles all but vanished under her blush. Turning, she threw herself into Eden's arms again. "I'll miss you, Miss Carlbough."

"Oh, Roberta, I'll miss you, too."

"I'm coming back next year and bringing my cousin. Everyone says we're so much alike we should be sisters."

"Oh," Eden managed weakly. "Wonderful." She hoped one winter was enough time to recharge.

"This was the best summer ever." Roberta gave one last squeeze as tears began to cloud Eden's eyes. "Bye!"

The front door was slamming behind her before Eden had taken the first step. "Roberta—"

"It was my best summer ever, too." Chase took her free hand before she could try for the door.

"Chase, let me go. I have to get back."

"Dry clothes. Though, as I may have mentioned before, you look wonderful wet and dripping."

"I'm not staying," she said, even as he tugged her toward the stairs.

"Since I just heard Delaney pull off, and your car's out of gas, I'd say you are." Because she was shivering now, he hurried her up. "And you're leaving puddles on the floor."

"Sorry." He propelled her through his bedroom. Eden had a fleeting impression of quiet colors and a brass bed before she was nudged into the adjoining bath. "Chase, this is very nice of you, but if you could just drive me back—"

"After you've had a hot shower and changed."

A hot shower. He could have offered her sable and emeralds and not tempted her half so much. Eden hadn't had a hot shower since the first week of June. "No, I really think I should get back."

But the door was already closing behind him.

Eden stared at it; then, her lower lip caught between her teeth, she looked back at the tub. Nothing she'd ever seen in her life had seemed so beautiful, so desirable. It took her less than ten seconds to give in.

"Since I'm here anyway…" she mumbled, and began to peel out of her clothes.

The first sizzle of hot spray stole her breath. Then, with a sigh of pure greed, she luxuriated in it. It was sinful, she thought as the water sluiced over her head. It was heaven.

Fifteen minutes later, she turned the taps off, but not without regret. On the rack beside the tub was a thick, thirsty bath towel. She wrapped herself in it and decided it was nearly as good as the shower. Then she noticed her clothes were gone.

For a moment, she only frowned at the empty rail where she'd hung them. Then she gripped the towel tighter. He must have come in and taken them while she was in the shower. Lips pursed, Eden studied the frosted glass doors and wondered how opaque they really were.

Be practical, she told herself. Chase had come in and taken her clothes because they needed to be dried. He was simply being a considerate host. Still, her nerves drummed a bit as she lifted the navy-blue robe from the hook on the back of the door.

It was his, of course. His scent clung to the material so that she felt he was all but in the room with her as she drew it on. It was warm and thick, but she shivered once as she secured the belt.

It was practical, she reminded herself. The robe was nothing more than an adequate covering until her clothes were dry again. But she tilted her head so that her chin rubbed along the collar.

Fighting off the mood, she took the towel and rubbed the mist away from the mirror. What she saw was enough to erase any romantic fantasies from her mind. True, the hot water from the shower had brought some color to her cheeks, but she hadn't even a trace of mascara left to darken her lashes. With the color of the robe to enhance them, her eyes dominated her face. She looked as though she'd been saved just before going under for the third time. Her hair was wet, curling in little tendrils around her face. Eden dragged a hand through it a few times, but couldn't bring it to order without a brush.

Charming, she thought before she pulled the door open. In Chase's bedroom she paused, wanting to look, wanting even more to touch something that belonged to him. With a shake of her head, she hurried through the bedroom and down the stairs. It was only when she stopped in the doorway of the front room and saw him that her nerves returned in full force.

He looked so right, so at ease in his workshirt and jeans as he stood in front of a nineteenth-century cabinet pouring brandy from a crystal decanter. She'd come to realize that it was his contradictions, as much as anything else, that appealed to her. At the moment, reasons didn't matter. She loved him. Now she had to get through this last encounter before burying herself in the winter months.

He turned and saw her. He'd known she was there, had felt her there, but had needed a moment. When he'd come into the bath to take her wet clothes, she'd been humming. He'd only seen a shadow of her behind the glass but had wanted, more than he could remember wanting anything, to push the barrier aside and take her. To hold her with her skin wet and warm, her eyes huge and aware.

He wanted her as much, as sharply, now as she stood in the doorway dwarfed by his robe.

So he'd taken a moment, for the simple reason that he had to be sure he could speak.

"Better?"

"Yes, thanks." Her hand reached automatically for

the lapels of the robe and fidgeted there. He crossed the room to offer her a snifter.

"Drink. This should ward off the danger of wet feet."

As she took the glass, Chase closed the doors at her back. Eden found herself gripping the snifter with both hands. She lifted it slowly, hoping the brandy would clear her head.

"I'm sorry about all this." She made certain her tone was as polite and as distant as she could manage. She kept her back to the doors.

"No trouble." He wanted to shake her. "Why don't you sit down?"

"No, I'm fine." But when he continued to stand in front of her, she felt it necessary to move. She walked to the window, where the rain was still pouring from the sky. "I don't suppose this can keep up for long."

"No, it can't." The amusement he was beginning to feel came out in his voice. Wary, Eden turned back to him. "In fact, I'm amazed it's gone on this long." Setting his brandy aside, he went to her. "It's time we stopped it, Eden. Time you stopped backing away."

She gave a quick shake of her head and skirted around him. "I don't know what you mean."

"The hell you don't." He was behind her quickly, and there was nowhere to run. He took the snifter from her nerveless fingers before turning her to face him again. Slowly, deliberately, he gathered her hair in his hands, drawing it back until her face was unframed. There was a flash of fear in her eyes, but beneath it, waiting, was the need he'd wanted to see.

"We stood here once before, and I told you then it was too late."

The sun had been streaming through the glass then. Now the rain was lashing against it. As she stood there, Eden felt past and present overlap. "We stood here once before, and you kissed me."

His mouth found hers. Like the storm, the kiss was fierce and urgent. He'd expected hesitation and found demand. He'd expected fear and found passion. Drawing her closer, he found hunger and need and shimmering desire. What he had yet to find, what he discovered he needed most, was acceptance.

Trust me. He wanted to shout it at her, but her hands were in his hair, entangling him and pulling him to her.

The rain beat against the windowpanes. Thunder walked across the sky. Eden was whirling in her own private storm. She wanted him, wanted to feel him peeling the robe from her shoulders and touching her. She wanted that first delirious sensation of skin meeting skin. She wanted to give her love to him where it could be alive and free, but knew she had to keep it locked inside, secret, lonely.

"Chase. We can't go on like this." She turned her head away. "I can't go on like this. I have to leave. People are waiting for me."

"You're not going anywhere. Not this time." He slid a hand up her throat. His patience was at an end.

She sensed it and backed away. "Candy will be wondering where I am. I'd like to have my clothes now."

"No."

"No?"

"No," he said again as he lifted his brandy. "Candy won't be wondering where you are, because I phoned her and told her you weren't coming back. She said you weren't to worry, that things were under control. And no—" he sipped his brandy "—you can't have your clothes. Can I get you something else?"

"You phoned her?" All the fear, all the anxiety, drained away to make room for temper. Her eyes darkened, losing their fragility. Chase almost smiled. He loved the cool woman, the nervous one, the determined one, but he adored the Viking.

"Yeah. Got a problem with that?"

"Where did you possibly get the idea that you had a right to make my decisions for me?" She pushed a hand, covered by the cuff of his robe, against his chest. "You had no business calling Candy, or anyone else. More, you had no business assuming that I'd stay here with you."

"I'm not assuming anything. You are staying here. With me."

"Guess again." This time, when she shoved, there was enough power behind it to take him back a step. He knew that if he hadn't already been mad about her, he would have fallen in love at that moment. "God, but I'm sick to death of dealing with overbearing, dictatorial men who think all they have to do is want something to have it."

"You're not dealing with Eric now, Eden." His voice was soft, perhaps a shade too soft. "You're not dealing with other men, but with me. Only me."

"Wrong again, because I'm through dealing with you. Give me my clothes."

He set the snifter down very carefully. "No."

Her mouth would have fallen open if her jaw hadn't been clenched so tightly. "All right, I'll walk back in this." Ready to carry out her threat, she marched to the door and yanked it open. Squat lay across the threshold.

As they spotted each other, he rose on his haunches with what Eden was certain was a leer. She took one more step, then, cursing herself for a coward, turned back.

"Are you going to call off that beast?"

Chase looked down at Squat, knowing the dog would do nothing more dangerous than slobber on her bare feet. Hooking his thumb in his pocket, he smiled. "He's had his shots."

"Terrific." With her mind set on one purpose, she strode to the window. "I'll go out this way then." Kneeling on the window seat, she began to struggle with the sash. When Chase caught her around the waist, she turned on him.

"Take your hands off me. I said I was leaving, and I meant it." She took a swing, surprising them both when it landed hard in his gut. "Here, you want your robe back. I don't need it. I'll walk the three miles naked." To prove her point, she began fighting the knot at the belt.

"I wouldn't do that." As much for his sake as hers, he caught her hands. "If you do, we won't spend much time talking this through."

"I'm not spending any time at all." She squirmed until they both went down on the cushions of the window seat. "I don't have anything else to say to you." She managed to kick until the robe was hitched up to her thighs. "Except that you have the manners of a pig, and I can't wait until I'm hundreds of miles away from you. I decided the other night, when I was given the choice between a boring fool and a hardheaded clod, that I'd rather join a convent. Now take your hands off me, or I swear, I'll hurt you. No one, but no one, pushes me around."

With that, she put all her energy into one last shove. It sent them both tumbling off the cushions and onto the floor. As he had done once before, Chase rolled with her until he had her pinned beneath him. He stared at her now as he had then, while she fought to get her breath back.

"Oh God, Eden, I love you." Laughing at them both, he crushed his lips to hers.

She didn't fight the kiss. She didn't even move, though her fingers stiffened under his. Each breath took such an effort that she thought her heart had slowed down to nothing. When she could speak again, she did so carefully.

"I'd appreciate it if you'd say that again."

"I love you." He watched her eyes close and felt that quick twinge of panic. "Listen to me, Eden. I know you've been hurt, but you have to trust me. I've watched you take charge of your life this summer. It hasn't been the easiest thing I've ever done to stand back and give you the space you needed to do that."

She opened her eyes again. Her heart wasn't beating at a slow rhythm now, but seemed capable of bursting out of her chest. "Was that what you were doing?"

"I understood that you needed to prove something to yourself. And I think I knew that until you had, you wouldn't be ready to share whatever that was with me."

"Chase—"

"Don't say anything yet." He brought her hand to his lips. "Eden, I know you're used to certain things, a certain way of life. If that's what you need, I'll find a way to give it to you. But if you give me a chance, I can make you happy here."

She swallowed, afraid of misunderstanding. "Chase,

are you saying you'd move back to Philadelphia if I asked you to?"

"I'm saying I'd move anywhere if it was important to you, but I'm not letting you go back alone, Eden. Summers aren't enough."

Her breath came out quietly. "What do you want from me?"

"Everything." He pressed his lips to her hand again, but his eyes were no longer calm. "A lifetime, starting now. Love, arguments, children. Marry me, Eden. Give me six months to make you happy here. If I can't, we'll go anywhere you like. Just don't back away."

"I'm not backing away." Her fingers entwined with his. "And I don't want to be anyplace but here."

She saw the change in his eyes even as his fingers tightened on hers. "If I touch you now, there's no going back."

"You've already told me it was too late." She drew him down to her. Passion and promises merged as they strained closer. She felt again that she had the world in the palm of her hand and held it tightly. "Don't ever let me go. Oh, Chase, I could feel my heart breaking when I thought of leaving here today, leaving you when I loved you so much."

"You wouldn't have gotten far."

Her lips curved at that. Perhaps, in some areas, she could accept a trace of arrogance. "You'd have come after me?"

"I'd have come after you so fast I'd have been there before you."

She felt pleasure grow, and glow. "And begged?"

His brow lifted at the glint in her eyes. "Let's just say I'd have left little doubt as to how much I wanted you."

"And crawled," she said, twining her arms around his neck. "I'm almost sorry I missed that. Maybe you could do it now."

He took a quick nip at her ear. "Don't press your luck."

Laughing, she held on. "One day this will be gray," she murmured as she trailed her fingers through his hair. "And I still won't be able to keep my hands out of it." She drew his head back to look at him, and this time there was no laughter, only love. "I've waited for you all my life."

He buried his face in her throat, fighting back the need to make her his, then and there. With Eden it would be perfect, it would be everything dreams were made of. He drew away to trace the line of her cheekbone. "You know, I wanted to murder Eric when I saw him with his hands on you."

"I didn't know how to explain when I saw you there. Then, later…" Her brow arched. "Well, you behaved very badly."

"You were magnificent. You scared Eric to death."

"And you?"

"You only made me want you more." He tasted her again, feeling the wild, sweet thrill only she had ever brought to him. "I had plans to kidnap you from camp. Bless Roberta for making it easy."

"I hope she's not upset you're going to marry me instead. You have a neat dog, and you're kind of cute." She pressed her lips to the sensitive area just below his ear.

"She understood perfectly. In fact, she approves."

Eden stopped her lazy exploration of his throat. "Approves? You mean you told her you were going to marry me?"

"Sure I did."

"Before you asked me?"

Grinning, Chase leaned down to nip at her bottom lip. "I figured Squat and I could convince you."

"And if I'd said no?"

"You didn't."

"There's still time to change my mind." He touched his lips to hers again, letting them linger and warm. "Well," she said with a sigh, "maybe just this once I'll let you get away with it."

* * * * *

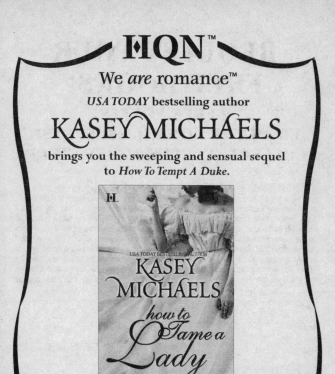

REQUEST YOUR FREE BOOKS!

2 FREE NOVELS
FROM THE ROMANCE/SUSPENSE
COLLECTION PLUS 2 FREE GIFTS!

YES! Please send me 2 FREE novels from the Romance/Suspense Collection and my 2 FREE gifts (gifts are worth about $10). After receiving them, if I don't wish to receive any more books, I can return the shipping statement marked "cancel." If I don't cancel, I will receive 4 brand-new novels every month and be billed just $5.74 per book in the U.S. or $6.24 per book in Canada. That's a savings of at least 28% off the cover price. It's quite a bargain! Shipping and handling is just 50¢ per book.* I understand that accepting the 2 free books and gifts places me under no obligation to buy anything. I can always return a shipment and cancel at any time. Even if I never buy another book from the Reader Service, the two free books and gifts are mine to keep forever.

185 MDN EYNQ   385 MDN EYN2

Name	(PLEASE PRINT)	
Address		Apt. #
City	State/Prov.	Zip/Postal Code

Signature (if under 18, a parent or guardian must sign)

Mail to **The Reader Service:**
IN U.S.A.: P.O. Box 1867, Buffalo, NY 14240-1867
IN CANADA: P.O. Box 609, Fort Erie, Ontario L2A 5X3

Not valid to current subscribers of the Romance Collection,
the Suspense Collection or the Romance/Suspense Collection.

Want to try two free books from another line?
Call 1-800-873-8635 or visit www.morefreebooks.com.

* Terms and prices subject to change without notice. Prices do not include applicable taxes. Sales tax applicable in N.Y. Canadian residents will be charged applicable provincial taxes and GST. Offer not valid in Quebec. This offer is limited to one order per household. All orders subject to approval. Credit or debit balances in a customer's account(s) may be offset by any other outstanding balance owed by or to the customer. Please allow 4 to 6 weeks for delivery. Offer available while quantities last.

Your Privacy: Harlequin is committed to protecting your privacy. Our Privacy Policy is available online at www.eHarlequin.com or upon request from the Reader Service. From time to time we make our lists of customers available to reputable third parties who may have a product or service of interest to you. If you would prefer we not share your name and address, please check here. ☐

BOB09

In 2009 Harlequin celebrates
60 years of pure reading pleasure!

We're marking this occasion by offering
16 **FREE** full books to download and read.

Visit

www.HarlequinCelebrates.com

to choose from a variety of
great romance stories
that are absolutely **FREE!**

(Total approximate retail value of $60)

We invite you to visit and share the Web site
with your friends, family
and anyone who enjoys reading.

NORA ROBERTS

(limited quantities available)

TOTAL AMOUNT	$	_____
POSTAGE & HANDLING	$	_____
($1.00 FOR 1 BOOK, 50¢ for each additional)		
APPLICABLE TAXES*	$	_____
TOTAL PAYABLE	$	_____

(check or money order—please do not send cash)

To order, complete this form and send it, along with a check or money order for the total above, payable to Harlequin Books, to: **In the U.S.:** 3010 Walden Avenue, P.O. Box 9077, Buffalo, NY 14269-9077; **In Canada:** P.O. Box 636, Fort Erie, Ontario, L2A 5X3.

Name: _____
Address: _____ City: _____
State/Prov.: _____ Zip/Postal Code: _____
Account Number (if applicable): _____

075 CSAS

*New York residents remit applicable sales taxes.
*Canadian residents remit applicable GST and provincial taxes.

Silhouette®
Where love comes alive™

Visit Silhouette Books at www.eHarlequin.com   PSNR1009BL